KILLER AMONG THE VINES

a Wine & Dine mystery

GEMMA HALLIDAY

KILLED AMONG THE VINES

Dedicated to Grandpa.
Wish you were here to read it. I hope it would make you laugh.

CHAPTER ONE

"Emmy, I'm telling you there is a thief among us!" My mother stabbed the air with her fork for emphasis, a long spinach noodle falling off the end and onto her plate.

I shook my head in the near-empty dining room of the Sonoma Acres assisted living facility. "Mom, I don't think anyone is stealing from you."

"Not me. Mrs. Borstein." Mom frowned, her artfully plucked eyebrows pulling together beneath her bangs. We both shared the same blue eyes and golden blonde hair, though hers was liberally shot with silvery grey these days. "Haven't you been listening?"

I had to admit, my mind might have wandered once or twice during dinner. Not that I wasn't totally enthralled with Mom's tales of Dorothy Chapman's bunions and the way ninety-year-old Mr. Horowitz was flirting with the new widow who had just moved into 4B. But I'd tried a new recipe out that day, and I was savoring each bite, thinking I'd almost gotten it right—but not quite yet. It was a copycat of the Walnut Mushroom Au Gratin that had been my mom's favorite dish at the Good Earth restaurant. She'd taken me to lunch there at least once a week when I was a kid. They'd long since closed most of their locations, and I'd thought it would be a nice treat to recreate a culinary memory for her. While the spinach noodles and crunchy water chestnuts reminded me of the restaurant version, something about the sauce was a little tangier than the original. Maybe I'd added too much sherry.

"Emmy?"

"Hmm?" I slurped a noodle, sauce smacking me in the chin.

"I said Mrs. Borstein's photo did not just get up and walk out on its own." Mom twirled more noodles on her fork.

"What photo?" I asked, taking a sip from my wineglass. Along with the pasta dish, I'd pulled from our cellar a bottle of our Zinfandel. A little taste of home from our family run winery.

"It was of Mrs. Borstein's grandnephew. And someone took it."

"Why would anyone want a photo of Mrs. Borstein's nephew?"

"Grandnephew. And I don't know why." She shrugged. "Maybe they have a thing for redheads."

"If he's that hot, why haven't you hooked me up?" I teased.

Mom shot me a look. "My point is the photo is missing."

"Mom, Mrs. Borstein is eighty-three and has cataracts. Isn't it possible that she might have just misplaced the photo herself?"

But Mom was undeterred, shaking her head so hard that her blonde hair shimmied across her shoulders. "No, Mrs. Borstein has looked everywhere for it. And it's not the only thing that's gone missing here!"

"Did she lose a picture of her dog too?" I joked.

"Mabel Marston said her needlepoint pillow went missing last week."

"Has she checked the lost and found?" I asked, taking another sip.

Mom set her fork down on her plate with a clatter and shot me a look. "You're not taking me seriously, are you?"

"Whatever gave you that idea?" I smiled at her and blinked my eyes innocently.

"Come on, Emmy. I've got dementia—I'm not stupid."

I choked back a bittersweet laugh at the feistiness in my mom's voice. While it was true early onset dementia had her in an assisted living facility much too young, one thing the disease had not robbed her of was a sense of humor. While we'd certainly had bad days where she barely recognized her own daughter, there were good days—like today—where she could laugh about the tragedy that was stealing her mind away from her so young. I'll admit, it was harder for me to find humor in it, but for her sake, I tried not to show it.

"Okay, okay," I conceded, setting my wineglass down. "So who do you—and Mrs. Borstein and Mabel Marston—think is the mastermind behind these thefts?"

She shook her head, her pink lips going into a thin line. "I don't know."

"The staff?" I asked.

Mom picked up her fork again. "I'd hate to think so."

"So, maybe another resident?"

"Maybe," Mom said, shrugging her shoulders. Now that we were pointing fingers, some of the certainty seemed to be waning. "Or maybe a visitor? Someone who came to see one of the residents?"

"Or maybe a cat burglar, sneaking over the azaleas at night to steal away with personal knickknacks and fancy bedding."

"You're mocking me again, aren't you?" Mom gave me the same narrowed eyed look I'd gotten with every less than stellar report card throughout my childhood.

"I wouldn't dare," I replied, shoving a big bite of noodles into my mouth to cover up the lie.

"Anyway, I was thinking maybe you could mention it to your boyfriend."

I froze mid-chew. "Boyfriend?"

Mom nodded, not making eye contact. "That policeman."

I finally regained control of my jaw and finished my bite. I swallowed before answering. "You've been talking to Conchita." Who was our house manager at Oak Valley Vineyards as well as self-appointed den mother to all. And apparently chief gossip.

"Well, I have to! My own daughter doesn't tell me she's dating someone new."

"We're not dating," I argued. "Well, okay, yes, we've dated. Some. A few times. But he's not my boyfriend."

Truth was, it was hard to categorize exactly what Grant was.

Detective Christopher Grant was a detective in the Sonoma County Sheriff's Office VCI unit—violent crimes investigations. Which meant his world consisted of hardened criminals, calloused actions, and all things from the seedier side of life. He'd moved to Wine Country from San Francisco after he'd been involved in a shooting. After an internal affairs investigation, no charges had been brought against Grant, but it had been highly suggested he transfer for a change of scenery. Ordered, even. Grant had never really told me much about the incident, but I had a feeling that "no charges" and "innocent" were not exactly the same thing.

Our paths had first crossed in his professional capacity when there'd been a death at my winery, though more often these days they crossed for reasons of a more personal nature. And while I was greatly enjoying all of those personal encounters, I wasn't sure how long I expected them to last or if they'd ever progress to a point where we'd be ready for a label as commitment assuming as "boyfriend."

"Well, Conchita tells me that you have been spending a lot of time with him lately," Mom pressed.

I shrugged. "I've spent *some* time with him."

"Conchita says it's a lot."

"Conchita has a tendency to exaggerate." And a big mouth.

"You know she's just looking out for you," my mom said.

I sighed. I did. When Mom had gotten sick, Conchita had wasted no time stepping into the role of mother hen. Which, while it was sometimes a little more intrusive into my personal life than I might have liked, it was also a welcomed comfort more often than not. So it was hard to be mad at her.

"So, when do I get to meet this hot cop of yours?" Mom said, waggling her eyebrows up and down.

Hard, but not impossible.

"He's not *mine*," I protested.

"Conchita says he's handsome," Mom prodded.

I couldn't help a grin as I pictured his square jaw, dark eyes dancing with little golden flecks, and broad shoulders. "He is."

Mom's face broke into a big smile. "And you like him."

The goofy grin on my face made it hard to deny that one. "Yes, I like him," I admitted.

Mom opened her mouth to interrogate more, but I ran right over her.

"But," I cautioned, "we're not that serious."

She shut her mouth, the frown reappearing. "Oh."

She looked so disappointed, my guilt riddled heart added, "At least not yet."

She tilted her head from side to side, mentally weighing that statement. "Okay, well, see where it goes. Maybe it will get serious at some point."

"Maybe," I hedged.

"You know, your father had to work hard to win me over," she said, shoveling more of the creamy noodles into her mouth.

"Really?" I asked. As far back as I ever remembered, Mom and Dad had been adorably in love. She'd been devastated when he'd passed away when I was twelve and had never looked at another man since, as far as I knew.

"Oh yeah. The first time I met him, I thought he was a stalker. Followed me home from work, and I almost called the police."

"I'm glad you didn't."

"So was he," she said with a laugh. "Anyway, give your detective time. Maybe he'll grow on you."

That was honestly what I was afraid of. That he'd grow on me so much I'd wish he was more the settling down type than he was. But I just nodded. "Maybe."

"So how are the Sirah grapes coming along this year?" Mom asked, switching gears. Thankfully.

"Well," I told her honestly, "we've had a little root rot with all the rain this year, but Hector's confident he's got it under control." Hector was our vineyard manager, Conchita's husband, and a long-time fixture at the winery who had taught me everything I knew about grapes.

Mom gave me a wide grin. "You've become quite the vintner, Emmy."

I laughed. While I'd grown up at the winery, it had never been my dream to run it. In my early twenties I'd left home to study at the CIA—just not *that* CIA. The Culinary Institute of America, though the LA Times had once called my food "to die for." I'd dreamt of one day opening my own restaurant, but when Mom had gotten sick and the winery had been in trouble, those dreams had taken a back seat. I'd come home to assume control over the operations at Oak Valley Vineyards, and while I did sometimes miss the idea of commanding a large kitchen full of chefs and getting that glowing review in Zagat, I'd never regretted the decision. Oak Valley was home, and it was where I belonged. And, as Mom had said, my vintner skills were improving.

"Did I tell you I hired on a security guard?" I said, licking cheesy gooey deliciousness off my fork.

"Oh?" Mom asked.

I nodded. "Thought it might be a good idea. You know, after the unpleasantness last year." Unfortunately, Grant had been to my winery on more than one occasion in a professional capacity. Something I did not want a repeat of.

"Can you afford that?" Mom asked, crunching down on a walnut.

Barely. But I didn't want to worry her, so I just nodded. "Sure."

"So business has been good?" Mom asked.

I bit my lip. "We're surviving," I said, feeling guilty for lying to her.

With the recent pandemic having shut down wineries in Sonoma for months, our bottom line was sinking lower and lower this year. Much lower and it would be below water.

But, again, not something I wanted to worry Mom with.

"I have an appointment with Gene Schultz tomorrow," I told her. "My accountant. He's looking at some funding options for us." He'd been able to get panels of investors to back us through hard times before, and I was hoping he could pull it off again.

Mom nodded. "That's sounds promising."

"Things will pick up," I told her with false optimism. "They always do in the spring."

"Right. Wedding season is coming up, isn't it?"

I nodded. "We have a few bookings already."

"The winery really is the most picturesque place to get married. I'm sure you'll be swamped soon."

"From your lips to brides' ears," I said, raising my glass in a toast.

"Anyway, did I tell you what happened to Mrs. Borstein?" Mom asked, her eyes alight with the thrill of good gossip.

I felt my heart clench the way it always did when one of her good moments lulled me into forgetting a bad one was right around the corner. "Yes," I said softly. "You did."

"I did?" A look of confusion crossed her features.

I nodded. "That she misplaced a photograph of her nephew."

"Oh." She got a far-off look in her eyes, as if trying to conjure up the memory of ten minutes ago that was lost already.

We sat in silence for a beat before she shook her head and picked up her fork again. "Anyway, it wasn't misplaced. It was stolen. Might be something you could mention to your cop friend."

I swallowed down the lump in my throat and nodded. "Sure. I'll tell him." I gave her a smile that I was sure didn't reach my eyes. What can I say? I was a vintner, not an actress.

* * *

It was dark by the time we finished off the last of the pasta and the bottle of Oak Valley Vineyards Zin. I'd just shoved the empty casserole dish I'd brought dinner in into the front passenger seat of my Jeep, when my phone rang. I glanced down at the readout before answering, seeing the name of Bill Buckley, the security guard I'd recently hired, flash across the screen. I swiped to take the call.

"Hello?" I answered.

"Ms. Oak, it's Bill," he said, his voice sounding a little breathless.

"Everything okay, Bill?" I asked.

"Yeah. Probably."

"Probably?" I asked, concern setting in immediately.

"The silent alarm was tripped in the south vineyard."

"What tripped it?" I asked, hearing urgency seep into my voice as I turned my car on and backed out of the parking lot.

"I'm on my way to check it out now," he said. "But it's probably nothing. Just deer."

Which was likely. We'd had problems with deer in the past at Oak Valley, and despite new fencing, they were constant pests.

On the other hand, we'd also had intruders on the grounds, who we'd mistakenly dismissed as deer, so I wasn't as quick as Bill was to think the best.

"I'm just leaving town now," I told him, pulling onto the main road. "I'll be there in twenty minutes."

Which was a lie. I made it in fifteen, going just slightly over the speed limit the entire way. By the time I finally pulled up the winding, tree-lined drive to the winery and parked in the lot in front of the main building, my mind had had plenty of opportunity to conjure up all sorts of worst case scenarios. "Possibly deer" had turned into a whole gang of thieves, breaking in and making off with every vintage bottle in our cellar. I left my casserole dish in the car, sprinting toward the main winery doors and rushing into the tasting room.

My Sommelier, Jean Luc, and my winery manager, Eddie Bliss, were the only two people in the room, standing at the bar beside the large picture window that looked out onto the dark vineyard. They were a study in opposites, Jean Luc's tall thin frame a contrast to Eddie's stout, portly one. The Frenchman was dressed in his usual dark slacks and white dress shirt, looking both understated and elegant at the same time. While Eddie was awash with color—his maroon jacket accentuated by a bright turquoise ascot that matched the loud flowers on his bell-bottomed pants. I wasn't sure if he was the epitome of style or trying out for clown college. Both men looked up as I entered the room.

"Emmy, we were just debating which glass to use with Bordeaux—" Eddie started.

But I cut him off with a wave of my hands. "Where's Buckley?"

"Buckley?" Jean Luc asked in his thick French accent, his lips contorting into a frown beneath his sleek black mustache.

"Bill Buckley. The security guard," I said. "He called and said an alarm was tripped."

Jean Luc's eyebrow pulled down in a frown. "Zees eez the first I hear of it."

"Oh my!" Eddie said, his hand going to his mouth.

"You haven't seen him?" I asked.

They both shook their heads. "No," Eddie answered. "Not since earlier when he clocked in."

I felt myself frowning to match Jean Luc's expression. "He didn't say anything to you about the alarm?"

They both shook their heads again.

"Where did it go off?" Eddie asked.

"South vineyard," I said, pulling my phone from my pocket and dialing Buckley's number. "Bill said he was going to check it out."

I waited silently while it rang on the other end. I could see the concern growing in the pit of my stomach mirrored in the faces of my two employees as we all waited for Buckley to answer.

Six rings in, it went to voicemail.

"Well?" Jean Luc asked.

I stabbed my phone off. "He's not answering."

We all turned to look out the window at the dark vineyard, seeming serene and still in the moonlight.

"I'm going to go look for him," I decided.

"I'll go with you," Eddie offered, pulling out his phone and turning on the flashlight app.

While I wasn't sure what the two of us would do if there really were an intruder on the grounds, I was grateful we'd be a duo and not a solo. We left out the back door, heading through the courtyard and across the meadow where we held our weddings against the backdrop of the vineyards. The south field was to our left and looked quiet and deserted. The air had a chilling bite to it, and the scent of dew and wet earth filled my nostrils as I inhaled deeply, fear as well as exertion making my breath come fast.

"Bill?" I called out, my voice sounding oddly loud in the still air.

A few birds in a nearby oak tree fluttered their wings, taking to the air. But no response from my security guard.

"Is anyone out here?" I tried again, hating that my voice held a shake to it.

"There!" Eddie said, pointing to our right and shining his flashlight in the direction.

"What?" I asked, eyes scanning the row of growing grapes as his beam illuminated them.

"I-I thought I saw something," he said, uncertainty in his voice now.

I licked my lips. "Buckley? Are you out here?"

The soft sound of crickets in the bushes to my left was all that I heard in reply.

"Maybe he went back inside," Eddie offered, his voice soft.

"Maybe." I pulled my phone out, trying his number again. Only this time as it rang in my ear, I also heard a faint echoing ring in the night.

My eyes shot to Eddie's. The look in them said he'd heard it too.

I pulled my phone from my ear, straining to hear the faint ringtone coming from between the rows of vines.

"Over there," Eddie stage whispered to me, nodding toward the left. His flashlight led the way as we carefully traversed the uneven ground toward the sound.

Only a few paces in, the ringing stopped, the call going to voicemail. I quickly hung up and dialed again, feeling that panic gather into a tight ball in my belly as we waited in the cool night air to hear the ringtone again.

Finally it echoed across the vines. Louder now. Closer.

Eddie took off at a near run this time, and I was just a quick step behind him, wishing I'd worn shoes that were more conducive to trekking through the mud. My heels were sinking and sticking in the earth, and I feared they would never be the same again.

The ringing was louder, and I expected to see Bill standing ahead of us any second, when Eddie stopped so suddenly that I almost ran into his back. I heard him gasp audibly. Then he spun to face me, his pallor ghostly white in the moonlight.

"What is it?" I asked, hearing the ringing come to an ominous end as I peeked around him, not waiting for a response.

And I realized why no one was picking up the phone. It was sitting in the mud next to a blossoming vine. And beside it was the outstretched hand of Bill Buckley, his body lying on the damp earth atop a large red pool of blood. And by the way his wide, glassy eyes were staring unseeing at the moonlit sky, I could tell that Buckley would never be answering his phone again.

Bill Buckley was dead.

CHAPTER TWO

"Name?" A uniformed officer with what was clearly a home haircut looked expectantly at me, fingers hovering over his electronic tablet as we stood in the meadow, watching crime scene techs crawl all over my vine covered hills.

"Emmeline Oak. Emmy," I amended.

"Address?"

"Here. I mean, I live in the cottage at the back of the winery."

"Phone number?"

I rattled off the digits, the act of reciting mundane information actually working to calm my nerves.

Some.

After Eddie and I had both screamed until our throats were raw, one of us had had the good sense to call 9-1-1. Probably Eddie, as my mind had been a whirlwind of fear, guilt, and horror at seeing my employee dead in my vineyard. Had he caught an intruder? What had tripped the alarm? Had there been an altercation? And where was the intruder now?

I'd been hovering near hysteria by the time the dispatcher on the other end of the line had said help was on the way and Jean Luc had come running from the winery, having heard our, as he put it, "blood curdling screams." The three of us had waited silently for the authorities, the only sound in the vineyard the 9-1-1 operator's voice repeatedly telling us to stay on the line and wait somewhere safe.

Safe. I'd always felt security and a sense of home at Oak Valley, but I wasn't sure I'd ever feel completely safe in those rows of blooming grape vines again.

"Ma'am, are you okay?" The officer cut into my thoughts, concern in his eyes below his slightly uneven bangs.

I realized I was shaking and wrapped my arms tightly around my middle. "Yeah. Sure. Fine."

"You're a terrible liar," a familiar voice said from behind me.

I spun to find myself looking up into the face of Detective Grant. Way up. He was well over six feet tall, with broad shoulders and chest that tapered to a perfect V at the waistband of his worn jeans. His hair was dark, his skin a warm sun-kissed tan, and his eyes were deep brown and creased at the corners when he smiled. And while his voice held a note of humor, at the moment he wasn't smiling, his eyes mirroring the concern in the uniformed officer's. "Hey," he said softly.

I licked my lips. "Hey," I squeaked out.

"You okay?"

Having already been called out as a liar, I shook my head in the negative.

Grant quickly closed the gap between us, wrapping his arms around me in a tight hug that I never wanted to end. He smelled like fabric softener and warm spicy aftershave, and the heat radiating from his chest felt so alive and strong that for a moment I could block out everything else that I'd seen that evening.

Only the moment ended too quickly, and Grant pulled back. "What happened?" he asked, his voice calm and even. While I could tell he was in cop mode, he was reining it in for my benefit.

I did some more lip licking, leaving them wet in the night air that was growing colder by the second. "I-I honestly don't know. We just found him like that."

"Do you know the victim?" he asked, eyes cutting to the south vineyard where a myriad of flashlight beams converged on the scene.

I nodded. "His name is Bill Buckley. He was my security guard."

"I'm sorry," Grant said, a new layer of sympathy in his voice at the thought I'd known the dead man.

I shook my head. "I'd just hired him. I mean, he'd only been here a little while."

"So you didn't know him well?"

"No." I felt guilt hit me again. "I mean, he showed up on time and had a decent looking résumé. I hadn't had a chance to get to know much more."

Grant nodded, and I could see him mentally taking notes. "When did he start working here?"

"I-I don't know. A couple of weeks ago, I guess. I could check my records." I nodded toward the winery buildings where my office was.

"Did you hire him through an agency?" Grant asked, pulling a notebook from his pocket. Though, unlike the uniformed officer, his was actually old school paper. He grabbed a ballpoint pen from his pocket to go with it, flipping to an empty page.

"No, he was freelance. David recommended him."

"David?" Grant's eyebrows rose. "Well, that should have given you a clue right there."

I could tell he was only half joking. David Allen lived in the guest house of his mother's abandoned estate just outside of town, and when he wasn't smoking pot and enjoying his trust-fund lifestyle, he spent his days painting dark violent artwork and card sharking the rich and oblivious at the local golf club. David had had my back enough times in the past that he was somewhere in the friend range of acquaintances. But he was enough of a wild card that I was always reminded of the phrase, *keep your friends close and your enemies closer.* Ninety percent of the time he seemed harmless enough. But the other ten percent of the time his wicked grin had me wondering what he was scheming.

So I almost didn't blame Grant's semi-joke at David's expense.

"David said his mom had used Buckley a couple of times for events at her place," I told Grant. "He said Buckley did a good job for her."

"Did David know Buckley personally?"

"I don't think so. Not that he mentioned to me anyway."

"You run a background check on Buckley before you hired him?"

"No. But Buckley said he was a retired police officer."

Grant nodded, his gaze going toward the myriad of flashlight beams again. "A lot of these private security guys are. Did he mention any friends or family in the area to you?"

I shook my head. "No." I tried hard not to picture a crying widow and little fatherless Buckley juniors, that guilt growing by the second. "But you could ask Eddie. He was usually here when Buckley clocked in. He might have mentioned something to him."

Grant nodded again. "I think someone is taking his statement now."

I hesitated to ask, but part of me just had to know… "Do you know how he died?"

Grant gave me a dubious look, as if he wasn't sure I seemed strong enough to handle the details.

I squared my shoulders, hoping my posture looked hardened enough to take it. While I wasn't sure I totally pulled it off, it must have been enough to convince Grant I wouldn't pass out, as he said, "Gunshot wound to the chest."

I cringed. "Please tell me he didn't suffer."

Grant shook his head. "We'll need ballistic to confirm, but it looks like it was a .22 caliber. Something like that? He would have died instantly."

Thank goodness for small favors.

"Buckley called me earlier. He said something tripped the alarm. He was going to investigate it," I said, quickly relaying to Grant the brief last conversation I'd had with the dead man before driving home. "You think whoever shot Buckley tripped it?" I asked when I'd finished.

Grant looked out at the vineyard again. "I don't know. Does your security system have cameras?"

I nodded. "But only around the building. Nothing that would cover the vineyards."

"We'll look over footage just in case."

I nodded. "Why would anyone be in my vineyard? With a gun?"

"Could be hunters."

"Here?" I glanced around the winery grounds which, while we were about twenty minutes outside of downtown, was hardly the wilderness. "Hunting what? Merlot?"

The corner of Grant's mouth ticked up at my attempt at humor. "Could have been teenagers. Looking for small game—rabbits, even young deer."

"But they wouldn't have mistaken Buckley for a rabbit," I reasoned.

"It's also possible we're looking at a potential intruder. Maybe Buckley surprised them."

I thought back to the image of Buckley's body on the ground. "His phone was out. Like it had been in his hand maybe. It was on the ground next to him. Maybe he was calling for help?"

"CSI has bagged it, and we'll be checking his phone records." He paused. "We're also checking the buildings for any sign of a break-in."

"Have you found any?"

"Not yet." Grant looked down at his notebook. "Anyone else on the property tonight?"

"Just Eddie and Jean Luc when I got here."

"What about Conchita and Hector?" Grant asked. As he knew, they lived in a small house just on the other side of the ridge.

I shook my head. "They're away for the weekend. Taking some time off before wedding season hits."

Grant frowned. "Emmy, I don't think you should be here alone tonight."

By the tone of his voice, I could tell that was not an amorous invitation. "Why?" I asked. "You don't think whoever did this would come back?"

Again Grant looked like he was hesitant to lay the truth on me. "There's a possibility this wasn't random."

"What do you mean?" I asked, hearing the fear back in my voice.

"I mean, until we know whether Buckley was responding to someone simply looking to make off with some valuables or to someone who broke onto the grounds with the intent to harm, you should be careful."

"Intent to harm…me?" I said, his meaning sinking in. "You think whoever did this came here to harm *me*?"

Grant shook his head. "I don't know, Emmy, but it *is* your winery."

"No." I shook my head, the denial more instinctive than anything. "Who would do that? Why? I don't have any enemies."

"Are you sure about that?" Grant asked.

I paused. "Yes." No. Especially with the way he was looking at me. Like he almost didn't want to let me out of his sight.

"I'd feel better if you weren't alone tonight. I don't want to take any chances."

A shiver ran down my spine that had nothing to do with the cold night air. I nodded dumbly.

Grant looked up at the hillside that seemed to be filling with more and more law enforcement personnel. "You can stay at my place, but I'm going to be held up here for quite a bit."

Normally the invitation to sleep over would have sent tingly warm feelings to all the right places. But in that moment, all I felt was numb. Numb with guilt, with fear, and with a distinct sense of vulnerability that was making me just as nervous about spending the night with Grant as it was spending the night alone at my home that was now a crime scene. I was starting to shiver again when I heard a female voice calling my name.

"Emmy!" I turned to see my best friend, Ava Barnett, running toward me through the tasting room doors. "Ohmigosh, areyouokay?" she asked all in a rush. She tackled me in a hug that smelled like her peachy lotion before waiting for a response.

I felt myself hiccup back a sob as I melted into her embrace.

Ava and I had been best friends since high school, and while our lives had sometimes taken us down different paths since then—mine to culinary school and hers to opening her own jewelry store where she sold her handmade sterling silver creations—as soon as I'd come home to take over the winery, it had been like no time had passed in our friendship. Ava had the same blonde hair as I did, and we were both an average size eight. Even if my hair was a little more on the frizzing-in-the-humidity side and hers was more on the straight-and-glossy-at-all-times side, and my size eight had a little more padding in the hips from my love of all things edible and hers had a little more muscle definition from her love of the outdoors.

Muscles that were currently squeezing the life out of me.

"I an't eeth," I told her.

"What?"

"I said I can't breathe," I repeated as she released me and took a step back.

"Ohmigosh, Eddie called and told me what happened," Ava said, her eyes going from me to Grant. "That your security guy passed away in the vineyard?"

Passed away was a nice way to put it. Much more peaceful sounding than the scene Eddie and I had stumbled upon. I tried to block out the image as I nodded. "It's true. He's dead." I quickly gave her the condensed version of events as Grant put his notebook away.

"Honey, I'm so sorry," Ava said, laying a hand on my arm and giving it a squeeze.

"Thanks," I managed to get out through the tears starting to back up again at her genuine sympathy.

Grant cleared his throat. "I was just telling Emmy that I don't think she should stay here alone tonight."

"Well, of course not!" Ava said, rubbing her hand up and down my cold arms. "You're staying with me tonight."

I glanced at Grant. I thought I saw a flicker of disappointment in his eyes, but he quickly covered it. "I think that's a good idea."

"You're sure?" I asked him, feeling a smidge of disappointment myself.

But he nodded confidently. "I'm going to be tied up here for a while. You shouldn't be alone."

It was two against one. Clearly I was going to Ava's that night. I nodded my agreement. "Sure."

Grant's eyes roved over me, looking like he wished he could do more. "I'll call you later."

"Sure," I said again. The one word must have sounded about as *unsure* as I felt, as he leaned in and pulled me into another tight hug before dropping a peck on my cheek.

* * *

The ride to Ava's felt longer than it ever had, and I fell asleep twice in the car, my head lulling in the passenger seat of her vintage GTO. The surge of adrenaline at finding the dead man had ebbed, leaving in its wake both emotional and physical exhaustion. As soon as we got to Ava's loft apartment above her shop, Silver Girl, I flopped onto her living room futon and passed out, barely even registering the soft quilt that Ava laid lovingly over me before tiptoeing off to her bedroom herself.

The next morning I was awaked by sunshine streaming through Ava's blinds in sharp ribbons of light and the sound of hushed voices in the small kitchen behind me.

"You think she's okay?"

"No. Who would be okay after seeing that?"

"Murder in the vineyard. Who do the police think did it?"

"Emmy said Grant thinks it could be personal."

"It's possible. Emmy can be hard to get along with."

"I can hear you," I called from beneath the quilt. I propped myself up into a seated position to glare over the top of the sofa at the two less-than-quiet gossipers.

Ava and David Allen sat at the kitchen table with a couple of mugs of coffee in hand.

David gave me a crooked grin. "'Morning, sunshine."

I shot Ava a look. "What's *he* doing here?"

"He called me as soon as he saw the news this morning," Ava said, rising from the table to grab another mug from her cupboard.

"I rushed right over to make sure you weren't traumatized," David said, only a small hint of sarcasm in his voice. He was dressed in his usual attire of worn jeans, dangerous looking combat boots, and a black T-shirt, this one touting some brand of whiskey. His dark hair was cut long, falling into his eyes that were twinkling with a teasing light in my direction.

"I'm fine," I told him, yawning as I joined them at the table. "And I am *not* hard to get along with."

David's grin grew. "I had a feeling you were awake over there."

Ava handed me the cup of coffee and as I took the first grateful sip, the fragrant Columbian beans soothed away any irritation I might have felt at her letting David in.

"Seriously though—you okay, Ems?" David asked.

And the sincerity in his voice served to wash away any irritation I had at *him* for the previous comment. I nodded, not trusting my voice until I'd swallowed another warm sip of heavily creamed coffee. "Yeah. I'm fine."

David gave me a dubious look.

"I *will be* fine," I amended. "Which is more than I can say for Buckley," I mumbled, feeling guilt gnaw at me again.

"The *Sonoma Index-Tribune* said he was shot sometime around nine last night," David said.

"What else did they say?" I asked, steeling myself for the worst. The local press and I had a bit of a love-hate relationship—they loved to report about every mishap at my winery, and I hated to read about it.

"Not a whole lot of other details, really. Just that an alarm had been tripped and when Buckley went to investigate, a 'killer among the vines' shot him at the 'deadliest little winery in Sonoma,'" he quoted.

"Bradley Wu was the reporter I take it?" The man had a flair for the dramatic.

David nodded. "He also reminded readers that this wasn't the first 'victim in the vineyard' at Oak Valley.'"

I winced. Unfortunately, that was true.

"I'm sorry, honey," Ava said. "Did you know Buckley well?"

I shook my head. "I only hired him two weeks ago." I nodded toward David. "On your recommendation."

Ava turned to David. "You said he worked for your mom, right?" she asked, setting a plastic carton of blueberry muffins on the table between us. While they were a far cry from Conchita's homemade variety, I gratefully grabbed one and peeled the paper off as David answered.

"He did. She had him work security at a couple of her weekend parties last year."

"Do you know if he had any family?" I asked.

David frowned, thinking back. "I think he mentioned living with a girlfriend."

"No kids?" I asked, hopeful that at least he wasn't leaving behind orphans.

David shrugged and shook his head. "I don't know. But, like I said, I only saw the guy a couple of times."

"Poor thing," Ava said, nibbling her muffin. "The girlfriend."

I nodded, the pastry sticking in my throat. "I feel awful."

"Why? You didn't shoot the guy," David said.

"Yeah, but he died on my property. Working for me. Possibly protecting me." That last thought had the shiver from the night before running up my spine again.

"It's not your fault," Ava said, covering one of my hands with hers. "You had no idea some random person waving a gun around would be in your vineyard."

"*If* it was random," David pointed out.

Ava shot him a look. "Not helping, David."

"What? I'm just saying." He put his hands up innocently. "Maybe someone had it in for our Emmy, here."

Ava frowned and opened her mouth to scold him again, but he ran right over her.

"Or, maybe someone had it in for *Buckley*."

Ava shut her mouth. She cocked an eyebrow at me. "Maybe. I mean, they did kill *him* and not you, right?"

I swallowed, the words *kill* and *you* being so close together in a sentence making me nervous. "I guess so. But why would anyone want to kill Buckley?"

David shrugged. "Maybe he was a crappy security guard."

"Maybe things weren't going well with the girlfriend," Ava said.

"Maybe he had a gambling problem and owed the wrong people money," David floated.

"Maybe some criminal he busted back when he was a cop had it in for him," Ava added.

"That's a whole lot of maybes," I pointed out, crumbling blueberry muffin on the wooden table. I sighed loudly. "I have an appointment with Schultz at one. My accountant," I clarified for David's benefit. "He's trying to secure us funding, but I can't imagine this incident being splashed all over the news is going to help his efforts."

"Sorry, honey," Ava said again.

"And it's going to be terrible for wedding season. I mean, who wants to get married where someone just died?"

Ava gave me a sympathetic look. David sipped his coffee, looking appropriately subdued.

I shook my head. "That's an awful thing to think, isn't it?" I looked up at my friends for confirmation. "I mean, a man is dead and I'm worried about my bookings."

Ava put her hand over mine again. "This was not your fault," she repeated.

I sucked in a breath. "I know." I lifted my eyes to meet Ava's. "I *do*. But, at the very least, I feel like I should pay my respects to Buckley's girlfriend, you know?"

"Good idea," David said. "The girlfriend is always the first suspect."

I shot him a look. "I meant to give her my condolences."

"I'll go with you," Ava decided, finishing the last of her coffee.

We both looked at David.

He held up his hands in an innocent gesture again. "Sorry, grief isn't really my thing. Besides, I've got a midmorning game at the Links."

"Who's the unlucky victim this time?" I asked, knowing full well he meant a poker game at the Sonoma Links golf club where he planned to fleece some unsuspecting soul, and not a round of golf.

"Doug Groudin," David said, getting up from the table. "Of the Groudin Gallery."

Ava cocked her head at him. "Aren't you doing a show there this week?"

David nodded. "I am. And the outcome of this game will determine if I'm showing five pieces or ten." He gave us a wink.

Ava laughed. "Poor Groudin. You might own the gallery by the time you're done with him."

"If I play my cards right. Pun intended," David added with a grin. "Anyway, call me later and let me know how it goes with the girlfriend interrogation."

"Condolences!" I said again. Only, he'd already shut the door behind him and probably didn't hear me.

"These were terrible," Ava said, gesturing to the muffin stumps still sitting on their paper wrappers on the table. "I miss Conchita's. When's she coming back?"

"Monday," I said, rising and helping her toss the leftovers into the trash.

"I could starve by then."

I couldn't help a laugh. "Tell you what—let's get a couple of showers, and I'll spring for croissants at the Half Calf on the way to console the girlfriend."

"Sold!"

CHAPTER THREE

As Ava showered, I logged into my email account and found the paperwork Buckley had filed with me when I'd hired him, noting his home address was an apartment on the outskirts of town. Google Maps said it would only take a few minutes to get there, so I didn't rush through showering and borrowing a clean outfit from Ava's closet. Even though the cargo capris were a little more snug on my hips than Ava's, paired with a loose floral top and my own heels from the night before (minus the mud I'd had to scrub off of them), the outfit didn't look half bad. Maybe not quite as put together as Ava's boho chic sundress, denim jacket, and chunky sandals, but presentable at least.

We stopped quickly at the Half Calf next door—a cute coffee shop with a logo of a cartoon cow enjoying a latte while lounging on a crescent moon—and grabbed a couple of croissants and the café's signature caramel flan lattes to go. Ten minutes later we pulled up in front of Buckley's building, a three story structure with a sign outside that said it was the Shady Meadows.

Unfortunately for the occupants, there was no shade and no meadow.

The building itself was a dull beige stucco that at one time could have been white or yellow depending on if the grime or the sun bleaching had won that particular war. It was a no-frills rectangular structure with covered car parks along the bottom tier beside a large green dumpster that looked to have hit capacity several bags ago. A rusted metal staircase stood next to the dumpster, and one sad square of brown lawn sat beside it, masquerading as landscaping.

"Depressing place," Ava mumbled as we parked in a spot marked *Visi_or*. They were missing a *T*.

"Well, Buckley didn't exactly make a lot." I frowned, biting my lip. "I know because I was signing his checks."

"I'm sure you paid what you could."

I nodded, following her as she tested the bottom stair carefully before ascending to the second floor. "Speaking of which—I wonder who I should send his last check to?"

Ava shrugged. "Let's ask the girlfriend," she said as we hit the second floor landing. Buckley's apartment was 2C, which ended up being three down from the staircase.

As we passed 2A I could hear pounding bass music from inside, and 2B seemed to be cooking a morning curry, if the scents coming through the walls were any indication. 2C's door looked just like the last two—peeling grey paint, letters that had been stuck on slightly crooked, peephole caked with enough grime that I doubted anyone could peep through it. I was just about to knock, when the raised voices from inside made me pause.

Ava shot me a look, clearly hearing them too. "That doesn't sound good," she mumbled.

A man's voice was shouting. The actual words were hard to make out, but the tone was clearly anger. A woman's voice replied—volume lower but cracking as if there were tears behind it.

"Maybe we should come back later," Ava suggested.

I nodded and turned to go.

But that was as far as we got before the door to 2C flew open and a man ran through it, nearly plowing us down.

"Jamie!" the female voice called, and a second later a woman in her mid-to-late 40s appeared in the doorway. "Jamie, wait!"

"Leave me alone!" the guy yelled back, and I realized that while his voice was deep, he looked to be little more than a teenager rather than a full grown man. He was dressed in a black leather jacket with a painted image of a skull and a red rose on the back. His short dark hair was gelled into dangerous spikes, and I watched his denim clad legs run down the stairs, taking them two at a time.

"Jamie!" the woman called once more. But even she seemed to realize how useless the attempt was as he disappeared from view. She sighed in resignation, her eyes flitting to us, seeming to realize for the first time that she had an audience. "I'm sorry, can I help you?"

I licked my lips, feeling distinctly intrusive. "Uh, hi. I'm Emmy Oak. I, uh, own Oak Valley Vineyards. Where Bill Buckley worked."

At the sound of his name, the woman winced, fine lines around her mouth pinching tightly.

"We came by to offer our condolences," Ava jumped in, her voice soft and sympathetic. "We're so sorry for your loss."

The woman sucked in a breath and nodded. "Thanks. Would you like to come in?"

She didn't wait for an answer before leading the way into the apartment.

As we stepped inside I could tell the interior was every bit as small and unappealing as the outside of the building indicated. Brown carpet marked with several darker brown stains spanned across the small living room to our right, where a TV was playing the Cooking Network on mute. A mustard colored sofa that was covered in a clashing hot pink afghan—probably in an effort to cover more stains—sat in front of the TV. A cracked leather recliner sat next to the sofa, a peach colored apron thrown over one of the arms. A low wooden coffee table took up the rest of the room, the top covered in dirty dishes and a cardboard pizza box.

"Sorry," the woman said, clearing the table. "Jamie left the place kind of a mess this morning."

"No need to apologize. I'm sure it's all been a shock," Ava said, sitting gingerly on the sofa.

"Jamie is your…son?" I guessed, as the woman gave up on the table, setting the dishes into a pile on top of the pizza box.

"Yes," she answered. Up close I could tell she was older than I'd originally thought, probably closer to fifty. Her brown hair pulled back in a low ponytail was starting to streak with grey. Her dark eyes had grey circles etched under them, and I could only imagine the type of sleepless night she'd had. I could see fine lines at the corners of her eyes and creases at her mouth.

She was dressed in a pair of jeans and a navy sweatshirt that didn't look like she'd been expecting company. "Jamie is…very upset about Bill."

"His father?" I asked.

"Oh, no." She let out a laugh that held zero humor. "No. A point which Jamie's made *several* times." She sent us a sad smile. "Jamie's at a…difficult age."

"Teenagers often are," Ava said.

The woman turned her attention to Ava. "I'm sorry, I didn't get your name?"

"Ava Barnett. I'm a friend of Emmy's."

She nodded, shaking Ava's outstretched hand. "Sheila Connolly." She turned back toward me. "You said you were Bill's employer?"

"Briefly," I told her. "I, uh, had just hired him on at the winery."

"Right," Sheila said. "Bill had been looking for work for a while."

"Oh?" I asked. "Had business been slow?"

"Very," she said, again giving that self-deprecating laugh. "Not a lot of parties being thrown these days. Not even in posh wine country."

I nodded. "I understand. The winery has been affected too."

She gave me a look like someone who owned a winery couldn't possibly understand how hard it had been for someone living in Shady Meadows.

I cleared my throat awkwardly. "Uh, anyway, we just wanted to offer our condolences. I'm…I'm just so sorry about what happened last night."

"Me too." Sheila sat back in the leather chair, causing it to creak in protest as she pulled a pack of cigarettes from a pocket on the side. "You mind?" she asked.

I shook my head, though she didn't wait for my answer before pulling a stick out and lighting it.

I saw Ava's nose twitch out the corner of my eye, but she was polite enough not to say anything. The woman had just lost her boyfriend—if smoking in her own home made her feel better, who were we to argue?

Even if I did breathe just a little shallower.

"Poor Bill. I always knew something like this would happen," Sheila went on, blowing a plume of smoke up toward the dull beige ceiling.

"You did?" I asked.

"Well, maybe not *this*. But trouble followed Bill like a dang dog."

Ava shot me a look, and I could almost hear her mind kicking into *Charlie's Angels* gear—the one where she imagined us as kick butt crime fighters with fabulous hair. "What sort of trouble?" she asked.

Sheila shrugged. "Any sort. All the time. He was a magnet for it. I mean, just look at his police record."

I bit my lip, regretting now that I hadn't. "Bill mentioned to me that he was a retired police officer."

Sheila's jaw worked back and forth with some emotion. "I suppose he didn't mention that his retirement was *forced*."

"Forced?" I shook my head. "No, he didn't."

"Yeah, well, I guess that wouldn't have looked real good on a résumé."

"Are you saying he was asked to leave?" Ava clarified.

Sheila nodded and took a long drag from her cigarette before answering. "I guess there's no point in trying to keep it quiet now."

"What happened?" I asked.

"This was before I knew him, mind you. I didn't meet him until after he left the force. But he told me he was caught taking bribes."

"Oh, wow," Ava said, her eyes cutting to mine again.

"Yeah, wow is right." Sheila shook her head. "It was stupid, and he should have known better. But," she added quickly, "he cooperated fully with Internal Affairs and agreed to take early retirement."

"Meaning, leave the force."

She nodded. "Without a pension."

"Ouch," Ava said.

"Right?" Sheila shook her head. "Painful. Between his odd security jobs, my waitressing, and Jamie's weekend job, we can just barely afford this palace," she said, heavy on the sarcasm.

I felt a niggle of guilt again that I couldn't have done more for him. But, honestly, the wage I'd been able to offer was already stretching our budget to the limit.

"But," Sheila went on, "the deal avoided criminal charges for Bill and a public scandal for the department. That's why he moved to Sonoma. To leave it all behind him and start over."

"When was this?" Ava asked.

She blew out a plume of smoke. "Like I said, before I met him. A couple years ago."

"So you met him after he moved here?" I asked.

She nodded. "He came into Ed's Diner one night." She gestured to the peach colored apron lying over the arm of her chair. "I usually work the dinner shift."

"Oh?" Ava asked. "Were you working last night?"

If I didn't know better, I'd say Ava was fishing for an alibi.

Luckily, if Sheila noticed, she didn't mention it. Instead she shook her head. "No, I was here. Waiting for Jamie to get home from God knows where. Wondering what the heck kind of trouble he was getting into with those friends of his." She frowned, her eyes going to the closed door her son had just exploded through.

"I'm sorry. Bill's death must have come as a shock to you both," Ava said.

She sniffed loudly, drawing her attention back to us. "Well, like I said. Trouble followed Bill everywhere."

"Did it follow him to Sonoma?" Ava asked.

"Hmm?" she asked, seemingly still lost in her own thoughts.

"His troubles. It sounds like Bill made quite a few enemies on the police force," Ava noted.

Sheila eyed my friend, taking a beat before answering. "Well, let's just say Bill didn't leave San Francisco with a lot of friends."

"San Francisco?" I asked.

She nodded. "Yeah. That's where he was on the force. SFPD."

My mind immediately went to Grant. He'd been SFPD before moving to Sonoma too. Though, of course, San Francisco was a huge place. There were probably thousands of police officers and several stations. Chances of their paths crossing were pretty slim.

"Anyone in particular unhappy with Bill?" Ava pressed.

Sheila shrugged. "Like I said, that was before my time."

"Did Bill keep in touch with any of them?" I asked, starting to feel like we were grasping at straws. The whole incident had happened two years ago. It seemed like Buckley had moved on.

Sheila shrugged. "Not really. I heard him talk about a partner a couple of times. But I never met him."

"Did they keep in touch?"

"Not that I know of. Then again, I didn't know Bill's every move." A sad looked crossed her face.

"I hope it doesn't sound indelicate right now," I started, but I had a feeling not much was too indelicate for Sheila. "But, I, uh, was wondering who I should send Bill's last check to? You?"

Sheila paused, something flashing behind her eyes. Then she shrugged. "We weren't married. So technically, his 'estate'"—she did air quotes around the word as she gave the room as disdainful glance again—"goes to someone else. Who, I don't know."

"He didn't have any family?" Ava asked.

She shook her head. "No one close. There was just the ex."

"He had an ex-wife?" I clarified.

Sheila nodded. "Carmen. Works at Nadia's Nails in Napa."

"Did they get along?"

Sheila laughed, the sound turning into a hacking cough at the end. "Yeah, no. She was a thorn in Bill's side from the day I met him."

"Oh?" Ava asked, leaning forward. "So they *didn't* get along."

"Not in the least. She always had her hand out, always looking for more money. Her alimony was bleeding us dry."

"Did she and Bill argue about that?" Ava shot me that knowing look again, one that had seventies crime fighter written all over it.

Sheila shrugged. "Look, don't get me wrong, here. Bill was no saint. He was a…a difficult man sometimes. He couldn't always see someone else's side." Her eyes got a far off look in them that was distinctly sad. As if she had often been that "someone else" in his life. She sniffed suddenly and shook her head. "But Carmen was a piece of work. You know she left him as soon as Internal Affairs started investigating him?"

I shook my head. Clearly I had known very little about my employee.

"Yeah. No loyalty whatsoever. I got no respect for that!" she said, stabbing her cigarette at me for emphasis.

"I take it she didn't know about the bribes before then?" Ava asked.

Sheila shrugged. "I dunno. You'd have to ask her. It's not like Bill told me much. I mean, what was I? Just his girlfriend." Again she got that sad look in her eyes, and I felt my heart go out to her—not only for her loss but for what had clearly not been a model relationship.

"I'm sorry," I told her.

She shrugged again. "Look, Bill might not have been perfect, but what can you do? He was what I had. I was trying to make it work."

"I understand," Ava said, sympathy in her voice again. "Relationships are complicated."

Sheila nodded. "Yeah. Complicated." She stabbed her cigarette butt out on one of the dirty dishes piled in front of her. "Jamie's never really had a man around. I'd hoped Bill would fill that void, you know? Male role model."

"Were they close?" Ava asked.

"Hardly." Sheila eyed her packet of cigarettes again but refrained from reaching for it. "Bill was…a strong personality. And so is Jamie. They clashed. But I always held out hope that at some point Jamie would come around." She looked tired, and I again wondered if she'd had any sleep the night before at all—

first up worrying about where her son was then getting the news about Buckley.

"I'm so sorry again for your loss," I said, honestly meaning it.

The sad look remained, but she just shrugged again and repeated, "What can you do?"

"Did Jamie ever say where he was last night?" Ava asked.

Sheila tore her gaze from the cigarettes to Ava. "What do you mean?"

"You said you were waiting for Jamie to get home from somewhere. Did he ever tell you where that was?"

Sheila's face sagged into that resigned, tired look again. "Sure. Same place he always is. 'Out.'"

* * *

"Well that was just sad," Ava said as we walked back to her car.

"Very." I nodded, giving Shady Meadows a backward glance. "On so many levels."

"It definitely sounds like Buckley was no angel, though," Ava noted.

"No." I pursed my lips. "I wonder if Grant knows about Buckley's past. The bribery charges?"

"He was SFPD too, right?" Ava asked.

I nodded. "Of course, San Francisco's a big place, but maybe their paths crossed."

"You think the bribery charges had anything to do with Buckley's death?" Ava asked.

I bit my lip. "Honestly, I don't know."

"Okay, let's say that this wasn't a random break-in gone wrong at the winery," Ava said, unlocking her car and getting in.

"I like that idea." I slid into the passenger seat.

"Let's say it was personal. Someone was there with the intention to kill."

"Liking it less."

"But it sounds like *Buckley* had more enemies than you do. What if someone knew he had started working at your winery, knew he'd likely be patrolling the vineyards late at night, alone, and took advantage of that."

I nodded. "Okay, I can see that." I paused. "And you think that someone was from his past? Someone who had to do with the bribery in San Francisco?"

Ava shrugged. "Possibly. She mentioned a partner. Maybe he was angry at Buckley? Felt betrayed?"

"I don't know. Two years feels like a long time to wait for revenge."

"Okay, what about the ex-wife?"

"What about her?"

"Sheila said she was a real piece of work."

"According to the *girlfriend,*" I pointed out. "Sheila wouldn't exactly be neutral on Buckley's ex-wife, would she?"

"Maybe not," Ava conceded. "But didn't she say the ex was always looking for money? Maybe Buckley wasn't paying up?"

I nodded. "I suppose. I mean, it sounds like he was hard up for money."

"He gets behind on alimony payments, she demands money, they fight, she shoots him."

"If she brought a gun with her, it doesn't feel like this was a crime of passion."

Ava shrugged. "Maybe she brought it along to threaten him? Or maybe her plan was to kill him all along." She paused. "Didn't Sheila say she worked at a nail salon?"

I nodded. "Nadia's Nails," I said, grabbing my phone and typing the name in. A minute later I had a number for the salon in Napa. I quickly swiped to call and listened to it ring on the other end.

"Nadia's Nails?" a slightly nasally female voice answered.

"Uh, hi. I was wondering if you could let me know when Carmen Buckley might be in?"

"She's here now. Would you like to make an appointment?"

"She's there now? Like, today?" I asked, shooting Ava a look. Clearly the woman wasn't in mourning for her dead ex-husband if she'd gone into work.

"Yeah," the woman said, sounding a little irritated at having to repeat herself. "She's here, but her afternoon is filling up fast. You want to see her?"

"Uh, yes. Please," I said, shooting a questioning look to Ava.

She shrugged. "I could use a pedicure."

"Can we book two pedicures?" I asked the woman on the phone.

"Sure. Her first opening is at two thirty. That work?"

I looked down at the dash clock. It was almost noon now.

"Perfect," I told her, giving her my name and number before I hung up. I turned to Ava. "Is it just me, or is it odd she'd be doing nails the day after her husband is shot to death?"

"*Ex*-husband," Ava reminded me. "And I guess that all depends on how ugly the divorce was." She paused. "And, come to think of it, if she was the one who did the shooting."

CHAPTER FOUR

Ava drove me back to Oak Valley with a promise to pick me up again later for our trip to Napa to Nadia's Nails. I tried hard to ignore the squad cars and CSI van still sitting in my lot as I quickly ducked into my office to get my paperwork in order for my meeting with my accountant, Gene Schultz. I thought about grabbing a quick glass of Zin to fortify my nerves but decided against it. I had a strict(ish) policy to (almost) never drink before happy hour. Instead, I made my way around the back to my cottage for a quick makeup refresh and grabbed a sandwich from the kitchen before heading back out to meet my accountant.

Schultz's office was on the top floor of a tall cement and glass high rise. The sheer size of the building always made me a little intimidated, as if hammering home that the people who worked here knew what they were doing when it came to money, and me—living in a small cottage that was barely big enough to even qualify as cozy—did not. I guess it was true what they said—size did matter.

I rode the elevator up to the top floor, tapping my fingers against my thigh the entire time. By the time Schultz's receptionist led me down the hall and into his private office, I could feel the nerves dancing in my belly.

"Emmy! Great to see you, kid!" Schultz said jovially, rising from behind his desk to greet me. His dark hair was starting to go grey, but thanks to his excellent esthetician his face was still virtually line free. His suits were tailored, his hands manicured, and his smile whiter than a toothpaste commercial.

"Hi, Gene," I said, doing an air kiss routine with him.

"Well, looks like you've been in the press again, huh?" He eyed an electronic tablet on his desktop, the page open to the *Sonoma Index-Tribune* website.

I cringed. "Bradley Wu tends to exaggerate."

"Sure. Sure." Schultz picked up the tablet, scrolling through the article. "'Deadliest little winery in Sonoma.' Second 'victim in the vineyard.' Oh, I particularly like this one. The man was found 'dead on the vine.'" Schultz looked at me. "All lies, I assume?"

I blew out a long breath. "No. All true. Unfortunately." I sank down into the leather chair in front of Schultz's desk.

"This is not good for business, Emmy."

"Tell me something I don't know, Gene," I shot back.

"Okay, how about this—the funding was a no-go."

My stomach dropped. "What do you mean?"

"I mean, this"—he gestured to the paper again—"is a huge deterrent to anyone looking to invest in a winery."

I licked my lips. "It's just a little bad press. It will blow over."

"Like a hurricane."

I cringed. He was right. My balance sheets were bad enough, but add "crime scene" to the winery description and even I wouldn't have wanted to invest in it. "Okay, so I'll just have to tighten the belt a little this season."

But Schultz was still shaking his head at me. "Honey, you're already wearing a corset."

"What does that mean?"

"It means there is no more tightening left. You're broke, Emmy."

I licked my lips. "You mean, we're nearly broke."

"No, kid, I mean you're there. You've been running in the red every month this year—"

"That's not my fault. The shutdown had our doors closed!"

"—and you know your margins were thin to being with."

I bit my lip. I did. "How broke are we?"

"*You,*" he said, putting a distinct emphasis on the pronoun, "have just enough left in your accounts to make payroll this month."

"One month? But I-I can't lay every one off like that." My mind immediately filled with images of Jean Luc and Eddie, who had become like my family. Not to mention Hector and Conchita, who had been fixtures at the winery for as long as I could remember. Heck, I'd been the flower girl at their wedding!

"Well, you can't continue to pay them either," Schultz argued. "Not unless they work for grapes."

I shook my head. "Okay, so what do we do?"

"You need cash, kid, and you need it quick."

"We have a couple of weddings booked at the end of the month," I said.

"You sure?" he asked, his eyes going down to the article. "No chance they'll cancel."

I licked my lips. "No. Probably not."

"And are you going to be able to book a couple more the next month?"

I glared at the tablet and sighed. "No. Probably not."

"I rest my case."

"Okay, so what about a small business loan?" I asked, not ready to give up yet.

"That depends. You have enough money to make the interest payments on a bank loan?"

"Apparently not," I mumbled. "Okay, so what then?"

Schultz gave me a long look. "If it were me, I'd seriously look at some of those offers you've had to buy the place."

My stomach clenched. Yes, we'd had a couple of offers. Both were from big corporate giants in the region who gobbled up little family wineries like ours and spit them out into generic, bargain priced wines. Grapes from a dozen or more small vineyards all mixed together so that the nuances of the different crops were completely lost. And the soul of Oak Valley would be lost right along with it.

I fought back fear clogging my throat.

"Not an option," I told him, jutting my chin out with defiance. "What else can we do?"

Schultz blew out a puff of air through his teeth. "You're as stubborn as your mother."

"Thank you."

"That was *not* a compliment." He narrowed his eyes at me. "Fine. If you don't want to sell—"

"I don't!"

"—and you don't want to close the winery doors—"

"I definitely don't!"

"—then you're going to need to get an infusion of cash from someone. You're going to need to take on a partner with deep pockets and a lot of faith."

"Partner?" That thought was almost as abhorrent as selling. "No, Oak Valley has always been family run and owned. I can't give up a part of that." I shook my head. "Have you tried looking for more corporate investors? There are tons of venture capital firms in Silicon Valley."

"Sure. And they all like to see balance sheets that have a lot less red than yours. Let's face it, as an investment, you're a losing proposition."

"But won't a partner see it the same way?" I asked, hearing the desperation in my voice.

Schultz shrugged. "Maybe. But I'd guess there are plenty of wealthy guys in the Bay Area who'd like to fancy themselves winery owners."

"*Part* owners."

"Sure." The way he waved that detail off didn't fill me with a lot of confidence about this plan. "Find someone who wants a hobby. Wants to see his name on wine labels. Who has a fat bank account and needs a little pet project."

My stomach twisted again at the thought of my family's legacy being someone's "pet" project.

"You sure we can't get a loan?" I tried again.

Schultz gave me a sympathetic look. "Emmy, I know you love Oak Valley. But you've got to face reality." He stepped out from behind his desk to put a hand on my shoulder. "This is the end of the line."

* * *

I left Schultz with my stomach so clenched it was in knots and a heck of a headache brewing. One month. Even if I could somehow manage to fully book the winery for wedding season, it wouldn't matter—we'd never last that long. As much as I hated the idea of giving up a portion of Oak Valley to a stranger who wanted to play weekend vintner, Schultz was right. I had no other options.

I tried not to dwell on that depressing thought as I drove back to Oak Valley. I was almost home when my phone rang, my mother's face coming up on the display.

"Hi, Mom," I said, putting her on speaker.

"Emmy, I'm so glad I caught you. Are you busy?"

"No, just on my way to the winery," I said, trying to infuse my voice with as much cheerfulness as I could force for her benefit. "Why? What's up?"

"It's happened again!"

"What's happened?" I asked, pulling off the main road and winding up the oak-lined driveway.

"Another theft!" She paused. "I did tell you about the thief here, right?"

"You did. The great Sonoma Acres caper."

"Emmy, I'm serious." I could tell by her tone that she was. I knew that tone. It had told me to clean my room and eat my veggies every day of my childhood.

"So, what was it this time?" I asked, parking in the lot. I averted my eyes from the police vehicles, trying not to telegraph through the phone that something was amiss here.

"Oscar Worthington's cat."

I frowned as I stepped from my Jeep, my heels crunching in the gravel. "I thought they didn't allow pets at the Acres?"

"They don't. I mean, it's not real. Well, it was real, but it's not anymore."

I bit my lip. "Mom, are you feeling okay today?"

"Yes, I'm fine." She took in a deep breath, a technique I knew her doctor had said helped ground her in the now. "What I mean is the cat is stuffed."

"So, a toy cat?"

"Oh, what do they call it? Taxidermy?"

"You mean he had his actual *pet* cat stuffed?" Ew.

"Well, after it died, of course. But, yes. Mrs. Pettigrew."

"Mrs. Pettigrew stuffed it?"

"No, the cat's name is Mrs. Pettigrew. Emmy, try to pay attention."

Believe me, I was. "Okay, so Oscar misplaced his stuffed pet cat, Mrs. Pettigrew."

"*Not* misplaced. It was stolen!" She said it with such aplomb that I expected a detective in a seersucker to appear.

"Who on earth would want Oscar's dead cat?"

"If we knew that, we'd know who the thief is." Her tone said I was still slow to catch on here.

"Mom, have you talked to any of the staff about this?" I asked, opening the doors to the main winery building and pushing inside. I ducked my head in the tasting room, but sadly Jean Luc was the only occupant, idly polishing glasses. I gave him a small wave before walking back down the hall toward the kitchen.

"Yes, I have talked to the staff. In fact, I marched Oscar right down to the administration office and helped him file a complaint."

"And what did they say?"

There was a pause on the other end. "That Oscar probably misplaced Mrs. Pettigrew," she admitted.

"Well, there you have it," I said, setting my purse down on the kitchen counter and opening the fridge. Which was depressingly bare. I hadn't had time to shop, and Conchita was still away. Ava was right. We might starve before she got home.

"Look, Emmy, I know you think we're just a bunch of old demented people."

"I don't think you're *old*."

"Ha. Ha," Mom said, though I could hear a hint of actual humor in her voice at my teasing. "But there really is someone stealing from residents here. And I know you don't think anyone would care about Mrs. Borstein's photos or Mable Marston's pillow or Mrs. Pettigrew. But the people here do. They don't have a lot, Emmy. These things have sentimental value."

I felt my heartstrings being pulled taut. Probably because my mother knew exactly where to pull from. "Fine. I will mention the thefts to Grant and see what he thinks."

"Thank you!"

"But I can't promise you that he can do anything," I hedged. "He's VCI. *Violent* Crimes Investigations. Missing taxidermy is hardly his forte." I didn't add that he was also busy investigating a homicide at our winery at current. But if Mom hadn't heard the news yet, I was not going to be the one to drop that on her. At least not until I could promise the person responsible was not still at large.

Speaking of which…

"Mom, I have to go," I told her, glancing at the large wine-barrel clock on the kitchen wall. "Ava's picking me up in a few minutes."

"Oh? Where are you off to?"

"Pedicures," I told her, leaving out the fact they were likely to go with a side of interrogation.

"Well, that sounds like a nice afternoon," she said, perking up. "Enjoy yourself. And don't forget to talk to your cop!"

"I won't," I told her, giving her a couple of phone kisses and a promise to visit again soon before hanging up.

CHAPTER FIVE

Nadia's Nails was located in a strip mall just off Jefferson in the heart of Napa. It was a small salon sandwiched between a yarn store and a bagel shop, with several signs out front offering discounted gels and mani-pedi specials. A bell rang over the door as Ava and I pushed inside, and a petite brunette greeted us from behind a tall front counter.

"Welcome to Nadia's Nails," she said in the same nasally voice I'd heard on the phone. "How can I help you today?"

"We called earlier to see Carmen," I said, giving the woman our names.

"Sure. Why don't you pick out your colors and I'll see if they have chairs ready for you," she said, gesturing to a wall of nail polish bottles to our right before disappearing deeper into the salon to ready our spots.

"I feel kind of bad," I told Ava, browsing the plethora of pink and red shades.

"Why?" she asked, grabbing a bottle of a sparkly purple color.

"The woman just lost someone close to her. And she's doing our nails."

Ava shot me a look. "Okay, this guilt thing? Not a cute look on you."

I grinned. "I just…"

"I know, I know. You have a big heart, and you feel bad about what happened. But it wasn't your fault."

I opened my mouth to protest, but she didn't let me.

"End of story. No more guilt." She paused, looking past me to the main room where the brunette was gesturing us in. "Now, let's go see if maybe it *was* the ex-wife's fault."

I followed her as we wound through half a dozen large pedicure chairs to two at the end with full bubbling footbaths in front of them. Once the brunette had settled us, two ladies emerged from the back room wearing black aprons and pushing little carts full of nail goodies. A younger blonde took up a spot in front of me, and a rounder, older woman with a head of obviously dyed red hair sat in front of Ava.

"I'm Penny," the blonde told me, a faint European accent in her voice.

"Emmy. Nice to meet you," I told her as she guided my feet into the tub of warm, bubbling water.

The older woman picked up Ava's bottle of "Plum Dream" nail polish.

"You're going with that color?" She looked like she'd smelled something foul, clearly betraying her thoughts on the color.

"Why?" Ava asked. "Not good?"

"Between you and me, honey, it's gonna make it look like you slammed all ten toes in a doorjamb." The faux redhead set the plum aside. "I see you as more of a peach color."

Ava shrugged. "Okay, I'll go with your recommendation..." She paused, looking down at the nametag on the woman's apron. "...Carmen." Ava shot me a meaningful look.

Carmen looked to be a few years older than Sheila and a few notches feistier. Her makeup was heavy, her midsection thick, and her own nails a hot pink that clashed with her bright red hair as she pulled it back into a knot at the nape of her neck.

"Peach Passion," Carmen said decisively. "Trust me, you'll look great."

"Thanks," Ava said, settling back in her chair. "Carmen Buckley... You wouldn't happen to be related to Bill Buckley, would you?"

The woman's hands froze for a split second, but it was long enough to see that the name had jarred her. "Used to be. I had the displeasure of being Bill's wife. Why, you know him?"

"Not personally," Ava said quickly. "But he worked for Emmy." She gestured to me.

"I own the winery where he..." I trailed off not sure how to delicately put it. "Uh, where he worked security. I'm so sorry for your loss," I told her.

Her gaze flickered away from Ava's submerged toes to me. "I appreciate the sentiment, but, believe me, it's no loss. World's a brighter place today."

"Carmen," Penny chided softly, shooting a concerned look my way.

"What? I should pretend to be sad the putz is dead?" Carmen shook her head. "Nothing doing."

"I take it things did not end well between you?" Ava asked, again shooting me one of those meaningful glances that said Charlie's most diligent Angel was on the case.

"Not in the least." Carmen motioned for Ava to put one of her feet up on a towel-covered pillow then began attacking her cuticles. "Things didn't start well between us, didn't go well in the middle years, and they sure as heck didn't end well."

"You shouldn't speak ill of the dead," Penny said, looking embarrassed.

"Please. I tell it like it is. I told that cop as much, too," Carmen said.

"Cop?" I asked. "The police have been to see you?" Which meant either Grant had been notifying even Buckley's ex-next-of-kin of his death personally or he'd also wondered how ugly the divorce had been between them.

Carmen nodded. "Yeah, some detective showed up at my front door before my shift started. Not a bad way to start the day though, I gotta say. He was some sugary sweet eye candy."

I felt my cheeks heat.

"I take it you mean Detective Grant," Ava said with a grin.

"Yeah, can't say I paid much attention to the name. But the booty on that guy? Now *that* I'd remember."

Ava stifled a laugh.

"I'd let him frisk me any day, if you know what I mean?" Carmen winked at Penny.

Penny blushed, keeping her attention on my toes.

"Uh, what did the detective want?" I asked.

Carmen shrugged. "Just told me Bill was dead. Wanted to know about his friends in the area. Family. That sort of thing."

"What did you tell him?" Ava asked.

"That he didn't have any. Family or friends. Like I said, Bill was a total putz, through and through." She glanced at me again. "I take it he didn't work for you long?"

"Actually, no. I just hired him a couple weeks ago."

"Yeah, I figured. Any longer than that and you would have realized what kind of guy he was." She cackled. "You heard about him bein' kicked off the force?" she asked me.

I nodded. "I heard he admitted to taking bribes?"

"That's right. Being paid to 'look the other way,'" she said, doing air quotes with her hot pink nails, "about an illegal business operating on his beat. What a moron." She shook her head.

"That's when you two split up?" Ava asked.

"Darn right! Like I was gonna stick around married to a dirty cop. Look, he had it all. A good job, a pension coming. Me!" She ran her hands up and down her body to encompass all of her assets. "Okay, so he wasn't the sharpest tool in the shed and he'd been passed up for detective a few times, but he had a nice, steady job. Then he had to go screw the whole thing up. Can you believe it? How dumb is that guy?"

"Very," Penny mumbled. Clearly this wasn't the first time she'd heard this particular rant.

"Not, mind you," Carmen said, waving a pair of nail clippers in her right hand, " that I hated the idea of a little cash on the side. Hey, if someone was offerin', I'd a taken it too. But *I* wouldn't have gotten caught. Moron."

"How *did* he get caught?" Ava asked, wincing only slightly at how vigorous her pedicure was getting the more worked up Carmen got talking about her ex.

"Dumb luck. Seemed the only kind that Bill had." She chuckled at her own joke. "Some off-duty officer saw Bill getting paid off. Brought IA into it, and it was all downhill from there."

"I understand Bill cooperated with the authorities, though?" I put in. "Agreed to forgo his pension and retire quietly from the force."

"Without even consulting me!" She threw her hands up, splashing droplets of water on Penny.

"He didn't tell you about the investigation?"

"Well, he had little choice but to come clean about that. But that pension was supposed to be for both of us. I was counting on that for my retirement too, you know. Then he goes and blows it. And where did all that bribery money go, I ask you?"

I shook my head. I hadn't even thought to ask that question. "I don't know."

"Yeah, me neither. It's not like he lavished any of it on his darling wife, that I can tell ya."

"So, you think he still had it?" Ava asked, eyes cutting to me.

"I do. And I had my divorce lawyer looking high and low for it. Never found a freakin' dime though." She leaned down, grabbing a small bottle of peach colored nail polish from her cart and shaking it. "That jerk was sitting on a pile of dirty money, squirreled away, and had the nerve to be behind on his alimony payments to me."

"Internal Affairs never found the money either?" I asked.

"Nah. They asked, but Bill told them he spent it all." Carmen started applying color to Ava's toenails.

"You think he was lying?" Ava said, eying her toes.

Carmen nodded. "Absolutely. Bill never came home with no fancy clothes, no cars, no watches. We lived like paupers, for crying out loud. I tell you, if he spent it, it was on thin air."

I thought about the place Buckley had been living with Sheila. It hadn't looked like he'd been spending it on her either. Then again, if he'd lied to IA, he'd want to make sure he was well off the police's radar before dipping into his ill-gotten fund.

"Speaking of money," I said, "I actually have Buckley's last check that should go to someone. Do you know who his heir might be?"

"Heir?" Carmen threw her head back and laughed. "Well, la-di-da, doesn't that sound fancy." Then she paused, narrowing her eyes shrewdly at me. "How big is the check?"

"Not that big," I conceded. "But it rightfully belongs to someone."

Carmen clicked her teeth, still eyeing me. "With all the alimony he owed me, I'd say it should go to me."

I bit my lip, hesitant to commit to that. While she might have a point about being owed something, I was pretty sure there was a legal channel for all of this. "Do you know if Buckley had a will? Or a lawyer?"

She shrugged. "Barry Levinson was his divorce attorney," she offered. "Little weasel of a man. I wouldn't be surprised if someone decided to shoot him one day too."

"Carmen," Penny chided under her breath again. She shot me an apologetic smile as she opened the bottle of rose colored polish I'd chosen.

But Carmen just shrugged. "Just saying. The world could do with a few less lawyers, right?"

I figured it was a rhetorical question, so I didn't bother answering. Neither did Penny, her eyes firmly on my toes.

"I'm curious," Ava said, her voice taking on a deceptively innocent tone. "Did the police ask you where you were last night?"

Carmen looked up at her and gave a smirk. "You mean where I was when Bill was killed?"

"I didn't mean to insinuate—" Ava started to backpedal.

But Carmen waved her concerns off. "Look, I might have dreamed of ending his miserable little life fifty different ways. But I didn't shoot the guy." She paused, a cold look suddenly coming over her eyes. "Pity. I'm sure whoever did felt immense satisfaction when they pulled that trigger."

For a second she looked like she might be fantasizing about the scene, her eyes on the blank wall above our heads as her mouth curved up into a creepy smile.

I felt a chill run up my spine, thinking I could easily imagine her doing it as well.

"Any idea who might have wanted to?" Ava pressed. "Pull the trigger, so to speak?"

Carmen shook her head, as if shaking herself out of her murderous thoughts. "Well, he made enemies of pretty much the entire SFPD. His partner, his captain, IA, heck, even his own lawyer wanted to strangle the guy at one point. Bill just had a knack for making friends."

His girlfriend had said much the same thing, even if she hadn't been quite so blunt about it.

"But I was at Horatio's, if you wanna know," Carmen said, finishing Ava's last baby toenail and capping the bottle. "That Italian place on 1st?"

"I've been there," Ava said. "Great pasta."

"I wouldn't know. Never made it past drinks."

"What happened?" I asked.

"Got stood up. Can you believe it?" She shook her head. "Sitting there waiting at the bar for an hour for this guy to show."

"The one from online?" Penny asked. "With the yorkie?"

Carmen nodded.

"Bummer. His pictures were cute. So was his dog."

"Probably all fake," Carmen said, fanning Ava's toes. "Men, they're all putzes."

Penny shrugged, finishing off the last of my toenails.

"Do you know Buckley's girlfriend?" Ava asked. "Sheila?"

Carmen shook her head. "The current one? Not really. I mean, I've met her. Anytime Bill wanted to try duckin' my alimony payments, he'd have her say he wasn't home."

"Was he really behind?" Penny asked.

Carmen nodded. "Always. Ever since the divorce, he's been dead broke. I was the glue holding that poop-show together." She cackled again at her own joke before turning to Ava. "Why do you want to know about Sheila?"

Ava shrugged. "Just curious what their relationship was like."

Carmen shook her head. "You mean, did she finally get fed up enough with him to kill him?"

"No, I—"

"Relax. I'm joking." Carmen laughed again. "No, Sheila's a doormat. She'd put up with anything Bill did. Or anyone."

"Wait—you mean Bill was unfaithful to her?"

Carmen shrugged. "I don't know. One can only assume. I mean, a leopard don't change his spots."

"You're saying he was unfaithful to *you*," I clarified.

"Why do you think we broke up?"

"I thought it was over the bribery scandal," Ava said.

"Well, sure. But I guess you don't know who he was taking bribes from, huh?"

She glanced at Penny, and I got the feeling the poor girl had heard this story several times before too.

"No," Ava admitted. "Who was he taking them from?"

"Katy Kline," she said, dropping the name like it was a bombshell.

Unfortunately, it was a dud, as I was drawing a blank. I looked to Ava, who seemed as clueless as I was. "Who is Katy Kline?"

"The famous madame?" Carmen said, trying to jog our memories.

"Madame? As in…"

"As in she ran a high priced escort service," Carmen said. "She was all over the papers a couple of years ago when the police raided her place and arrested her."

"I guess I missed that," I mumbled.

"Yeah, well, it was Bill's testimony to IA that took her down."

"So, Katy was the one bribing Bill?"

Carmen nodded. "She'd slip him a little a cash on the side to make sure he looked the other way about her business." She paused. "Only, I come to find out that not *all* of Bill's payments came in the form of cash, if you know what I mean."

Unfortunately, I did. So did Penny, as I could see her blushing so hard she matched my pink nail polish.

"Yeah," Carmen said, helping Ava slip her chunky sandals back on, "like I said, he was a first rate putz. Good riddance."

* * *

"If I ever get that bitter, please push me off a cliff or something," Ava said as we left Nadia's Nails.

I stifled a laugh. "If I ever contemplate marrying someone like Buckley, push *me* off a cliff."

"He doesn't seem like he was the most stand-up guy, does he?"

I shook my head, frowning. "Apparently, I'm not the best judge of character."

"Don't be so hard on yourself. You were hiring him as a security guard—not looking at him as a potential suitor."

"Still." I shook my head. "Okay, so the ex-wife clearly wasn't a fan."

"You think?" Ava laughed. "What was that line about immense satisfaction from pulling the trigger?"

"Downright chilling. I hope Penny never gets on her bad side."

"Carmen was right about one thing, though," Ava said as we got into her GTO.

"What's that?"

"The peach does look really cute." She wiggled her toes in her sandals.

I looked down. "Agreed. But just because she knows her colors, that doesn't mean she didn't also kill her ex-husband."

"Her alibi was pretty thin," Ava agreed, tucking her purse down at her feet before turning on the car.

"Emaciated," I agreed.

"I mean, she was alone at the bar."

I nodded. "And we only have her word for it that she was supposed to meet anyone at all."

"So maybe she made up a fake date, goes to the bar and orders a drink to establish some alibi, then she drives to Oak Valley and shoots Buckley. Why?"

I bit my lip. "The satisfaction of pulling the trigger?" I quoted.

Ava shrugged, backing out of the lot. "I dunno. I mean, why not kill him when she found out he was sleeping with prostitutes two years ago? Why now?"

"Great question," I conceded. "Money? The bribery cash she never saw? Or the back alimony payments he owed her?"

"I can see her being angry about that, but why shoot him? I mean, he's not gonna catch up on payments now, is he?"

"No." I looked out the window, watching the storefronts of downtown give way to sprawling oaks and green fields full of ripening grapes in the early afternoon sunshine. "Okay, here's an idea—what about the madame?"

"The supposedly infamous Katy Kline," Ava said.

"Carmen said it was Buckley's testimony that led to her arrest. Maybe she wanted to get back at Buckley."

Ava took a beat to think about that one before nodding. "I suppose it's possible. Carmen made it sound like we should know who she is, but I've never heard of her before. You?"

I shook my head. "I'll admit, I don't follow the news that closely though." I pulled out my phone, googling the name as Ava jumped on the 12 toward Oak Valley. Several sites came up, most of them news outlets covering the madame's arrest in San Francisco two years ago. I clicked the first link, reading out loud to Ava as she drove.

"It says here Katy Kline was running an escort service out of her brother's butcher shop."

"Eww. I can think of nowhere *less* amorous than a room full of animal carcasses. Let's hope they didn't actually…you know…do *business* there."

I scrunched up my nose, trying to get that picture out of my head. "The article says she was arrested after her name came up in connection with another investigation."

"The investigation into Buckley," Ava supplied.

"It doesn't say here. But if the police were trying to keep the whole bribery thing quiet, I doubt it would."

"What else does it say?" Ava asked, eyes flickering momentarily from the windshield to my phone.

"She apparently had a network of over a dozen girls working for her."

"Wow. I wonder what happened to them."

"Doesn't say here." I hit the back button, trying a different link to another new story. "This one says she 'cooperated with police' for a reduced sentence. She pled guilty and was sentenced to four years in prison."

"Ouch. That's reduced?"

"I guess." I glanced up at her. "Why? Is that a lot?"

Ava shook her head. "I don't know. But it's not like she killed anyone—she just charged for a little something-something."

"Which is illegal," I pointed out.

"Did the guys who paid for it get arrested? Did Buckley? Why is it always the woman who gets the short end, huh? And guys like Buckley go free."

"Well, don't feel too bad for her," I said, scrolling down another article. This one dated much more recently. "She's not serving all four years. In fact, she's not serving any time at all anymore. Katy Kline was let out on parole."

Ava's eyebrows rose. "Now we're getting somewhere. When?"

"Two months ago."

"Interesting timing!" Ava made a right, pulling off the main road toward Oak Valley Vineyards. "Okay, so Katy's paroled, tracks down Buckley, finds him working at your winery, and kills him out of revenge for ratting her out."

"I could see that." I shook my head. "Why do it at my winery? Why couldn't the killer have tracked him down somewhere else?"

"Really. I'd wager it wouldn't have been the first homicide Shady Meadows has ever seen," Ava said, pulling up the long winding drive toward Oak Valley.

Only, as she did, someone came barreling down the driveway, the roar of a motorcycle hitting my ears a split second before the flash of chrome and steel came into my vision.

Coming down the center of the road at terrifying speeds.

Right toward us.

CHAPTER SIX

"Look out!" I screamed, my fingers instinctively grabbing at the dashboard.

"Holy crap!" Ava swerved, the car jerking to the right on the wide bend.

My body slammed against the side of the car, my head connecting painfully with the window. Then I flopped to the left, as Ava struggled to regain control of the fishtailing car. She came precariously close to one of the hundred year old oak trees lining the drive, the bumper kissing the bark as she swerved again.

I heard the motorcycle fly past us, the engine growling menacingly, as the driver narrowly missed Ava's GTO. While he was going fast enough to be a blur as he passed us, I spun in my seat to get a look at him out the rear window and caught the image of a skull and a red rose on the back of his black leather jacket before he disappeared from sight.

"Holy crap, holy crap, holy crap," Ava chanted beside me as she finally regained control of the swerving vehicle. "That guy could have killed us!"

"That *guy* was Jamie Connolly!"

"Who?" Ava asked, coming to the top of the drive and slowly easing her car into a parking space in the lot.

"Sheila Connolly's son," I reminded her.

Ava frowned as she shut off the engine. "Are you sure?"

"He was wearing the same leather jacket I saw on the kid at Sheila's this morning."

Ava slowly pried her hands off the steering wheel, and I could see that they were shaking. I didn't blame her. My entire body felt a little unsteady, not to mention my head was suddenly throbbing.

"Well, Sheila needs to give him a few tips on road safety," Ava said.

"Among other things," I mumbled getting out of the car and leading the way toward the main winery buildings. "What do you think he was doing here?"

"Great question," she said as she followed me inside. "One I think we should discuss over a steadying glass of wine?"

"Agreed." It was close enough to happy hour.

Unfortunately, it was also nearly empty in my tasting room. Just one person sat at the bar with his back to us, chatting amiably with Jean Luc. The lack of patrons immediately served to remind me of the conversation I'd had with Schultz that afternoon. I tried to shove it to the back of my mind as I made my way to the bar.

Where I quickly realized the one "customer" was not actually a paying one.

"There's my Ems," David Allen said, spinning to face us as Ava and I took the empty barstools beside him. "And the lovely Ava. Where have you two ladies been?"

"Getting pedicures," Ava told him, holding out her foot and wiggling her peachy toes as evidence.

David gave her a raised eyebrow. "I see our mood has lightened considerably since this morning."

"We were at Nadia's Nails in Napa," Ava explained. "Buckley's ex-wife works there."

"Ah," David said sagely. "So we did conduct some interrogations."

"Conversation," I corrected as Jean Luc silently poured Ava and me two glasses of our house Chardonnay. I nodded a thank-you, and he stepped away to clean some already clean glasses at the end of the bar, where he wouldn't look like he was eavesdropping, as Ava quickly filled David in on what we'd learned that day.

"Carmen Buckley definitely had motive and opportunity," Ava ended with.

"So we think the ex-wife was so angry she showed up here with a gun?" David asked, sipping his wine.

"Possibly," Ava said. "I mean, I could totally see her shooting him and walking away happy as a clam."

"She all but told us she would," I said. "In fact, I think she was even daydreaming about it."

David swirled his wine in his glass, making it tear pleasingly down the sides. "I don't see what she'd have to gain from killing him, though."

"Satisfaction of revenge?" Ava tried on.

"Possibly. But if we're talking revenge, I feel like the madame has a bigger grudge."

"Katy Kline. And that's true," Ava conceded. "Thanks to Buckley, she spent two years in jail."

"Well, to be fair, it was thanks to her illegal business," I noted.

Ava scoffed and turned to David. "You think it's fair that she was sentenced to jail for four years just for supplying a service?"

"Not in the least," he said, the corner of his lip curling upward. "Sounds like a lovely service. In fact I—"

"Stop." I put my hands up. "I don't want to hear anymore."

David's grin widened. "I was going to say I fully support a woman's right to make a living however she sees fit."

I shot him a look. I'd bet money I didn't have that was *not* what he'd been about to say.

"Anyway," I went on, "there's also another person who didn't get along with Buckley."

"Oh?" David asked, sipping at his Chardonnay again.

I nodded. "His girlfriend's son. Jamie Connolly."

"A kid?" David frowned. "That's very *Bad Seed*."

"He's a teenager," Ava explained.

"Late teens, if I had to guess," I added.

"And he almost ran us off the road with his motorcycle just now," Ava said.

Jean Luc, who had clearly been pretending not to listen until then, gasped. "Off zee road?

David frowned. "What happened?"

Ava quickly relayed the encounter we'd had on the winding driveway.

"What was 'e even doing 'ere?" Jean Luc asked, all pretense at minding his own business abandoned.

"That's what I'd like to know," I said. "He didn't come inside?"

Jean Luc shook his head. "I would 'ave thrown 'im out if 'e did. Twenty-one and over."

"You said he had dark hair. Leather jacket?" David asked, still frowning.

I nodded. "Yes. Why?"

"I think I might have seen him."

We all turned in his direction.

"When I pulled in," David explained. "There was someone standing just out there. In the vineyard." He nodded toward the picture window.

"What was he doing?" I asked.

David shrugged. "Honestly, just standing there. I figured he was some morbid curiosity seeker, you know? Read about the shooting and wanted to get a look at the crime scene."

"Or he was returning to the scene of his own crime," Ava suggested. She swiveled on her stool to face me. "You remember Sheila said she was waiting for Jamie to come home when Buckley died?"

I nodded. "Yeah. He told her he'd been 'out.'"

"Maybe 'out' killing his mom's overbearing boyfriend."

"I don't know. You really think a kid would do that?" David asked.

"You didn't see this *kid,*" Ava told him. "Lots of leather, fast motorcycle, mouthy."

"Sounds like you just described *my* teenage years." David grinned.

I tried to picture him as a rebellious teenager. Which wasn't that hard since he was currently a rebellious thirty-something who dressed like a teenager. His jeans had holes at the knees, his black T-shirt featured some band I didn't know, and his black boots looked like exactly the kind one would wear while riding on a motorcycle like the one that had nearly run us off the road. Even if I knew for a fact that David drove his mother's old Rolls Royce and not a shiny chrome death machine.

"Teenagers can be impulsive," I noted. "Sheila said Buckley and Jamie clashed. Maybe they clashed hard enough that Jamie decided to get rid of the guy once and for all."

"Maybe they argued over something before Buckley came to work that day," Ava suggested. "Something important enough that Jamie lost it."

"Still." David shrugged. "Offing your stepfather would be pretty cold."

I paused, knowing he wasn't just talking about Jamie. I'd first met David when *his* stepfather had died in my cellar. There'd even been a point where I'd suspected David might have had something to do with it. While it had come out that someone else entirely had done his stepfather in, that didn't mean David hadn't still had ample reason to have wanted to do it himself.

"Sheila and Buckley weren't married," Ava noted. "So, not stepfather. Yet."

"Maybe he wanted to keep it that way," I added.

"Or maybe he feels completely broken up at the death of someone close to him and wanted to come see where Buckley spent his last moments," David said, playing devil's advocate. "Teens have feelings too, you know."

I pursed my lips together, suddenly feeling insensitive. "You're right."

"Could you say that a little louder, my dear?" David put a hand behind his ear and grinned teasingly at me.

"So how did your poker game go?" I asked, changing the subject. Lest I had to admit he was right twice.

"Just the way I'd hoped." David's grin grew.

"So you beat Mr. Gallery Owner?" Ava asked.

David nodded. "I let him win a couple of early rounds, but in the end, I walked away with a guaranteed space for a dozen pieces at the showing."

"Wow, nicely done," Ava said, raising her glass in a salute.

"Do you have that many paintings ready?" I asked.

David shrugged. "Almost. I'm putting the finishing touches on a couple, and I've got another one that I think I can finish in time. If enough inspiration strikes."

"Well, if you ever need a muse, I hire out by the hour," Ava joked, giving him a mock curtsey.

"Careful," David said with a grin. "You can get arrested for that. Just ask Katy Kline."

I was about to point out the differences between *madame* and *muse* when my phone trilled from my purse. I pulled it out to see Grant's name flashing across the screen.

"Hey," I said, after swiping to take the call.

"Hey, yourself" came Grant's deep voice. "You at the winery?"

"I am," I told him, stepping away to the relative privacy at the back of the room. "Why?"

"I was just about to head up that way to release the crime scene."

I cringed at my winery being referred to that way, but the word "release" was a good sign. "I take it that means CSI is done?"

"They are. They're just packing up now."

I glanced out the window to see the truth of that statement—the van that had been sitting in my parking lot all day was finally pulling down the drive.

"Anyway, I wanted to see if you were free for dinner," Grant went on.

"You mean, wanted to see if I'd cook you dinner?" I asked, grinning.

Grant laughed. "Guilty as charged. But, if you're busy, I could pick something up on the way?"

"Not busy," I said, glancing back at Ava and David at the bar. "But I am sorely low on supplies. Conchita's still away, and I haven't had a chance to go shopping."

"Tell you what," Grant said. "Text me a list, and I'll pick up whatever you need on my way over."

"Done," I said, already mentally going over dinner options. Cooking was an activity that always had a calming effect on me, and after the last couple of days, I could use some calm. Not to mention, the company wouldn't be bad either.

"Great, I'll see you soon," Grant said before hanging up.

I slipped my phone into my pocket as I rejoined my friends.

"Everything okay?" Ava asked.

I nodded. "That was Grant. He's releasing the crime scene, and I'm cooking him dinner."

David gave me a raised eyebrow. "I take it that's our cue to leave?"

I shook my head and drained the last dribbles of Chardonnay from my glass. "Not at all. Feel free to stay and drink." I gave him a pointed look. "Here. Not with us."

David chuckled, though it had a bit of a self-deprecating edge. "I wouldn't dream of crashing your date, Ems."

"Good," Ava joked. "Because she wouldn't dream of inviting you." She turned to me. "But I do expect all the details in the morning," she said with a twinkle in her eyes.

"Sorry, kids," I told them, slinging my purse over my shoulder as I made my way across the room. "I don't cook and tell."

* * *

After mentally going through several recipes, I settled on texting Grant the ingredients to make Creamy Pork Marsala. I already had garlic and onion, so I chopped those, along with some baby lettuce and field greens, to make a nice accompanying side salad and then made my way down the stone pathway to the cellar to pull a bottle of Pinot Noir while I waited for him to arrive.

My grandmother and namesake, the first Emmeline Oak, had long ago dubbed our underground cellar The Cave. Which, in reality, it pretty much was, dug deep into the cool earth to house our most precious commodities—the Pinot Noir, Chardonnay, Pinot Blanc, Zinfandel, and a few cases of a small run Petite Sirah that bore the Oak Valley Vineyards label. I tried not to let bittersweet feelings intrude as I grabbed a bottle of Pinot from one of the hand-made wooden racks. It might be among the last bottles to bear that label. Even if I could find a partner to help with our financial situation, as Schultz had said, he'd likely come with strings attached—like putting his own name on our labels. Or doing away with the old cellar altogether in favor of some temperature-controlled smart cellar he could control with an app.

Of course, having to sell Oak Valley would be worse.

Both options made my chest feel heavy. I'd not only let my employees down, but also the generations of Oaks who had kept the winery going for years before me. Of course, they hadn't had to contend with social media, the internet, and cheap bargain wines with catchy names like Nifty Dollar Fifty.

I turned off the lights and shut the cellar door, hoping to shut down the internal voice calling me a failure along with it.

As I made my way back to the kitchen, the sun was sinking below the horizon, bathing the entire valley in soft hues of gold and pink. Long shadows of the oak trees spanned across the meadow, and the fragrant scent of grapes that had been baking all day in the warm spring sunshine wafted toward me on a light breeze. I drank it all in, letting the natural beauty and serenity of the place fill me.

"There you are."

Grant's voice intruded into my mini meditation, and I turned to find him silhouetted in the kitchen doorway.

"Hey," I said, quickly crossing to him and giving him a light peck on the cheek. "Sorry. I was just grabbing something to go with the pork."

Grant grinned down at me. "That is definitely not something to be sorry about." He led the way back into the kitchen, pulling a pair of wineglasses down from the cupboard. He'd been in the large commercial kitchen attached to the winery enough times that he knew his way around it well. It gave me a warm feeling that he felt so at home there.

"So, how was your day?" he asked. He grabbed a corkscrew and opened the wine while I peeked in the grocery bag he'd deposited on my countertops.

"Good." I pulled out a pair of pork chops and some heavy cream. "Busy."

"Oh?" Grant asked. "Doing what?"

I paused. "Ava and I got pedicures," I told him honestly.

He glanced down at my pink-painted toes. Bare now, as I'd long ago kicked off my heels, having been at their mercy for the last two days.

"Very nice," he said, handing me a glass of Pinot Noir as he nodded approvingly. "Glad you were able to relax a little today."

I sipped my wine to cover the guilt at not being completely forthright about my activities that day. Not that I had to hide them. I could go wherever I wanted and talk to whomever I pleased. I just wasn't sure Grant would be totally thrilled with those wheres and whos, and who wanted to argue before the main course?

I grabbed a pan and added olive oil, letting it heat slightly before adding the pork chops.

"So, our vineyard is now free of the police presence?" I asked, pulling some sliced mushrooms from his grocery bag.

"The crime scene techs are done," he answered, leaning over my shoulder to peer at the sizzling chops in the pan. "They got all they could from the vineyard. But I'm leaving an officer on the grounds for tonight."

"Why?" I asked, spinning to face him.

His expression gave nothing away. "I'd feel better having someone here."

I bit my lip. Meaning he was afraid someone with not-so-nice intentions was still out there. Or, more accurately, might end up here. I involuntarily swallowed. "You didn't find anything to indicate that I was…that someone might come back to…"

"No," Grant said quickly. He took a step toward me, closing the gap between us. "We have found no indications that you specifically were targeted."

I nodded, letting out a breath I hadn't realized I'd been holding. "Good."

"For all we know," he went on, "this was just a random trespasser."

"Did you find any evidence of random trespassers? Like, any broken fences or anything?"

He shook his head slowly. "No, but that doesn't necessarily mean they didn't just walk onto the property."

"It also doesn't mean Buckley's death was random and not intentional. And deliberate."

Grant frowned. "Do you know something, Emmy?"

"No." I strategically turned my back to him, chopping some parsley for a garnish.

"Uh-huh."

"It's just that...well, Buckley wasn't really well liked," I said, wishing my voice sounded more casual than it did.

"I thought you said he seemed fine to you."

"Well, he did. To me. But I didn't know him well."

"But you've been talking to people who did," Grant said slowly, reading between the lines.

I sighed. I should have known I couldn't put one past the detective.

"Okay, fine," I admitted as I flipped the chops in the pan. "Yes. I have been talking to some people."

"Emmy..." Grant started.

But I didn't let him finish. "I wanted to give my condolences to his girlfriend. It was the least I could do."

Grant's features softened some. "Understandable."

"And I needed to know where to send his last check, so I might have visited his ex-wife."

"Uh-huh," he said, soundly a little less understanding.

"And his girlfriend's son showed up here, joy riding on his motorcycle."

"Emmy..."

"And did you know," I said, not letting him follow through with the warning I could clearly hear in that one word, "that Buckley was *forced* to retire from being a police officer?"

"Emmy!" This time it wasn't so much a warning as a threat.

I clamped my mouth shut. "What? Just saying. If anyone was targeted here, it's more likely Buckley than me."

Grant took a long sip from his wineglass and swallowed slowly. If I had to guess, I'd say he was employing some counting-to-ten anger management routine before he responded. "Emmy, I know you feel involved."

"Of course I do," I said hotly. "A man died at *my* winery."

"*Again*," he noted. No amusement in the word whatsoever.

"Not my fault," I said, pointing a spatula his way before I removed the pork from the pan and tossed in garlic, onions, and mushrooms.

"No, not your fault. But I want you to leave this to me."

"We all have things we want in life," I told him, finishing off the sauce with wine and cream. "That doesn't mean we're going to get them." I gave him a playful grin, trying to lighten the mood.

"Clearly," Grant mumbled as I scooped the pork chops and creamy Marsala sauce onto a plate and set it in front of him.

"Look, I just think it bears looking into is all," I said, taking the stool beside him with my plate as well.

"I promise you, I am looking into Buckley's death."

I swiveled to face him. "I know you are," I said, meaning it. What I was worried about was that he might not be looking in the right places. "But did you know that Buckley was caught taking bribes from a madame to keep quiet about her business?"

"Yeah." He shoved a bite of pork and mushroom into his mouth, chomping down hard. "I know all about the bribery. I was there."

I frowned. "What do you mean you were there? Like…when it happened?"

He nodded, eyes on his plate.

"You mean you were in San Francisco, right? Like, not as in there-there when Buckley was actually taking bribes?"

Grant let out a long breath through his nostrils, still not making eye contact. "I mean, I was working out of the same station as Buckley at the time."

"Wait—are you saying you knew Buckley?" I asked, trying to wrap my head around this news.

"Sort of."

"How do you *sort of* know someone?" I set my fork down, all attention on Grant. Or I should say, on his profile, as he still wasn't looking at me. "Either you do or you don't."

"Okay, fine. I met Buckley. Once or twice. Through his partner." The words came in short spurts, as if doling out as little info at a time as possible.

"Why didn't you say something?" I asked.

"Like what?" He stabbed at his salad.

"Look at me." A weird sensation bubbled up inside of me. It felt uneasy. Unsure.

Grant let out another long breath before his eyes slowly rose to meet mine. But when they did, their dark depths were completely void of any emotion, the little gold flecks giving nothing away. His entire expression was an unreadable blank.

"Why didn't you tell me you knew Buckley last night when I found him?"

"It didn't seem relevant."

"It didn't seem…" I trailed off, shaking my head. "There was a *dead man* in my vineyard, and you pretended you knew nothing about him!"

"I never said I didn't know who he was," Grant protested. Which was true enough but did nothing to chase that growing unease from my belly.

"You were asking me all kinds of questions about him," I said, reliving the conversation in my head.

"I wanted to know what you knew about him."

"So this was about questioning *me?*" My voice started to rise again, only this time the emotion behind it was anger and not guilt. Whatever I might have held back from Grant, apparently, he'd been holding back a whole lot more.

Grant sighed, his eyes going out the dark window to the rows of grapes where Buckley had been found. "Not *you* specifically. It was more about what he was telling people here. In Sonoma."

"So do you think his death has something to do with his former life as a police officer?"

"No," Grant said quickly.

Too quickly.

And his eyes were back on his plate again as if my pork Marsala was the most interesting thing he'd ever tasted.

"What do you know about Katy Kline?" I asked.

"Nothing." He shoved a bite into his mouth, as if looking for an excuse not to say more.

"She was the madame Buckley was taking bribes from," I said, trying to jog his memory.

"I know."

"Did you know she's out on parole now?"

He paused mid-chew, which indicated he had in fact *not* known that. Score one for the inquisitive blonde. But he quickly recovered, stabbing another piece of pork with his fork. "Who told you that?"

"Google." I shot him a *duh* look.

He chuckled and shook his head. "Should have guessed."

"But Buckley's ex-wife seems to think Buckley still had the bribery money hidden away somewhere."

"His ex-wife is a nutcase."

"So you knew her too?" That unease was back.

Grant's eyes flickered to mine before he answered, and I had the distinct feeling he was carefully crafting his response. "Met her once. After the case broke."

"But she could be right," I pressed. "I mean, no one ever found the bribery money, right?"

"Buckley told IA he spent it."

"And you believe that?"

Grant shrugged. "IA believed him."

"You said you knew Buckley's partner?" I asked slowly, picking my fork back up.

Grant nodded. "Mason Eckhart. We came up together as rookies."

"So you were close?"

Grant shrugged. "Used to be. Haven't talked to him in a while."

"What did Eckhart think of Buckley?"

"Not a fan," Grant said decisively.

"Oh?"

"Look, when IA started investigating Buckley, as his partner, Eckhart got dragged into the whole mess too. He didn't deserve that."

I pursed my lips. Grant had been the subject of an Internal Affairs investigation himself, and I could see the memory of that coloring his defense of Eckhart.

Grant had only ever shared the broad strokes of what had happened in San Francisco to prompt his transfer. I knew there'd been an arrest gone wrong and a fatal shooting, the circumstances of which had been murky enough that IA had gotten involved. So involved that when it was all over, Grant was in the comparatively sleepy Sonoma County, a distinct demotion from SFPD. Who had been shot and what the specifics were was something Grant had yet to share with me. And possibly never would. I could tell it was a subject that bothered him. I could tell that not only did he feel a hint of humiliation at being investigated by his own kind, but I'd also seen the guilt in his eyes when he'd talked about the death, even if he had, in the end, officially been cleared of any wrongdoing.

"Did Internal Affairs think Eckhart was taking bribes too?" I asked.

"He was Buckley's partner. They had to investigate. And Eckhart was benched while they did."

"But didn't Buckley cooperate? Confess to everything?"

Grant nodded. "He did. But even after he said he'd acted alone and Eckhart knew nothing, it was too late. Eckhart's reputation was tarnished."

"How so?" I asked, frowning. "I mean, Eckhart didn't know anything about it, right?"

"Sure. But how is he ever going to make detective when the guy doesn't even realize his partner is taking bribes right under his nose?"

"Good point." I nodded. "It does make him seem a little oblivious."

"Eckhart is a good guy," Grant said again.

"Sure." I pushed food around on my plate with my fork. "But I guess he'd have a good reason to hold a bit of a grudge against Buckley, huh? I mean, if Buckley really did tank his career?"

Grant shot me a look. "Don't."

"What?" I blinked in mock-innocence.

"Don't get involved."

"This feels like old territory. Once again, he died at my winery. I'm involved, like it or not."

"Yeah, well, don't involve Eckhart. He's one of the good guys."

While I could tell Grant believed that, I could also feel myself coming up against the blue wall of silence. Eckhart was a fellow officer—one apparently Grant had known for a long time.

And while I admired Grant's loyalty, I wasn't as sure as he was that it wasn't clouding his vision a little.

But since I didn't want to ruin dinner, I let it go. "So, I talked to my mom today," I told him.

"How's she doing?" While Grant had yet to meet her, he knew about her condition and living situation.

"She's doing well." I nodded. "Seems like she's having more good days than bad this month, so that's a plus."

"Cheers to that." Grant raised his glass before taking a sip.

"She did have a little favor to ask of you though," I said, watching him out of the corner of my eye.

"Me?" His eyebrows rose into his dark hair.

I nodded. "Apparently she—and some of the other residents at Sonoma Acres—are convinced there is a thief among them."

Grant grinned, some of his natural humor back now that we'd moved on to a less tense subject. "Oh, do tell."

"Well, a few things have gone missing."

"Could they just be misplaced?"

"That is exactly what I asked," I said. "But Mom is insistent there's malice behind it."

"Sounds like Mom's been watching too much TV."

I grinned. "She does have kind of an addiction to *Law & Order* reruns."

"Okay, so what kind of things are we talking?" Grant asked, picking up his wineglass again.

"Well, there was a picture in a frame. A needlework pillow…and a cat."

"A cat? That's hard to misplace." Grant took a sip of wine.

"Well, it was a dead cat."

Grant choked on his Pinot. "Excuse me?"

"Dead and stuffed."

He wrinkled up his nose in disgust.

"I know," I told him. "I'm with you. But apparently there is a deep sentimental attachment to Mrs. Pettigrew, which didn't end at death."

Grant laughed, shaking his head. "God, I hope I'm not that weird when I'm old."

"Everyone gets weird when they're old," I informed him. "They've earned the right."

Grant chuckled again. "Okay, so who does your mother think stole the stuffed cat?"

I shrugged. "She didn't know. But she was hoping…" I trailed off, giving him a pleading look.

Grant stopped chuckling. "Oh no. No, I'm not tracking down some guy's dead cat."

"I know," I said, holding up a hand. "You're busy. But maybe you could just send someone over there? Just to look around? Make sure this really is just a case of a few misplaced items?"

Grant let out a long breath. "Sounds like a waste of police resources."

"It would make my mom really happy," I said, giving him a big smile.

The corner of his mouth curved up slowly. "Fine. For Mom," he added.

"Thank you." I leaned over and gave him a kiss on the lips. Which lingered just long enough that my hormones started to stir.

"Hmm…" Grant moaned as I pulled back. "You know what you could do to *really* thank me?" he teased, his eyes going dark and bedroomy.

I gave him a playful swat on the arm. "Finish your dinner."

"Yes ma'am," he said, his eyes still crinkling and glinting with a teasing light. "But I'm definitely saving room for dessert."

Oh boy. Those hormones were suddenly wide awake.

CHAPTER SEVEN

Sunlight streamed through my window, shining unrelentingly on my face and breaking into a lovely dream about the taste of Pinot Noir on Grant's lips and the feel of his warm arms holding me all night long. I cracked one eye open, reluctantly letting go of the memory, though I couldn't help a smile at the sight of the pale morning light filtering through the branches of the stately oak tree outside my bedroom window. I could hear the faint sound of birds chirping as they nested nearby, and the sky was the proverbial cloudless blue.

I grinned as I stretched, working out the kinks of sleep. A grin that only faltered a little as I turned to my right and found the other half of my queen sized bed was empty. Instinctively I rolled over, finding the spot still warm and holding a lingering scent of Grant's aftershave. I nuzzled my nose into it, inhaling deeply, before I finally dragged myself from bed and into the shower.

Once I'd exhausted the hot water supply, I threw on a pair of jeans, a pale lilac T-shirt, and my favorite boots that were a worn brown leather that felt rustic even though the cut was all fashion. I capped the outfit off with a pair of silver crescent moon shaped earrings that Ava had given me last Christmas. After a little lipstick and mascara, I felt ready to face the day and wandered down the pathway toward the kitchen in search of coffee.

While my cottage had its own postage stamp–sized kitchen, with the winery's well-appointed commercial one just steps away, I rarely cooked in my own. And, as was the case currently, rarely kept it well stocked. I made a mental note to pick up some groceries while I was out that day as I went through the motions of brewing coffee. I toasted some bread and foraged in the refrigerator for the last of Conchita's homemade blackberry jam to go with it.

I took my breakfast down the hall to my office and nibbled while I answered a few emails (sadly, none looking to book Oak Valley for their weddings), went through my messages (just one from Schultz telling me he was still on the hunt for a suitable candidate to take a partnership role, which instantly soured the coffee in my stomach), and stared at my balance sheets, willing the red lines to turn black and tilt upward instead of plunging down like they'd fallen off a cliff. While Schultz was right—I barely had enough in my accounts to pay the bills—I did have one more payroll to get through. And as long as I had *anything* in my accounts, I was going to pay my employees.

Which still included one last check to Buckley. Small as it might be, it rightfully belonged to someone. I grabbed my phone, googling the name that Carmen had supplied the day before for Buckley's attorney, Barry Levinson. Okay, while I *mostly* wanted to talk to Buckley's attorney to do the right thing about the check, I might have *partly* wanted to learn more about Buckley's past…and if it had anything to do with his death.

A few clicks in, a splashy website provided a phone number for his office. It was a local one, and I tapped to dial it, putting my speakerphone on.

"Law offices of Levinson & Levine," a woman's voice answered on the second ring. "How may I direct your call?"

"I was hoping to speak with Barry Levinson," I told her.

"One moment, please," she said in a monotone. I heard soft music in a jazzy style playing as I was transferred through the phone system.

A beat later, a slightly younger woman's voice came over the line. "Mr. Levinson's office, how may I help you?"

"Hi. Is Mr. Levinson in?" I asked.

"May I ask what this is regarding?" the receptionist asked.

"It's about one of his clients. Well, former client, I guess now." I licked my lips. "Uh, Bill Buckley."

If the woman had heard the news of his demise, she didn't show it, just moving on to the next question on her gatekeeper's checklist. "May I have your name please?"

"Emmy Oak. I was Buckley's employer."

"Would you mind holding a moment?" Before I could agree or decline, the soft jazz was back.

I doodled on a piece of paper, drawing little concentric circles with my ballpoint pen while I waited. Finally, a couple of minutes later, the receptionist was back.

"I'm sorry, Mr. Levinson has client meetings all morning."

"Oh," I said, hearing the disappointment in my voice.

"But, he could squeeze you in this afternoon at three if that works for you?"

"Oh?" I asked, perking up. "Uh, yeah. Yes, that works fine," I told her, giving her my number and agreeing to meet at his office in downtown Sonoma later that day.

As soon as I hung up I decided another cup of coffee was in order before tackling the task of possibly the last payroll I'd be able to afford. I abandoned my desk for the kitchen and had just added copious amounts of sugar and cream to my cup, when my phone buzzed in my back pocket. I pulled it out to see Ava's face lighting up my screen and swiped to take the call.

"Hey," I said, sipping my coffee.

"Hey, yourself. I wasn't sure if you'd be up."

"It's ten thirty. Of course I'm up."

"Well, I know you had a date with Grant last night, so I was kind of hoping you slept in…" She trailed off, the tone in her voice hinting that actual *sleeping* was not what she was envisioning.

"I did not sleep in," I told her.

"Did Grant?"

"No," I said truthfully. "He was out early."

"So he did sleep *over*, right?"

I shook my head at my phone. "Okay, yes. We had a nice meal, and he stayed over."

"And?" she prompted. "Details!"

"And it was nice."

"Wow. You really don't know the meaning of the word details do you?"

I laughed in earnest. "Okay, it was *really* nice."

Ava blew out a breath on the other end. "I give up. It's useless trying to live vicariously through your relationship."

"I don't know if I'd call it a relationship," I hedged.

"No?" Ava asked, and I could hear her shifting on her futon. "I thought you really liked him."

"I do. I mean, yeah, he's great. I like him."

"But…?"

"I never said there was a *but*."

"Girl, it was bigger than Kim Kardashian's."

I couldn't help a chuckle. "Okay, fine. *But*, I'm just not sure how far this whole thing with Grant will go."

"What do you mean?" she asked, the concern clear in her voice despite her teasing.

"I mean…does Grant seem like the settling down type to you?"

She thought about that for a beat before answering. "I don't know. Maybe he just hasn't met the right woman to settle down with until now."

"Hmm," I said, sipping my coffee. "I don't know."

"Did he say something last night?" Ava asked. "Did something happen?"

"No." I paused, remembering our conversation from the night before. "I mean, not really. Nothing about us. It's just…he told me he knew Buckley."

"So they *did* cross paths in San Francisco after all."

I nodded. "Yeah, but why didn't he say anything before? I mean, why hide it?"

"Well, did you ask him before?" Ava asked.

"No. But doesn't it feel a little weird that he wouldn't have mentioned it?"

Ava sighed. "Kind of?"

"Yeah. That's what I thought." I took another sip from my coffee, but this one tasted bitter. "Grant also knew Buckley's former partner. Pretty well in fact," I said, filling her in on everything Grant had told me the night before.

"So you think Buckley's death really does have to do with the bribery scandal?"

"I don't know," I said honestly. "But I got the feeling Grant was holding something back. Especially when he talked about Eckhart."

"You think he was trying to protect Eckhart?"

I blew out a sigh. "Or maybe just cop instinct."

"If Buckley did derail Eckhart's career, I could see him still being angry at Buckley," Ava said.

"Not to mention feeling betrayed," I agreed.

"Maybe even betrayed and angry enough to want Buckley dead."

"But why wait two years?" I wondered out loud. "I mean, it seems like plenty of time to cool down."

"Maybe it's just now sinking in how badly his career has been affected?" Ava offered. "Maybe he was recently passed up for detective? Or maybe it's just been festering for two years and finally hit a boiling point?"

"Maybe," I hedged.

"So when are you picking me up?" Ava asked.

I raised my eyebrows at the phone. "Picking you up?"

"Uh, duh. To drive to San Francisco and talk to Eckhart?"

I shook my head. "Ava, he's a cop. You really think he's going to confess murder to a couple of nosey blondes?"

"I'm sorry—nosey? Unh-uh. We're dedicated to the truth and diligently following every lead until we find it."

I couldn't help a grin.

"Besides," she went on, "at the very least we could ask him about Katy Kline, the notorious madame who is coincidentally out on bail now."

I pursed my lips together, contemplating the logic in that move.

But the truth was, between depressing payroll paperwork or a road trip to the city, it was kind of a no-brainer.

"I'll be there in twenty," I promised her.

* * *

Buckley's former station was located in a two-story cement and brick building in a largely residential neighborhood of The City. While San Francisco might have boasted some of the most beautiful painted ladies and Victorian era buildings in the country, none of that intricate architecture was present in the utilitarian building squatting in the center of the block. I circled it three times before finding an empty spot on the street a block and a half down, beside a row of equally unimaginative homes stacked one upon the other like children's blocks. I put my parallel parking skills to the test, shimmying back and forth before finally connecting with the curb and shutting off the engine. We fed the meter and hoofed it back down the cracked sidewalk before walking to the front of the station.

The interior of which was about as unimpressive as the outside. Plastic chairs sat in rows in a waiting room, and lots of glass and chrome created cage-like barriers between the public and the uniformed officers manning the reception counters and desks. The overall effect was like being in a zoo, though looking around at the rough looking crowd filling the plastic chairs, I wasn't sure which side held the animals.

"Can I help you?" the woman in the uniform behind one of the cages asked. She had sleek black hair, pulled back in an elegant French braid, and pale smooth skin. With her clear blue eyes and painted red lips, she somehow reminded me more of Snow White than a hardened officer.

"Hi...Lana," I said, reading her name badge. "We were hoping to speak with Officer Eckhart."

"Is this in reference to an ongoing case?"

"Yes, it is," Ava said, emphatically nodding.

"Do you have a case number?"

"Oh." She turned a questioning look to me. I shrugged. "Uh, no. We don't. But it involved a former officer, Bill Buckley."

Lana frowned. "Buckley died in Sonoma, didn't he?" she said, clearly having kept up with recent news. "That's out of our jurisdiction."

"Right," Ava agreed. "But we, uh, thought maybe we could talk to Eckhart about it."

"So, this isn't about one of Officer Eckhart's cases?" Lana asked, narrowing her eyes at us.

"Not really," I confessed.

"But Emmy's boyfriend is an old friend of Eckhart's," Ava piped up.

I shot her a look.

"Your boyfriend?" Lana asked.

"Uh, well, we're just kind of dating…casually. I'm not sure I'd label." I realized Lana was not fishing for my relationship status so much as a name. I cleared my throat. "Uh, his name is Grant. Detective Christopher Grant."

"You're dating *Grant*?" The woman's whole demeanor changed, the suspicion in her eyes being replaced by a twinkle of amusement.

"Uh, yeah. You know him?" I asked.

"Oh, honey, we *all* knew Grant," she said with a laugh.

My turn to frown. "What's that supposed to mean?"

"Nothing, nothing," she said, backpedaling as she shook her head. "How is our Chris these days?"

I felt my frown deepen. I'd never known anyone to call Grant *Chris* before, let alone *our Chris*, and I suddenly wondered just how well she'd known him. "He's…fine. Good."

"Wow, it's been forever since I've seen Chris." She was smiling, still shaking her head. "In fact last time I saw him was at the Halloween bonfire a couple years ago. We all got so drunk that night." She laughed at the memory.

"Grant was drunk?" I didn't think I'd ever seen him drink more than a couple of glasses of wine or a single cocktail.

"Oh, yeah." She nodded, her braid swishing behind her. "Plastered enough to suggest we all go skinny dipping. Boy, was *that* a good idea." She giggled loudly.

Giggled. As if picturing my boyfriend naked.

I felt my eyes narrowing.

"Hey, did he ever tell you how he got that scar on his butt?" Lana asked.

I took a deep breath in, trying hard not to throttle the woman with the gun talking about my boyfriend's butt. "No," I said slowly. "What scar?"

"The one shaped like a little crescent moon right next to his—" She seemed to suddenly remember where she was and who she was talking to, as she shook her head and waved her hands. "Never mind. Anyway, it's a cute story. Ask him to tell you sometime."

"I'll do that," I ground out.

"Uh, anyway, is Officer Eckhart available?" Ava asked, pulling us back on track.

"Right. Sure." Lana wiped the smirk off her face with difficulty. "He's here. Let me just go see if he's free, huh?" she said, suddenly all helpful smiles after the trip down memory lane.

"This feels weird," I said to Ava once we were alone.

"What? Being in a police station?" she asked, glancing around at the caged walls.

"No. Going behind Grant's back like this. Talking to people who…"

"Have apparently seen him naked?" Ava finished for me.

"Yeah. That."

Ava shook her head. "Look, it's not like we're *sneaking* around. We're here in a police station in broad daylight. We're not doing anything wrong."

"I know. It just…feels intrusive. You know? Like…he's never told me about some moon scar."

Ava shrugged. "Maybe it just never came up."

"Seems to have come up with the fairest of us all," I muttered, gesturing to Lana's empty seat.

Ava snorted. "She does kinda look like Snow White."

"Anyway, I'm just not sure we should—"

But that was as far as I got before Lana reappeared, still all smiles. "Officer Eckhart says he has a few minutes free now. Wanna follow me back?"

"Absolutely," Ava said, giving me a nudge.

I shut my mouth, reluctantly following her as Lana buzzed us through a pair of security doors and led the way down a short hallway filled with lots of rooms filled with people in uniform doing what they did to protect and serve. She stopped at the second to last doorway on the left, gesturing toward it. "He's in there," she said before gliding back down the hall the way she'd come.

Ava and I stepped through the open doorway, Ava knocking on the doorframe as we did. "Officer Eckhart?"

The room was small, windowless, and just big enough to hold a gunmetal grey desk and a pair of upholstered chairs in front of it. A large, square monitor sat on the desk, perching like an ancient piece of machinery next to a handful of framed photos. Behind the desk sat a man in uniform, who rose as we entered the room.

"Hi. Come on in." His tone was welcoming to match his words. He looked to be a few years older than Grant, even if they had come up through the ranks together, and his dark hair was already dusted with hints of grey at the temples. Fine lines sat at the corners of his eyes as he smiled jovially at us. "Officer Mason Eckhart," he said, shaking hands with each of us in turn.

"Ava Barnett. And this is my friend Emmy Oak."

"Hi," I said.

Eckhart gestured to a pair of chairs in front of the desk for us to sit as he took his place behind it again. "Lana said you knew Grant?"

"Uh, yeah," I said. "I know him. I mean, we both know him, but I...well...know him better. I guess."

Eckhart gave me a funny look but let it go. "How is that old dog doing up in Wine Country?"

"Well," I said, clearing my throat in an attempt to clear out that sneaking-behind-his-back feeling. "He's well."

"I haven't heard from him in forever," Eckhart said, leaning back in his chair. "Guess he's too busy protecting all those precious grapes, huh?" He winked and chuckled at his own joke.

"He has been busy," I told him. "In fact, that's kind of why we're here."

"Oh?" Eckhart asked, jovial smile still in place.

"Grant is investigating the death of a former officer. Your partner, I believe. Bill Buckley?"

The smile finally faded. "Ah. I see."

"Has he been in contact with you about it?" I asked.

"Grant?" Eckhart shook his head. "No. But, I, uh, read about Buckley's death. Heck of a thing."

"He was actually killed in my vineyard," I told him.

"Really." Something unreadable flashed behind his eyes. "*Your* vineyard?"

I nodded. "My family owns Oak Valley Vineyards. I'd just hired Buckley to provide some extra security for me."

Eckhart let out a short laugh on a breath of air. "So Buckley was working as a security guard, huh?" He shook his head. "Poor Buckley."

"I take it you two didn't part on the best of terms," Ava said slowly.

"You could say that." Eckhart leaned back in his chair again, the pose deceptively casual as his eyes slowly went from Ava to me, as if assessing how much to share. "I'm assuming you know all about the reason Buckley left the force."

"I heard he was caught taking bribes," I said.

Eckhart nodded. "Hard to believe he'd be that stupid, but there you have it."

"What do you know about the woman who was bribing him?" Ava asked.

Eckhart turned his gaze toward her. "A modern day madame. I'm sure you two have read about her in the papers?"

I nodded politely, even though everything we knew had come from Google just the day before.

"She was running an escort service out of a storefront on our beat," Eckhart went on. "Drake's Butcher Shop. Guys would go in for a chuck roast and apparently come out with a happy ending, if you know what I mean." He chuckled again at his own wit.

"I'm assuming you didn't know this at the time," Ava said.

"No. Gosh, no. It just looked like one busy butcher shop to me. But, I guess Buckley got wind that it was more than that somehow, and well…" Eckhart's smile faded. "Well, he decided to capitalize on that intel."

"How long was this going on?" I asked.

Eckhart shrugged. "Few months. Maybe a year."

And right under Eckhart's nose. I could well see why he'd lost the respect of his fellow officers if he'd been oblivious the whole time.

"And you knew nothing about it until Internal Affairs started to investigate?" I pressed.

"No, I did not," he said emphatically, and I got the feeling it was a question he'd been asked to answer many times. "In fact, the first I heard of any of it was when I was called into IA's offices and put on suspension."

"Ouch. They suspended you just like that?" Ava asked.

"Just like that." Eckhart nodded. "But, you know, what can you do?"

"How long were you on suspension?"

"Six months."

Which was a lot longer than I'd envisioned. Somehow I'd had it in my mind that Buckley had been caught, confessed, and it had all gone away. "Was this without pay?" I clarified.

Eckhart sucked in a breath and let it out slowly. "Yeah. At the time. But it was all paid after the fact when Buckley admitted he'd worked alone. So, more like a paid vacation." He grinned and gestured to a framed photo on his desk that featured him in a grey vest and tall boots, standing beside a pine tree somewhere mountainous. "I did some fishing. Took a hunting trip with some friends. Ended up bagging a few rabbits even. So really"—he spread his hands wide—"no harm done in the end."

No harm, except that he was sitting behind a desk in officer blues while his peers, like Grant, had made detective.

"Did you and Buckley keep in touch?" I asked.

"No." He shook his head. "No, once I found out what he'd done, that was it. I was done with the guy."

"That must have been hard," Ava said, her voice laced with sympathy. "I mean, having someone you're so close to—someone you trust—betray you like that."

That flash of emotion flicked behind his eyes again, but he quickly covered it with a loud sniff and a shift in his seat. "Buckley betrayed us all. Everyone who wears the uniform."

"But he was *your* partner," I said, trying to mirror Ava's tone.

Though I wasn't sure it quite worked, as his gaze whipped my way.

"How did you say you know Grant, again?" Eckhart asked, suspicion entering into his tone.

"She's dating him," Ava said.

Eckhart's eyebrows rose. "That so?"

I nodded, feeling more than a little self-conscious under his assessing gaze. "Well, we're…friends."

He smirked. "Yeah, Grant always did have a lot of *friends*."

Lana's flawless face suddenly popped into my mind, and I resisted the urge to ask if she'd been among them.

"Grant tell you we were rookies together?" Eckhart asked.

I nodded. "He spoke very highly of you," I said honestly.

"Yeah?" Eckhart smiled and nodded. "Well, Grant was a heck of an officer himself. Had kind of his own playbook, if you know what I mean."

"Oh?" I asked, not able to stem my curiosity. "How so?"

"Just that the guy knew how to work the system. Play the game."

While the trite allusions were fun, my blank expression must have told him I wasn't quite getting his meaning.

"Grant knew exactly how to get the confessions he needed. Where to look for the evidence and get it to stick."

A distinctly uncomfortable feeling started to creep into the pit of my stomach. "You mean he worked hard?" I clarified.

There was that smirk again. "I mean he worked *smart*."

I wasn't sure exactly what he was insinuating, but that feeling in my gut was growing.

"He tell you why he moved to Sonoma?" Eckhart asked, and I could have sworn there was something of a taunt in his smile this time.

I licked my lips, sending an uneasy glance Ava's way. "He said there was a shooting."

Eckhart nodded. "There was. Did he tell you it was a kid?"

"Grant shot a kid?" Ava breathed out on a gasp.

My stomach dropped, and I suddenly had the urge to plug my ears as Eckhart continued nodding.

"Some gangbanger. Playing all tough, but it turned out he was only seventeen."

Grant had *not* told me this. He'd told me he'd shot a man and he hadn't regretted it. Knowing that man was just a teenager left me with mixed feelings.

"Do you know what happened?" Ava asked, leaning forward in her seat.

Part of me didn't want to know more, but I couldn't not listen.

"We were at this house in the Tenderloin."

"You were there?" I asked.

Eckhart nodded. "It was supposed to be a routine arrest. Buckley and I were there as backup."

"Buckley was there too," I said. Another detail Grant had failed to mention.

"We thought we were going in for one guy, but it turned out a bunch of them were inside. They started shooting at us as soon as they saw blue. We shot back. In the end…the kid was dead, and it was Grant's bullet."

"Well, it sounds like it was clearly self-defense," Ava said, and I loved her for defending Grant in that moment.

"Sure it was," Eckhart agreed.

I almost hated to ask… "So why the IA investigation?"

He shrugged. "When the dust settled, they couldn't find a gun on the kid."

I closed my eyes. Grant had shot an unarmed seventeen-year-old.

"I mean, it wasn't like the guy was *innocent*. He was covered in gang tattoos, and prints came back with a list of juvenile offenses starting as young as ten," Eckhart told us. "I don't know why IA had to jam Grant up so hard over it. He did a public service, if you asked me."

I bit my lip, wondering how Grant had felt about it. The way Eckhart was talking about him, like he'd had some vigilante justice in mind…that was not the Grant I'd come to know. Then again, I didn't know how Grant did his job. All I knew was the side he showed me. Did that mean Eckhart knew him better than I did? Or was Eckhart seeing what he wanted to?

Or trying to distract us all together from our original purpose in being here.

I sucked in a deep breath, shoving down the host of confusing emotions this visit had brought.

"What about Katy Kline?" I asked, getting back to her.

He turned to me. "Katy Kline?"

"The madame who was bribing Buckley to look the other way."

"I know who she is," Eckhart said, and I could hear a hint of impatience edging into his voice, signaling that we were on borrowed time.

"Did you know she's out on parole now?" Ava asked.

"Of course. I was at her parole hearing."

Of course. What were the chances we were delivering news to the man who had been unwittingly at the center of her demise?

"Do you know where she is now?" Ava asked.

"Not offhand, but it's in the system." He nodded toward the ancient computer monitor on his desk. "Condition of parole. They have to keep their parole officer updated on where they live, where they work, where they go." Eckhart looked from me to Ava, the suspicion back in his gaze. "Why do you want to know?"

Great question. I looked to Ava.

"Just curious. I mean, it's interesting timing—her being out on parole right before Buckley is killed."

His eyes narrowed. "Is Grant thinking Kline had something to do with Buckley's death?"

Was Grant thinking it? Doubtful. But I knew two blondes who were. I slowly nodded, already feeling guilty for the half truth. "Does it feel possible to you?"

He did some more eye narrowing and pursed his lips. "Who can ever say what people are capable of?"

Which was a very noncommittal answer.

"Capability aside," Ava jumped in. "Is it even possible? I mean, is she still in the Bay Area?"

Eckhart shrugged. "I can check." He turned to the computer, jiggling his mouse to wake it up. We waited in silence while he did a little clicking and typed Katy Kline's information into his system. A minute later he frowned at the screen.

"Huh."

"Huh what?" I asked, leaning forward even though the screen was still facing too far the other direction for me to see anything.

"Well, it says here Kline's got some sort of bakery business now. Katy's Cookies."

"That's a switch from selling…er, from her other profession," Ava mumbled.

"It is. She's switched locales too," Eckhart informed us, still frowning at the screen.

"So she's not in San Francisco anymore?" I asked, feeling her possibility as a suspect fizzle.

"No." Eckhart shook his head. Then he pried his eyes from the screen to meet mine, that flash of something running through them again so quickly that I had no chance to read it. "No, it says here that Katy's Cookies is on 2nd Street." He paused, infusing the next words with meaning. "In downtown Sonoma."

CHAPTER EIGHT

"So, Katy followed Buckley to Sonoma!" Ava said as we stepped back out of the station and into the cool air.

Even though it was well into the eighties in Wine Country, the coastal fog still enveloped The City in a perpetual chill. I inhaled the salty, moist air, hoping it would cleanse some of the discomfort I'd experienced in the station.

"Katy was *in* Sonoma at the same time as Buckley. That doesn't mean she followed him there," I pointed out as we walked the block and a half back to my Jeep.

"So you think it was just coincidence that she set up shop in the same place Buckley settled?"

"Maybe. I mean, Sonoma is a big place."

"Nuh-uh. Not that big," Ava countered. "Not so big they couldn't have had a chance encounter even if Katy hadn't known ahead of time that Buckley was living there."

I had to concede that point to her. "Okay, so Katy runs into Buckley..."

"...and it stirs up all the old anger over how Buckley put her behind bars. So Katy decides to get revenge for what Buckley did to her. She finds out that he's working at your winery. Alone. At night," Ava said, clearly on a roll with this theory. "And she decides it's the perfect place to take him out!"

It all sounded plausible. Too plausible. That chill was back, and as we got back to my car, I immediately cranked up the heater to stave it off.

"So, in this scenario, how does Katy find out Buckley is working for me?"

Ava thought about that a beat as she pulled a tube of lipstick from her purse and touched up her makeup in the visor mirror. "Maybe she ran into Buckley and he told her?"

"I don't know. I can't see them being that chummy." I pulled away from the curb. Carefully, as a Prius and an ancient Dodge Dart had boxed me in since I'd parked.

"Well, maybe Katy ran into someone Buckley knew. Like, maybe she had a meal at the diner where his girlfriend, Sheila, works? Maybe they got to talking, and who knows?"

I nodded. "Yeah, I guess I could see that."

"Or maybe Katy got her nails done at Nadia's and Carmen started talking about her ex."

"That I could *definitely* see. Carmen is very light on the filter."

Ava laughed. "And *light* is generous."

I merged onto the 101 freeway, heading north back to Wine Country. "So, I guess there's just one question left."

"What's that?" Ava asked.

"Do we want cookies before or after lunch?"

* * *

Katy's Cookies was a small storefront in a strip mall anchored by a CVS and a bagel shop. Between them sat several mom and pop establishments, including a dry cleaner and a sandwich place with a big grinning pickle in their window. They all seemed to be doing a pretty brisk business, if the lack of parking in the lot was any indication. After spot-stalking a woman with a loaded shopping cart and three kids to her minivan, we finally got a parking place and locked my Jeep before heading toward Katy's Cookies.

Which, unlike the other shops along the sidewalk, seemed distinctly empty. I wondered if maybe Katy's reputation had preceded her into town and turned customers off to her baked goods.

A bell jingled above the door as Ava and I pushed inside. A long counter took up the bulk of the back wall, its glass cases showing off gift baskets of all sizes filled with cookies. To our right sat several more shelves lined with baskets and tins—

some bearing *Get Well Soon* wishes and others sporting stick balloons that read *Happy Birthday*. All of them were filled with cellophane wrapped cookies in a variety of shapes, colors, and sizes. Two empty sets of white tables and chairs sat in the center of the room, facing the window that looked out onto the parking lot. The walls were painted in a cheery yellow, and the white tile floors clean, if clearly not new.

At the sound of our arrival, a middle aged woman appeared from the back of the shop to stand behind the counter, tying a pink apron on as she did.

"May I help you?" she asked in a cheerful tone that matched the overall vibe of the place.

"Hi," Ava said, stepping up the counter. "We're looking for Katy Kline."

"You found her," the woman told us, giving us a wide smile that caused creases to form at the corners of her eyes.

"*You*'re Katy Kline?" I asked, taking in the woman before me. I wasn't sure what I'd been expecting, but the term "madame" conjured up images of black leather or sexy lace and slinky Jessica Rabbit style dresses. The woman before me was short, round, and looked like someone's mom. She wore little makeup, and the silver streaks in her sandy brown hair, styled in a feathered bob, clearly betrayed her age. Nothing about her said *sex*, from her plaid shirt and wide-legged jeans down to the sensible shoes on her feet.

"Katy Kline, you betcha," Katy replied, nonplussed by the question. "Can I interest you ladies in a cookie sample?"

"Uh, sure," I said, sending a glance Ava's way. From the raised pair of eyebrows she was giving Katy, I'd say the woman's appearance hadn't lived up to Ava's imagination either.

"I just pulled a tray of Oatmeal Raisin Cookies from the oven," Katy said, ducking into the back again. "If you're lucky, they'll still be warm."

Ava cleared her throat. "Uh, have you been in business here long?"

"Oh, a couple of months now. We do a lot of delivery orders. Gift baskets are our biggest sellers." She came back into the room with two cookies held in white paper. "Here. Give these a try."

"Thanks." Ava grabbed one of the proffered samples and took a small bite.

I did the same, the sweet brown sugar and spicy cinnamon mingling perfectly as the warm raisins melted onto my tongue. "Wow, this is good."

"Thank you." Katy beamed. "My mother's recipe. I know it's not as popular as chocolate chip, but I've always been an oatmeal raisin fan."

While I would have probably picked chocolate myself, I had to admit these were good enough to change my mind.

I leaned toward the glass case, seeing a basket of oatmeal raisin and snickerdoodles accompanied by a cute little teddy bear holding a sign that read *Thinking of You.* "Maybe I should get one for my mom," I said. I glanced at Ava. "I really haven't been visiting as much as I should lately."

Ava nodded, licking the last of the cookie crumbs from her fingers. "I think she'd love that."

"We can customize something for her," Katy said. "Delivery is free."

"You've sold me." I pointed to the bear. "Something like that is perfect."

Katy pulled out a notepad. "What's your mom's address?"

I rattled it off for her, along with the name to go on the basket.

"You said the shop's only been open a couple of months. Are you new to Sonoma as well?" Ava said, as Katy took my credit card and rang up the order.

"Yep. Gorgeous area. Pricey, but everyone has been so welcoming. I feel right at home."

"Have you been to Ed's Diner yet?" Ava asked. She shot me a side-eye glance, referencing the restaurant that Sheila Connolly had told us she'd worked at.

"Can't say I have." Katy shook her head. "Any good?"

Ava nodded. "Sure. What about Nadia's Nails? Over in Napa?"

Katy frowned. "No." She paused, suspicion suddenly clouding her pleasant smile as she handed my credit card back to me. "Why do you ask?"

Ava shrugged. "Oh, no reason. I just thought maybe you might have run into a mutual acquaintance there."

"Mutual acquaintance?" The suspicion was more than a hint now.

"Carmen Buckley."

At the name Buckley, all pleasantness dropped from her features, and I got a glimpse of the hardness that two years in prison could create. Her jaw clenched, the pleasantness in her eyes going dark. "You're an acquaintance of Carmen Buckley?" she asked. Though it came out more as an accusation than a question.

I stepped forward. "Actually, I knew Bill. He, uh, he worked for me," I confessed. "At my winery."

Katy cocked her head to the side. "That's where he was killed, right? At a winery? That's what they said on the news."

I nodded. "Unfortunately, yes. He was working security that night." I watched her reaction, trying to feel out if this was news to her or if she'd already known because she'd been there. Shooting him.

"Terrible tragedy," she said, though her voice was a deadpan monotone that conveyed no emotion behind the words.

"You knew Buckley, right?" Ava asked. "When he was a police officer in San Francisco?"

Katy's eyes flickered to the door, as if worried some other customer might overhear. But considering no one else had so much as even looked in the windows since we'd arrived, she just let out a sigh before answering. "Yes. I mean, it's public record, right? It's not like it's a secret." She set her lips in a thin line, a dark gaze going from Ava to me. "I led a life of crime at one point. I was caught, I paid my debt to society, and now I'm a reformed person."

The statement sounded like a cliché taken straight from some TV crime drama, but as I glanced around her cheery yellow cookie shop, I had to admit it did look like she'd turned over a new leaf.

"From selling nooky to cookies, huh?" Ava joked.

The corner of Katy's mouth curved up, but the smile didn't quite reach her eyes. "Something like that."

"It was Buckley's testimony that ended your other career, wasn't it?" I asked.

"More than testimony." She scoffed. "He led the police right to my door."

"That must have been upsetting," Ava said.

"You think?" Katy's jaw clenched again, and even the thick layer of sarcasm couldn't cover the genuine anger I felt radiating off her.

"Right," Ava said. "Clearly upsetting."

Katy smirked and shook her head. "Look, yes, of course I was upset with Buckley. I paid him to keep his mouth shut, and what did he do? Blab everything to the police."

"And you ended up in jail."

"But I did my time. I've paid my debt to society," she repeated, "and I've moved on." She gestured around her to the empty cookie shop as evidence of that.

"Still, you must not have been a Buckley fan?"

"I didn't shed a tear when I heard he was dead, if that's what you mean."

"What made you choose Sonoma to open up a shop?" I asked.

"I like wine." She crossed her arms over her chest in an unconsciously defensive gesture.

"Did you know that Buckley was living in Sonoma?" I asked slowly.

"Was he." Again her tone was a deadpan that was neither a question nor an answer. "Small world."

"So small one would assume you'd run into each other eventually," Ava pointed out.

She shrugged. "Maybe eventually. But I've only been here a couple of months."

"Right. Interesting timing."

"Excuse me?" She narrowed her eyes, the soccer mom pleasantness replaced by the former inmate suspicion again.

"I just think it's an interesting coincidence that Buckley is killed right after you move to town," Ava said.

"I did *not* kill Buckley," she said hotly, taking a step around the counter. "I haven't seen him since my trial, and if I never saw him again, that would have been too soon."

"I'm curious," I said. "How much did you pay Buckley?"

"What?" she asked, her attention diverting from Ava's thinly veiled accusations to me.

"The money you gave him to keep quiet about your escort business. How much was it?"

She sucked in a breath, the question seeming to calm the anger that had been bubbling up inside of her. "Over the course of the year? Probably around a hundred grand."

I blinked at her. "A hundred thousand dollars?"

She shrugged. "Give or take."

I was so in the wrong business.

"You must have really been raking it in," Ava said.

"I did okay." She grinned in a way that said she'd done a whole lot better than okay. "But it's all gone now. What wasn't seized when I was arrested was spent on my useless lawyer."

"Then where did you get the start-up money to open this place?" I asked.

"Not that it's anyone's business, but I got a loan," she told me. "From family. My brother sold his butcher shop and had some cash sitting around."

"The butcher shop you used to run your other business out of?" Ava clarified.

She shrugged. "What can I say? The place wasn't nearly as popular without my girls' services on the menu."

"So your brother invested in your cookie business?" Ava said.

She nodded. "Why not?"

"I hate to say it, but it seems pretty quiet in here," Ava pointed out.

Katy shrugged again. "Like I said, most of our business is delivery." She nodded toward the glass case. "Our baskets are very popular."

As if on cue, the bell over the door jingled and a tall man in a blue T-shirt that read *Katy's Cookies* walked in.

His shoulders were broad, his hips slim, and his tanned arms rippling with biceps that strained against the tight T-shirt. His blond hair was artfully tussled back from his chiseled features, and his blue eyes looked so bright that they had to be contacts.

"Allison Beech loved the friendship basket—" The guy paused, realizing Katy had customers. "Oh. Sorry. I didn't know you were with someone." His eyes flickered to me before resting on Ava. And giving her a slow up and down that curved the corners of his mouth upward.

"Hi." Ava waved.

"My nephew, Derek. He does deliveries for me," Katy said.

"Hey." Derek held up a hand in greeting. "Have you tried the oatmeal raisin yet? They're really good."

"They have," Katy said before either of us had a chance to answer. "And they were just leaving." She gave us a pointed look.

"Right," I agreed, turning to go.

"Hope you come back soon," Derek said. Though the way his eyes were firmly on Ava's retreating backside, it was clear he was only talking to one of us.

"Dang, I may need a cookie basket delivery," Ava mumbled as we stepped back out into the sunshine.

"Down, girl. I don't think his Aunty Katy was a fan."

"Well, she was less of a fan of Buckley's. Did you see the way that vein in her neck started to bulge when we mentioned his name?"

I nodded, threading our way through the aisles of cars in the parking lot. "And I'm having a hard time believing she didn't know Buckley was in town before she saw him on the news."

"The question is, did she intentionally follow him here to kill him, or was it just a coincidence that they both liked wine?"

"I wish I knew." I unlocked my Jeep. "But she apparently had a hundred thousand reasons to be mad at Buckley. That's a lot to pay someone to be quiet."

"Especially someone who then sang like a proverbial canary," Ava added.

"I had no idea we were talking about so much money." I slipped into the driver's seat and turned the car on.

"Money no one has ever seen," Ava said, giving me a meaningful glance. "Carmen said her lawyer looked for it, but she neglected to say how much it was. What if she actually *did* find it."

"And killed Buckley for it?" I asked.

"People have killed for a lot less."

That was true. A hundred grand could do a lot for someone who lived off tips from pedicures. While Nadia's Nails was a nice enough place, I could imagine a hundred thousand dollars was far more than Carmen would see in a year. Possibly even two or three.

My phone buzzed from my pocket. I pulled it out to see David's name on the display.

"Hey, David," I said, putting it on speaker.

"Hey, Ems. Where are you?"

"2nd Street," I said, backing out of the parking space.

"Is Ava with you?"

"I'm here," she piped up. "Why?"

"Because I thought I'd invite the two of you to join me for lunch at the Links."

I raised an eyebrow Ava's way. "And you're buying?" I asked, knowing that the prices at the golf club were high enough to cover the prestigious ambiance.

"I am," he confirmed.

"May I ask the occasion?" I asked as I pulled out of the parking lot.

David chuckled on the other end. "Well, I just happened to run into someone here I thought you might like to talk to."

He was purposely drawing this out for drama's sake.

"Okay, I'll bite. Who?"

"Jamie Connolly. Bill Buckley's almost-stepson."

Ava and I shared a look across the car interior. "Jamie Connolly is a member at the Links?"

"Not member. He works here. He's a weekend server on the back nine veranda."

I nodded, remembering Sheila had mentioned a weekend job when we'd met her.

"So, what do you say?" David asked. "Fancy a Cobb salad on the veranda, ladies?"

I made a right at the light. "We'll be right there."

CHAPTER NINE

The Sonoma Links was located on several manicured acres just outside of town, consisting of lush golfing greens, a large clubhouse with an indoor lounge, dining rooms, several meeting and club rooms, and a spacious veranda, where ladies who lunch could sip cocktails and gossip while eyeing the hot golf pros. The unspoken dress code ranged from slacks and golf shirts, to breezy sundresses, and even a few business suits for those who enjoyed the club more for its prestige than physical pursuits.

David Allen stuck out like a cactus among lilies, sitting at the edge of the veranda in a black T-shirt and jeans—ripped at the knees and splattered along the thighs in oil paints of various colors. His combat boots were crossed at the ankles, and his arms were casually cradling the back of his head as he leaned back in his dark sunglasses, obviously enjoying the midday sunshine.

"Hey," Ava said as we approached his table. "Thanks for the invite."

David lifted his shades but didn't straighten up in his seat on our account. "Ladies." He nodded from Ava to me. "I took the liberty of ordering a rosé."

I noticed three glasses on the table and a chilled bottle in a silver ice bucket on a stand to his right.

"Sounds wonderful," Ava said.

"You come from the studio?" I asked, gesturing to the paint on his jeans.

He nodded. "Just putting a couple finishing touches on a piece."

"For your show tomorrow night?" Ava asked, reaching for the chilled rosé.

"Possibly." David held his glass out to her. "I'm still debating whether to show this particular piece or not."

"I'm surprised they let you in this place looking like that," I said, knowing from personal experience that the clerks who manned the front desk were more gatekeepers than greeters.

David's face broke into his trademark sardonic smile. "Honey, with how much I spend here, they'd let me in naked."

Ava snorted as she filled his glass. "I'd like to see that."

"Oh yeah?" His grin widened. "That can be arranged."

"Behave, children," I told them.

David winked at me but thankfully ceased flirting.

"You said Jamie was working here?" I asked, moving the subject on.

David nodded. Then gestured to our left with his head. "He's our server."

I glanced in the direction he indicated, seeing a tall guy in a pair of khaki pants and a blue polo shirt bearing the Links logo. He was presenting a pair of plates to two older ladies at the next table over. I honestly never would have recognized him out of his street clothes and in the uniform that blended in with every other young person working the club.

"Have you talked to him yet?" I asked.

"Just to order drinks. Thought I'd wait for Charlie's Angels to begin the interrogations." He sent us a teasing grin.

I rolled my eyes. But since the rosé looked delightful, and David was paying, I let it go. Instead, I filled my glass and had just taken my first fruity sparkling sip when Jamie made his way to our table.

"I see the rest of your party is here," he said, addressing David. "Are you all ready to order?"

"I think so," David decided, finally sitting up in his chair and folding his long legs back under the table. "Ladies first, though." He nodded to Ava.

"I'll take a chicken Caesar wrap," she decided, setting down her menu.

Jamie wrote the order on a little notebook then turned an expectant gaze my way.

Up close, I could see the same dark eyes his mother had, though his features were much more angular than hers. While he was polite enough to us paying guests, I could see something almost challenging in his demeanor and posture. As if in a constant state of trying to prove he belonged here.

"Uh, the Lobster Bisque please, " I said.

He nodded and wrote it down.

"And for you, sir?" he asked, and I thought I could almost detect a hint of sarcasm in the word *sir.* Granted, David did dress more like a teen than a country clubber.

"Let's go with the filet mignon."

I shot him a look. Had I known we were splurging, I would have ordered more. I was suddenly tempted to add an actual lobster tail to go with my soup.

"You only live once, right?" David said, giving me a wink.

"Sure." Jamie's face was totally void of emotion, giving only the bare minimum of social interaction that was required to earn his paycheck. He turned to go put our orders in.

But Ava piped up stop him. "Uh, you're Jamie, right?" she said.

He paused. "That's right. Was there something else, ma'am?"

"No, I just…well, I saw you the other day."

He frowned.

"Uh, at your apartment building." Ava nodded toward me. "Emmy and I were visiting your mom."

Jamie's eyes went from Ava to me, the frown between his brows deepening. "You know my mom?"

"Sort of. I mean, we've met her. I own the winery where…" I trailed off, not sure how hard Buckley's death had hit the boy.

But it turned out I hadn't needed to worry, as Jamie finished the thought for me. "You mean, where Bill got his brains blown out."

I saw Ava visibly wince.

But David chuckled. "Not a fan of the old man, huh?"

"He wasn't *my* old man," Jamie shot back.

"Sure, but he was dating your mom, wasn't he?" David pressed.

Jamie's jaw worked back and forth, but he didn't answer.

"How is she holding up?" I asked, trying to lighten the tone a little.

"She's fine," came his clipped answer. Then he quickly turned and all but stalked toward the kitchen to put our orders in.

"Well, he's a delight," Ava said, sipping her rosé.

"People grieve in all sorts of ways," I said, trying to give the kid the benefit of the doubt.

"Yeah, *that* was not grief," David said, swirling wine in his glass. "That was pure hatred."

I opened my mouth to protest, but David ran right over me.

"Just because the guy is dead does not mean he was a saint in life."

I shut my mouth. "You're right. Seems like he was far from it, actually." I quickly filled him in on our conversations that day with Eckhart and Katy Kline, ending with the theory that Buckley had been hiding a hundred thousand dollars' worth of ill-gotten gains.

"And no one has ever seen this money?" David asked when I was done.

I shook my head. "Buckley told IA he spent it."

"But it's possible he's been just sitting on it," Ava said.

"And you think it's why he was killed?" David asked.

Ava shrugged. "It's one theory. I could see Carmen killing him for it in a heartbeat."

"I could see her killing him for a twenty," I joked.

Ava laughed. "Agreed. She had a huge grudge against him."

"Well, if you think this is a grudge killing, I'd say the cookie queen has the better reason for revenge," David said. "Buckley put her away for how long?"

"Four years. But she only served two," Ava said.

"Don't count out his former partner, Eckhart, though," I added. "Buckley's greed derailed Eckhart's whole career."

"And there's still our server," Ava reminded us. "He's clearly not shedding a tear over his mom's boyfriend being out of the picture."

We all turned to look at Jamie as he took a drink order from a couple who'd just been seated near the doors. I noticed he was studiously avoiding looking in our direction. I halfway suspected he'd pawn our table off on another server.

"I forgot to ask how your meeting with Schultz went yesterday," David said, leaning back in his chair and turning his face toward the sunshine again. "You get the cash infusion you needed, Ems?"

"Ugh. No. Not even close," I mumbled. "Schultz says I need to take on a partner."

"Partner?" David frowned. "Why?"

"Short answer? Investors won't touch me with a ten foot pole."

"Honey." Ava sent me a sympathetic smile.

"Have they tasted your wines?" David asked.

I shook my head. "My wine has nothing to do with it. Unfortunately," I added, thinking I might have had a chance of winning them over if it had. "Our profits just aren't high enough. At least not high enough to outweigh the growing expenses, which have had us in the red all year long."

"Everyone's been in the red. They can't blame you for the governor's shutdown," David pointed out.

"No." I bit my lip. "But we weren't exactly thriving before that either," I confessed. "Anyway, without investors or getting deeper into debt I can't pay back, Schultz says finding a partner who wants a 'pet project' is my best bet."

"Ouch. He called Oak Valley a pet project?" Ava said.

I blew out a long breath. "Yeah. I know. My pride is just about flat lining."

"Sorry, Ems." David sat up and threw an arm around my shoulder, giving it a squeeze. "Something will come along. It always does."

"Sure," I said with entirely false optimism. I had a bad feeling the only thing that would be coming along was a weekend warrior with big ideas and very little knowledge to back them up. If I was lucky. If not...

I didn't even want to think about if not.

I shook that depressing thought as Jamie approached with a tray of plates in hand. Apparently, he had decided to brave our table again after all. Though I noticed as he silently doled the plates out, he avoided any eye contact.

"Thanks very much," I told him as he set my bisque in front of me. Which, I had to admit, looked delicious. The aroma of buttery lobster and briny tomato broth wafted up to me from my bowl, making me realize just how hungry I'd been.

Jamie grunted in response but averted his gaze as he set Ava's wrap in front of her.

"I'm sorry if we upset you earlier," Ava told him.

He squared his jaw but managed to grind out "Don't worry about it."

"I'm sure it's all been a shock," she went on. "In fact, I'm surprised the club didn't give you some time off."

"I don't need it," he said, all but throwing David's filet in front of him.

"It must be a lot to process," Ava said, her voice still sympathetic, despite his gruff demeanor.

He didn't answer, still averting his gaze as he gathered his tray back up in his hands.

I felt any opportunity to get more from him quickly slipping away.

"Your mother mentioned you were out," I said quickly.

Jamie finally lifted his eyes to meet mine.

"Uh, the night Buckley died," I clarified. "Your mom said you weren't at home. That she was waiting up for you."

His expression was unreadable, but his voice was clipped. "So?"

"So, I was wondering where you were."

Jamie's eyes narrowed, and he took a step closer, lowering his voice so it came out as a growl. "What is this, an interrogation?"

"No!" I protested. "No, I just… I know she was worried about you."

"You don't know anything about my mother!" he spat back.

"Well, since we're being frank here," David jumped in, "how about you tell us what you were doing at the winery?"

"I wasn't at your stupid winery!" Jamie said. "I was nowhere near that place when Bill died."

"So where were you?" David asked again. "When Bill died?"

"Out. With friends."

"What about the next day?" I asked.

Jamie's gaze shot to mine again.

"You *were* at my winery then. You almost ran us off the road."

He shrugged. "You should learn how to drive."

I opened my mouth to protest that it had been *him* who'd been driving like a maniac, but David jumped in again, his tone insistent. "What were you doing at the winery that day?"

Jamie clenched his back teeth together again, squaring his jaw. But the anger radiating off of him was tempered with another emotion this time. It looked a lot like fear in the way his breath was coming heavier, his eyes darting between us.

"I don't know what you're talking about," Jamie said. He spun and turned to go.

But David's hand shot out and caught the kid's arm, preventing his exit.

Jamie's eyes were full of fire, and for a moment I thought he might try to punch David right there on the golf club veranda.

"You were there," David said, his voice stern now, the jovial tone gone. "I saw you."

Jamie's heated gaze went from David to me, a murderous look in his eyes that I could easily see spilling over into actual action. Despite the warm sunshine, a chill ran up my spine.

"Let go of me!" He jerked his sleeve free, eyes darting around the veranda, as if trying to make sure he wasn't causing a scene. "You people might think you own the world, but you don't own me," he ground out.

Then he turned and stormed back to the kitchen.

"Well, I guess we won't be seeing a dessert menu," Ava said, staring after him.

"And he won't be seeing a tip," David said, his eyes hard as he watched the kid's retreating back.

* * *

Predictably, we did not see Jamie again while we finished our meal. In fact, the bill was brought out by another server altogether who told us Jamie was "on a break." Which was clearly code for avoiding any more questions that he didn't have good answers for.

"We could corner him in the break room?" Ava suggested as David paid the bill.

I shrugged. "You think it would do any good?"

"At least maybe we could get an alibi out of him."

"You won't," David said as the server walked away. "If he doesn't want you to know, he'll just lie."

"Well, he clearly has some anger issues," Ava said. "I could definitely see him snapping and…"

"'Blowing Buckley's brains out?'" David finished for her.

She shuddered as we rose from the table. "Who talks like that? I mean, the guy was basically his dad."

"Maybe that was what he wanted to avoid," I said.

"Or maybe it was about his mom," David offered as we made our way back through the club to the valet station.

"How so?" Ava asked.

"Well, we've established Buckley wasn't a pillar of moral fortitude," David said.

"Agreed," I added.

"Maybe he wasn't such a nice guy to Sheila Connolly. Maybe he did something or said something to her, and it pushed Jamie over the edge."

"He did seem defensive when we mentioned her," I agreed.

"And Buckley does have a history of cheating, if Carmen's to be believed." Ava turned to David. "Apparently not all of the bribes Buckley took from Katy were in the form of cash."

David grinned. "I've gotta meet this Cookie Katy."

"No," I told him emphatically. "You don't. Besides, she was more Soccer Mom than Lady of the Evening."

"Hmmm." David didn't sound convinced.

Ava tapped me on the arm. "I'm just gonna go powder my nose before we go." She gestured toward the ladies' room near the club entrance.

I nodded. "I'll get the car," I told her.

"So, where are you off to now?" David asked as we walked to the valet station.

"I have a meeting with Buckley's lawyer," I said, glancing at the time on my phone.

"Oh?" David raised an eyebrow my way.

"I need to find out where to send his last check. I figured his lawyer would know."

"Uh-huh." He gave me a funny look.

"What?"

"Nothing. It's just cute when you pretend you're not investigating a murder."

I opened my mouth to tell him how *un*-cute it was to call a grown woman cute, but my phone buzzing from my purse saved him. I pulled it out to see Grant's name lighting the display.

I paused. I'd been doing a bang-up job of not thinking about everything Eckhart had told me about Grant that morning. Not to mention Snow White and her cute little stories about Grant's derrière. But I wasn't sure how well I could keep my head in the sand during an actual conversation with Grant. Guilt at talking to his former colleagues behind his back mixed with a weird sensation of suddenly wondering just how well I knew him.

I swiped to decline the call and put the phone back in my purse.

I thought I'd been discreet, but I looked up to find David staring at me.

"We're screening the boyfriend now?" he asked, something unreadable in his voice.

I shook my head. "He's not my boyfriend."

"Oh? Trouble in paradise?"

"No. I mean, it's just...we're just taking things slow. Right now."

"Who's taking things slow?" Ava asked, rejoining us, shifting her purse onto her shoulder.

"Grant and Emmy apparently," David said, his voice still holding a quality I couldn't quite put my finger on.

Ava laughed. "Sure, if you call sleeping over slow," she joked.

David quirked an eyebrow at me. "So, you're screening him the morning after a sleepover?"

I licked my lips, wondering how my love life had suddenly become the subject of an interrogation. "It's hardly *morning*."

David's mouth curved into a slow grin. "Touché."

"We ready?" Ava asked, as my Jeep pulled to a stop in front of us.

"Very," I mumbled.

CHAPTER TEN

The law offices of Levinson & Levine were located in a three story building just off West Napa that looked like it had recently had a modern facelift and paint job. We parked in the small lot in back of the building and took the elevator up to the second floor, where the sleek modern theme was carried through to the interior. A reception area was outfitted in a pair of upholstered mid-century inspired grey chairs and a low yellow sofa. White stone tables held a vase of flowers and a stack of magazines, and a long black reception desk took up the back wall. Behind it sat a young redhead in a tight pencil skirt and blouse with about a thousand ruffles on the front.

"Welcome to Levinson & Levine, may I help you?" she asked all in one breath.

"Emmy Oak. I have an appointment to see Barry Levinson," I told her.

"Of course. One moment, please," she said, picking up her desk phone and pushing a couple of buttons. Then she spoke in hushed tones to the person on the other end before turning her pleasant smile on us again. "Mr. Levinson will be right out." She gestured to chairs.

"Thanks," I told her, taking a seat on one of them as Ava did the same.

We didn't have to wait long, as a couple of minutes later a short guy in a dark suit emerged from the back offices, his hand outstretched as he approached.

"Barry Levinson," he said, his voice loud and brusque. "Pleasure to meet you."

"Emmy Oak," I told him as he pumped my hand up and down with vigor. "And this is my friend, Ava Barnett."

"Barry Levinson," he repeated, shoving his hand at Ava.

"Hi," she said.

"Come on back to my office," he said, not waiting for a reply as he spun on his wingtips and led the way down a long hallway. For a short guy, he was quick, and I had to jog to keep up.

"So, Linda said you knew Bill Buckley, huh?" he asked.

"Uh, yes, I was his employer—"

"Heck of a thing," Levinson said, cutting me off. "A guy going like that."

"Yes, it was very—"

"Of course, I've known Bill for years," he went on. "He's had his share of legal troubles in the past, but no one deserves to go out like that, am I right?"

I paused a moment, waiting to see if he'd actually wait for me to answer this time. "Right."

He stopped abruptly outside the door to a large office near the end of the hall and spun to face us, gesturing into the room with one arm. "After you, ladies."

I gave him a polite nod as I stepped into the room and took a seat in one of two leather chairs in front of a wide wooden desk flanked by tall windows that overlooked the street. The desktop was piled high with various file folders and binders, two thin computer monitors, and several stacks of loose papers.

Levinson followed us into the room on a cloud of expensive cologne and sat behind the desk, leaning forward and clasping his hands on its top in front of him. "So, what can I do for you, Ms. Oak?"

"Well, for starters, you could tell me who Buckley's heir is," I said.

He raised his eyebrows at me. "You expecting an inheritance?" he joked.

I shook my head. "No, but I do owe him a paycheck for his last week with us. I'm wondering who I should send it to."

"Ah." He nodded. "Well, Buckley didn't have a will, so all of his assets will go into probate now before being dispersed. You can send the check to me, and I'll make sure it's included among those assets."

"But ultimately, they will be dispersed to someone, right?" I asked.

He nodded. "Next of kin." Levinson pulled a folder from his stack and flipped it open. "No kids, his parents both deceased. But it looks like he's got an older sister in Oregon. My guess is it will all go to her." He looked up. "Whatever is left after funeral costs and taxes, anyway."

"I'm guessing that's not a lot," I said, thinking of where he and Sheila had lived.

Levinson shook his head. "No. Not a lot."

"You think there will even be enough in Buckley's estate to cover funeral costs?" I asked, picturing Sheila Connolly's haggard face.

Levinson did a palms up and shrugged. "Up to the family what they want to do with that. But honestly? The guy was on the verge of bankruptcy. He was racking up credit card debt, his car was about to be repossessed, and he was way behind on his alimony payments."

"His ex-wife mentioned that," Ava said.

"Carmen?" Levinson narrowed his eyes. "You friends with her?"

"No," I said quickly, shaking my head. "Uh, but we did run into her recently."

"Poor you," he said with a laugh. "That woman is a whacko. I kid you not, she called my office ranting about one thing or another *every day* during their divorce. Every single day." He shook his head at the memory.

"What was she ranting about?" Ava asked, shooting me a knowing look.

"I don't know. Who paid attention?" he said, dismissing it.

"You know, Carmen mentioned something else when we talked to her," Ava started. "About money."

"Not surprised. It's her favorite subject," Levinson said, leaning back in his chair now.

"Specifically about the money Buckley took when he was on the force. The bribery money he was paid."

Levinson didn't say anything, but I could see his eyes narrow again ever so slightly.

"She said she never saw any of it," Ava added.

"Why should she?" He shrugged. "Hey, Buckley admitted he'd been wrong. He took bribes, he spent the money, he got caught."

"You sure he spent it?" I asked. "All of it?"

"That's what my client said."

Which did not exactly answer my question.

"Carmen said they lived a modest lifestyle. Buckley never brought home any fancy jewelry or clothes, no new cars. They never went on any vacations. She couldn't imagine what Buckley had spent it on."

"Carmen is a whacko," Levinson repeated. "I wouldn't put too much stock in anything she says."

"So, it isn't possible that Buckley tucked that money away for a rainy day?" Ava asked. "Maybe hid it somewhere, waiting for the attention to die down before spending it?"

Levinson's eyes narrowed again. "Lying to Internal Affairs and hiding bribery money? Now, that would be illegal, wouldn't it?"

The guy was a pro at avoiding direct answers.

"How did Buckley pay you?" Ava asked.

He frowned at the change of subject. "What?"

"If Buckley was in such dire financial straits, how was he able to pay your fees?"

Which was a great question. The modern décor and newly renovated building did not speak to a bargain law office.

"We had an arrangement," Levinson said. What that arrangement was, was not elaborated on as he leaned forward in his seat again. "Was there anything else other than the check?"

There was, but he was doing a heck of a job of avoiding all of it.

"Does Sheila get anything?" I asked, my mind again going to the sad image of her. "Anything of Buckley's at all?"

"Sheila?" He frowned.

"Buckley's girlfriend," I clarified. "They lived together."

"Sure, sure." He nodded in recognition. "Well, like I said, Buckley didn't have a will. I mean, why should he, right? He was young, healthy…"

"Didn't have a lot of assets to leave to anyone," Ava added.

"That too. Anyway, no, I don't think she could claim much of anything. Even if there was much to claim. Really, the only person who is likely to profit at all from Buckley's death is Crazy Carmen."

"Carmen?" I frowned. "I thought you said Buckley's sister would be considered his next of kin."

"Oh, she is. But Carmen's got the life insurance policy."

Ava and I shared a look.

Levinson must have seen it as he added, "Carmen didn't tell you about the life insurance policy?"

"No," I said. "She didn't."

"Ah." He looked from Ava to me, probably weighing how much to share. "Well, it was a term of their divorce. Since Carmen was getting alimony as long as Buckley was alive, she insisted on taking out a life insurance policy on him as well. In case anything ever happened to him on the job where he couldn't pay that alimony anymore."

Like now.

I felt my spidey senses tingling as I asked, "How much was the policy worth?"

Levinson smirked. "Five hundred thousand dollars. That whacko is now worth a cool half million."

* * *

"That settles it. Carmen is guilty," Ava said as we walked back to the car.

I laughed. "Just like that? Judge, jury, and executioner?"

"I didn't say she should be executed," Ava backtracked. "But I could have easily seen her killing Buckley just for the fun of it. Add in a half million dollars, and how could she resist?"

She wasn't wrong.

"She *did* fail to mention the life insurance policy when we talked to her," I conceded.

"And she had that shaky alibi," Ava noted. "Waiting in the restaurant bar for some guy who never showed up. Who can conveniently *not* back up her story."

"We should have asked for his name," I said, wishing we'd dug a little deeper as we both got into my Jeep.

"We should ask that now," Ava decided, already pulling out her phone and dialing. Two rings in, the nasally receptionist answered.

"Nadia's Nails, how may I help you?"

"Can I speak to Carmen, please?" Ava asked.

"No," came the reply. "Sorry, she's not here today."

"Oh. Well, do you know when she's scheduled to be there?"

"She was *scheduled* today," the woman said, not without a small hint of annoyance. "Called in sick at the last minute."

Ava raised both eyebrows in my direction. "Really? Sick?"

That spidey sense kicked into overdrive, and I suddenly wondered if she was out sick or out guilty.

"So she said," Nasally replied. "Anyway, can I book you an appointment with someone else?"

"Uh, no. Thanks," Ava said. "I don't suppose you could give me her phone number?"

There was a pause on the other end. "Yeah, we're really not supposed to give out personal information to clients."

"Oh, I'm not just a client," Ava assured her. "I'm…a friend. A good friend."

"Oh yeah?" came Nasally's reply. "Then how come you don't have her phone number?"

Touché.

"Look, if she's really sick, I just want to look in on her," Ava tried again.

"Sorry. Store policy." I could tell Nasally was going to stand firm on this one. "But I'd be happy to tell her you called." Which was going to be hard, as she hung up before Ava could even give her name.

"So much for that," Ava said, putting her phone back in her purse.

"You know," I said, thinking over what the lawyer had told us. "If Carmen knew she'd get the insurance money when Buckley died, the missing bribery money could have nothing to do with Buckley's death at all."

Ava scrunched up her nose. "So where do you think the missing money is?"

I shrugged. "I don't know." I glanced up at the lawyer's offices. "But did you see how Levinson evaded directly answering our questions about it?"

Ava nodded. "Yeah, I caught that too. You think Levinson knows where Buckley stashed it?"

I shrugged. "I don't know. But I don't think he believes Buckley spent it all."

"Neither do I," Ava decided. "If he had, wouldn't someone have noticed? I mean, a hundred grand is a lot of money. Even if you spread it out over some time. No one at the police department noticed anything different, and Carmen said he didn't spend any money at home. Unless he gave it away, he had to still have it."

"And he isn't striking me as the charitable type," I added. "So, where could Buckley have been hiding it?"

Ava shrugged. "Offshore accounts?"

I nodded. "Maybe. Seems sophisticated for Buckley, though."

"Coffee can in the backyard?" Ava suggested with a grin.

"If he had a backyard. He lived at Shady Meadows, remember."

"Okay, maybe under his mattress?"

"Wherever he hid it, maybe he finally needed it." I turned to Ava as I pulled on my seat belt. "Levinson said the shutdown had him in financial trouble. Maybe he finally felt like it was worth the risk to dip into his ill-gotten gains."

"You think that's what got him killed?" Ava asked.

I shrugged. "I mean, maybe someone realized Buckley had the cash still and killed him for it."

"Well, if we're talking about someone close to him, there's Sheila," Ava offered.

I thought back to our meeting with her. "She seemed pretty desperate for money." I paused. "But she's not the one who was at the crime scene the next day. Jamie was."

"Okay, so Jamie finds out his mom's boyfriend has been lying this whole time and sitting on a pile of cash. Maybe he finds Buckley's offshore account numbers or sees him digging up the coffee can," she added with a grin. "He's no fan of Buckley's anyway, so he goes where he knows he'll be alone and isolated, kills him, then takes the money."

I nodded. I could easily see it all playing out that way. "So, where's the money now?"

Ava shrugged. "Jamie must have it stashed somewhere."

"Most likely close to home. Probably still at Shady Meadows."

"Didn't Sheila say she usually worked the dinner shift at the diner?" Ava's eyes had that concerning twinkle in them as she glanced at the dash clock. "It's happy hour now. She's not home."

"I don't know..."

"And Jamie's at the Links. Their apartment should be deserted." The twinkle became downright dangerous.

"I'm not sure I like where you're going with this," I hedged.

"But do you like it less than investors giving the 'deadliest winery in town' a wide berth?" Ava reasoned.

I sighed and turned the car on. "You win. Let's go commit B&E."

CHAPTER ELEVEN

Shady Meadows was no less depressing in the early evening than it had been the previous morning. The sun setting behind the building cast long shadows across the ground that felt almost ominous in their gloom. Most of the outdoor lights looked either busted or burned out, leaving a single one casting pale light on the rusted staircase. It buzzed as we climbed up to the second floor, signaling that like most of the place, it too was on its last leg.

Not much had changed since our previous visit, though 2A seemed to be playing some heavy metal instead of the bassy hip hop from earlier, and 2B had upped the ante on the curry, the scents so strong I was sure it seeped through the walls of every unit.

We stopped outside the door to 2C, and Ava raised a hand and knocked. "Just in case Sheila called in sick," she said in a low voice.

We both listened, though no telltale footsteps echoed on the other side. In fact, no sounds came from within the apartment at all. The windows were dark, and I could tell no lights were on behind the thin curtains. The place looked as deserted as Ava had anticipated it to be.

"Now what?" I asked.

Ava shrugged then stuck a hand out and tried the knob. Predictably locked. Then she reached down and lifted the edge of the worn welcome mat. A roly-poly bug crawled out, but no key was conveniently stashed there.

"So how do we get in?" I asked.

Ava bit her lip, glancing up and down the hall. "I wonder if there's a super on site."

I shrugged. "I didn't see a sign, but that doesn't mean much."

Ava backtracked a few steps to the door to 2B, rapping sharply on it. A few minutes later it was opened, and the aroma of spices almost knocked me over. A short woman about my age with long dark hair stared back at us. She had a toddler attached to her hip, and her sweats looked like she'd just been on the losing end of a baby food battle. "What?" she asked impatiently, shifting the toddler.

"Hi!" Ava gave the woman a bright smile.

One that was returned with a scowl of suspicion.

"Uh, I was wondering if you could tell me if there's a super on the premises?" Ava went on. "I'm new to the building and forgot my key."

"Bottom floor, first apartment on the right," the woman said.

"Thanks so much. I really appreciate—"

But the door had already shut in her face.

"So much for being neighborly," Ava mumbled as we stepped away.

"To be fair, you're not really her neighbor," I pointed out as I followed her back down the stairs to the first floor.

We both stopped outside apartment 1A.

"What are you going to tell the super?" I asked. "I mean, he's gonna know you don't live there, right?"

Ava thought about that a beat. "Here." She pulled her small crossbody purse off her shoulder and handed it to me. "Put this in your bag," she said, gesturing to my larger purse, which was slung over my shoulder.

"Why?" I asked, complying.

She grinned, the twinkle back in her eyes. "Just trust me."

"That phrase never ends in a good idea—" I tried to warn her, but she was already knocking on 1A's door.

Heavy footsteps approached before the door swung open to reveal an older guy with ample belly and lots of grey hair sticking out in wild tufts from his head. And eyebrows. And nose. He was dressed in shorts, a white T-shirt, suspenders, and galoshes. The outfit was incongruous enough that I wondered just what sort of apartment emergency he'd been preparing for.

"Something you need?" he asked, his voice just slightly less irritated than 2B's had been. Clearly living in Shady Meadows was irritating enough that any slight intrusion was an annoyance.

"Hi," Ava said, giving him the same big bright smile. "I was hoping you could help me."

"With?" the guy asked, frowning as his gaze went from Ava to me.

"My uncle just passed away."

I shot her a look.

"Bill Buckley," she continued. "He lived in 2C."

"Oh, gee. Sorry. I didn't know he had a niece." The man looked appropriately sympathetic.

"Thanks," Ava said, giving him another smile, albeit a slightly more somber one. "But I was here earlier, giving my condolences to his girlfriend, Sheila, and I forgot my purse inside the apartment." She shrugged. "The grief. I just don't know where my head is at these days."

"Yeah. The grief." The guy nodded his hairy head. "Sorry for your loss."

"Thanks," Ava said again. "I just went to see if Sheila would let me in to grab it, but she's not home. I'd call her at work but…well, the number is stored in my phone, and my phone is in my purse, which is in the apartment." She pointed up toward the second floor.

The guy shook his head. "Modern conveniences, huh? No one knows numbers anymore. You know my kid didn't even know my number? Just has my face stored in his iPhone thing and swipes. What happens if someone takes his phone from him, I ask you?"

Ava nodded. "I agree. I plan to memorize some important numbers. But for now…" she said, looking upward again. "I was hoping maybe you could unlock the door to the apartment so I could just slip in and get my purse?"

He frowned. "I dunno. I really ain't supposed to let anyone in when residents aren't here."

"I hate to bother Sheila again," Ava said. "She's been through so much."

He thought about that for a beat. "Yeah. I hate to bother her too." I wasn't sure if it was because it would be intrusive or because he was lazy. But he nodded. "Okay, yeah, I could unlock it for you. I mean, you are family after all, right?"

"Absolutely." Ava gave him another winning smile as the guy grabbed a ring of keys from a hook just inside his apartment door and stepped out into the sunshine with us.

"Thanks so much. I really appreciate your help," Ava said.

"Wait." The guy paused midstep and turned to face her. "Maybe I should see some ID first."

Uh-oh.

"Uh, sure," Ava said. She paused. "It's in my purse."

The super's face broke into a self-deprecating grin. "Duh. Right."

As soon as the super's back was turned again, Ava let out a sigh of relief and rolled her eyes my way.

I stifled a grin. She'd missed her calling. Forget designing jewelry—she should have been an actress.

We followed the super up the flight of stairs and past the noise and stinky apartments to 2C. He fiddled with the keys a moment, looking for the right one, before he unlocked the door.

"Thank you so much. This is really kind," Ava said, pushing past him.

I gave him a wan smile and did the same.

"We'll just be a minute," Ava promised before she shut the door behind her.

"You think he really bought that?" I whispered once we were alone.

"Possibly. But I think the longer we give him to think about it, the flimsier it will feel." Ava glanced around the dimly lit apartment, the last rays of late afternoon sunlight coming through the worn curtains providing minimal light.

"Where do we start?" I asked. The small living room looked about the same as on our previous visit. The grungy furniture was still covered in afghans and stains, a few fast food wrappers had joined the pizza box on the coffee table, and the scent of cigarette smoke hung thick in the air. It was clear that Sheila hadn't been doing much housekeeping in her grief. A small kitchen sat on the other side of the apartment, dishes piled in the sink and some pots and pans still sitting on the stove bearing the greasy remains of meals past. A short hallway lay ahead of us, leading off to two bedrooms and a bathroom, whose door stood partially open to reveal a powder blue toilet and an old oak vanity.

"Let's try the bedrooms. If Jamie took the money, his room is the most likely place he'd stash it."

"If he took it. If Buckley still had it, it could be stashed anywhere," I reasoned, feeling more and more like this was a bad idea.

But Ava was already down the hallway, standing in front of two closed doors. She took the one on the left, opening it to reveal a queen-size bed covered in a floral duvet, a couple pieces of outdated mismatched furniture, and a pair of red sheets tacked over the windows as makeshift curtains. Women's clothing lay scattered over the unmade bed, and the floor was strewn with shoes, books, a few boxes against the wall, and a small space heater.

"Looks like Sheila's room."

"Sheila *and* Buckley's," I added.

Ava nodded before crossing the hall to open the door on the right, revealing what was clearly a teenager's room. The walls were plastered in posters of rock bands and sports cars, a twin bed was shoved up against the wall next to a small desk that looked like it served more as a clutter catcher than a place to study. More fast food wrappers littered the floor here, along with video games, a pair of broken headphones, and several pairs of shoes emitting a stale odor.

"Hey, you find that purse yet?" we heard the super call from the front door.

"Uh, no. Sheila must have tucked it away for me. Be just a minute!" Ava yelled.

"He's not gonna wait much longer," I cautioned.

"Then we better split up to look for the money. You take the master—I'll take Jamie's room."

Before I could protest, she was already in the teenager's room, riffling through his desk drawers.

I glanced toward the front room, expecting the super to lose patience any second, before quickly ducking into Sheila's and her former boyfriend's bedroom.

In addition to the queen bed, which took up most of the small space, there was a dresser on the far wall and a small desk wedged in the corner near the windows. On the top of the dresser sat an old, square style television with a built-in VCR. Which, judging by the layer of dust along the opening of it, got about as much use as one would expect of technology that was thirty years out of date. I opened the top drawer of the dresser, only to find several pairs of skimpy panties. I quickly closed it, feeling totally intrusive. Sheila Connolly had lost her boyfriend, her son was possibly a murderer, and now a stranger was going through her intimates drawer.

I shoved down an icky feeling and moved on to the desk.

Where the first thing I noticed was a large rectangular void in the dust on the top. Like something had been there before and was missing now. I glanced under the desk and noticed an indentation in the carpet, where something heavy had sat. "It looks like there was a computer in here," I called out to Ava.

She popped her head in the doorway. "You found a computer?"

"Negative. I found where a computer used to be." I gestured to the empty desk.

Ava pursed her lips. "You think the police took it?"

"Maybe. They'd need a warrant," I said, having spent enough time around Grant to know the basics of police procedure.

"Which means they'd have to have some reasonable idea that something incriminating was on there," Ava concluded. "Like, say, the number of a bank account in the Cayman Islands?"

"Or something that would incriminate Buckley's killer."

"Well, either way it's not here." Ava blew out a frustrated breath. She glanced around the room, eyes going to the boxes stacked on the floor. "What's in those?"

I shrugged. "I don't know. I haven't had a chance to look yet—"

"Hey!"

Ava and I froze at the sound of a woman's voice yelling from just outside the door.

"You hear that music?" the woman yelled, a slight accent coloring her English.

"Yeah, so what?" the super responded.

I let out a sigh of relief. The neighbor from 2B was talking to the super. Not Sheila catching us red-handed in her bedroom.

"Robby can't even get a nap. Can't you do something about it?" she said.

"I can talk to 'em, but hey, it's a free country, lady. They wanna play music…" The rest of the super's response trailed off as I heard him follow the woman down the hall to 2A's pulsating door.

"I'm guessing no luck with Jamie's room?" I whispered as Ava made a beeline for the boxes.

She shook her head. "I checked under the bed, in the closet." She paused to look up. "Totally gross, by the way. I found pizza that was ripe enough to grow legs."

I shuddered. "But no cash?"

She shook her head. "Nope. Granted, I'm not sure how big of a bundle we're talking, but I'm guessing bigger than a wallet."

I nodded. "So, if Jamie took the money, he doesn't have it stored here."

"Which doesn't mean he didn't take it," Ava pointed out. "I mean, he could have it stashed at a friend's house or with a girlfriend. Maybe it's even in an account somewhere."

"Like the Caymans," I said, glancing at the empty spot on the desk again.

"Whoa."

"What?" I moved over to Ava's side.

She nodded into the boxes. "Looks like Buckley was old school. These are financial files."

"Like actual paper ones?"

She nodded. "Look." She handed me a recent bank statement. For a moment I thought we'd hit pay dirt and found the missing money. Until I looked down at the balance. $115. It was worse than mine.

"Wow. They really *were* living hand to mouth," I noted. Though I noticed Sheila's name wasn't on the statement. If they'd been splitting the bills, they hadn't been commingling their money to do so.

"Anything else in there?" I asked, glancing back at the front door.

Ava flipped through a few more files. "Looks like some bills, tax returns." She pulled out another yellow file folder marked *Important* and opened it to reveal a photocopy of Buckley's birth certificate and a letter of commendation from his early days on the force.

"What's that?" I asked, pointing to a file marked *Insurance*. "Maybe the life insurance policy?"

Ava pulled it from the box and opened it.

Only instead of an insurance policy, a stack of photos fell out, spilling onto the carpeted floor.

We both scrambled to pick them up, and I hoped they weren't in any particular order before. There were a couple dozen 4x6 sized photos, like you'd print off from your camera or phone. All were on glossy photo paper, though some looked more vividly colored than others.

"What are these?" Ava asked, picking the first one up. It was of two women, one with her back to the camera, leaning forward to hand the other woman something across a counter.

"Wait—that's Katy's Cookies!" I pointed to the countertop we'd seen earlier that day.

Sure enough, as Ava flipped to the next photo, Katy's face was clearly visible as the other woman stepped to the right of the frame.

"So Buckley definitely knew she was in town," Ava mused.

"Which doesn't prove *she* knew *he* was," I noted, watching Ava shift to the next photo. Which looked to be a third shot of the same two women, this one capturing their profiles.

"Why would he be taking photos of her shop?" I wondered out loud.

"Maybe he was keeping tabs on her? Making sure she didn't violate her parole."

"Maybe. But I'm not sure why he'd care. I mean—why not let her parole officer handle that?"

"Who's this?" Ava said, shuffling through more photos. The next one was a different scene entirely. It looked to be some sort of party, several people in cocktail dresses and slacks holding glasses of wine and smiling.

I shrugged. "I dunno. Maybe some of Buckley's friends?"

"Or clients." Ava moved to the next photo and pointed to the corner, where we could clearly see part of Buckley's sleeve as he took the photo—a blue security uniform.

"So Buckley took some pictures of a party he was working security for? Why?"

Ava shrugged. "Maybe he wanted to remember it?"

"Wait, I know that guy." I stabbed a finger at the face of a man in the next photo. "That's James Atherton." I turned to Ava. "Remember he was married to Leah and then to Heather?" Leah was a friend of both Ava's and mine who owned a bakery in town called the Chocolate Bar. And Heather had been James's unlucky second wife, who had been killed after a wine and chocolate party Leah and I had thrown together. While I was sympathetic to James's widower status, that was about all I was sympathetic to about James Atherton. He worked at a large corporate winery in the area, and he was even more pretentious than the wines he sold.

"Why would Buckley be taking pictures of James Atherton at a party he was working?" Ava asked.

"Beats me. Maybe they were friends?"

Ava shifted the stack of photos, flipping to the next one.

And we both froze.

"If these are pictures of friends, then what is this doing here," Ava asked slowly.

I had no answer for that. Because the guy in the picture was Grant.

He was standing outside of some brick building, his phone to his ear, eyes going off in the opposite direction, like he wasn't aware he was being photographed.

Ava flipped to the next one and the next. Three more photos of Grant in various places and poses.

"You did say they knew each other, right?" Ava asked, clearly fishing for a way to explain them.

I nodded, my throat dry. "But only through Buckley's partner, Eckhart. Grant said he didn't really know Buckley."

"Maybe he was downplaying their friendship?" Ava asked.

"You mean lying to me," I croaked out. For some reason I couldn't take my eyes off the photos. Clearly *Buckley* had known *Grant*. Well enough to have pictures of him. Why? And why had Grant lied?

"You find that purse yet, lady?" the super's voice came from the front door.

Ava shoved the photos back into the file and put it in the box. "Yeah! Be right out!" she called, putting the lid back on it.

I pulled her purse out of my bag and handed it to her as we quickly slipped out of the bedroom and to the front door, where an impatient looking super was waiting. "What took you so long?" he asked.

"Sheila had it tucked away for me," Ava lied with a big smile on her face as we stepped outside. She held her handbag up. "Right here, see?"

The super frowned as he locked the door behind us, but clearly we'd taken up too much of his time already, so he just grunted as he turned and headed back toward the stairs.

Ava and I moved to follow him, but as we reached the bottom of the stairs, Ava stopped so abruptly that I almost slammed into her back. Then she spun and shoved me behind the overflowing dumpster.

"What the—?" I stopped as I looked past her and saw what had caused her shift in course.

Trudging across the parking lot with a scowl firmly in place was Jamie Connolly.

CHAPTER TWELVE

I ducked behind the trash bin, trying not to inhale too deeply, as Ava and I both squatted down low.

"Hey, you're Buckley's kid?" I heard the super call.

"No!" came Jamie's emphatic answer.

"He was living with your mom, though?" the older guy prompted.

"What of it?" It didn't sound as if Jamie's mood had improved any since we'd seen him at the Links. If anything, the hard edge was even more pronounced.

"His niece came by. You just missed her," the super said, his voice trailing off as he walked toward his apartment.

I held my breath and dared to peek out from behind the dumpster as I watched Jamie stare after the super.

But either he didn't care if Buckley had had a niece or just didn't care about people in general, as he just turned and stomped up the stairs, the scowl never changing.

I tried to think small, unnoticeable thoughts as I listened to him clomp up the flight of metal stairs and make his way down the hallway overhead. His footsteps paused, presumably outside the door to 2C as he unlocked it, and then I heard the sound of a door slamming shut.

"Let's go," Ava hissed in my ear.

She didn't need to tell me twice, as I was already up and running down the cracked pavement to the parking lot. My heart didn't stop pounding until I was safely inside my Jeep. Ava threw herself in the passenger seat beside me, and we both breathed deeply for a moment.

"That was way too close," Ava finally said.

"And pointless," I added, turning the car on. "We still have no idea if Buckley had the bribery money, let alone if it was what was worth killing over."

Ava looked disappointed for a moment before she said, "But we do know now that Buckley knew Katy was in town."

"I wonder why he was taking pictures of her," I thought out loud.

"Well, it looked like he was on the job in those party pictures. Maybe someone hired him to watch Katy?" Ava speculated. "Maybe even an old friend on the force?"

"Maybe." Which immediately made me think of Grant and the pictures Buckley had had of him. I was about to say more when my phone rang from my purse, making both of us jump.

I pulled it out and checked the readout.

Grant.

I froze, guilt washing over me. Did he know where we were? Had he been watching Buckley's place?

"Who is it?" Ava asked.

"Grant." The word stuck in my throat.

"Are you going to answer it?"

I took a deep breath and swiped the call on.

"Hey," I said, wishing my voice didn't sound like I'd just been caught with a hand in the cookie jar.

Luckily, if he noticed, he didn't indicate it. "Hey, Emmy," he replied. "Where are you?"

I licked my lips, shooting a glance at Ava. "Uh, why?"

"Just wondering if you were at the winery."

"Yyyyyes," I said, drawing the word out as if it might make it feel less terrible to lie to him.

"I was just finishing up with forensics and thought I'd pick up a pizza and swing by." He paused. "If you're not busy?"

"Uh, yeah." I cleared my throat. "I mean, no. No, I'm not busy."

"Good. See you in about half an hour?"

"Sure. I'll be there. *Here*," I amended.

He hung up, and I let out a long sigh. "I could never be a spy. I'm so not cut out to lead a double life."

"Honey, you're barely cut out to lead *one*," she joked.

I swatted her arm and laughed as I pointed my Jeep back toward downtown.

* * *

By the time I'd dropped Ava off at her loft above Silver Girl and I'd driven slightly faster than normal back home, I arrived at Oak Valley with just about ten minutes to spare. I quickly parked in the near-empty lot and made a beeline for my cottage at the back of the property.

Like most of the buildings on the site, the cottage had been built by my grandfather, long before I'd been born. It was what real estate agents like to call cozy and everyone else would call cramped, but to me it just felt like home. I quickly ran up the hand carved wooden stairs to my bedroom and shed my jeans and T-shirt in favor of something a little more romancy looking. I threw open my closet door, catching a glimpse of my bedside alarm clock as I did. Seven minutes to go. I grabbed my go-to little black dress, noting unhappily that it was a smidge tighter than usual with the post-shutdown layer of ice cream I was still holding on to around my hips. But, with a pair of flashy red heels and a slim silver necklace of Ava's creation, it looked pretty decent. I glanced at the clock. Five minutes.

I ducked into the bathroom to do a quick hair fluffing and makeup check, adding a layer of red lipstick to complement the shoes. Then I hightailed it back downstairs and out the door, taking the stone pathway to the kitchen. I had just grabbed a bottle of Pinot Noir from the wine chiller and had an opener in hand as I heard the crunch of car tires on gravel outside the window.

Perfect timing.

A moment later Grant's footsteps echoed down the hallway from the main entrance to the private kitchen. "Hello?" he called.

"In here!" I pulled down two glasses and poured wine into each as he approached.

"Hey," Grant said. He set a large pizza box down on the counter and came up behind me to place a soft kiss on my neck that instantly sent goosebumps down my arms. "Nice dress," he murmured into my hair.

"What, this old thing?" I said, turning around to face him. I held out a glass. "Pinot?"

"Please." He took it, a lazy smile on his face as he took a sip. "Quiet day here?" he asked.

"Hmm?" I opened the lid on the box. Pepperoni and olive. My favorite combo.

"Quiet day? At the winery?" Grant clarified.

"Oh. Uh, yeah." I nodded. "Real quiet."

He gave me a funny look. "Sorry."

"Sorry?" I asked, wondering if he meant he was sorry for prying or I should be sorry for holding back where I'd really been.

"Sorry it's been slow. Business will pick up soon."

"Oh." I told my telltale heart to stop beating so fast. "Yeah. Thanks." I cleared my throat. "Uh, so how was your day?" I grabbed a couple of plates from the cupboard, handing him one.

"Good. Busy." He pulled a slice of pizza from the box and took a bite before setting it on the plate.

"Oh? Make any headway on Buckley's case?" I asked as I loaded my own plate.

He slipped onto one of the barstools at the granite counter in the center of the room. "Some."

"And?" I took a seat next to him and bit into my ooey-gooey pizza. Heaven erupted on my tongue.

"And, we'll get there."

I rolled my eyes. "That tells me nothing."

"Exactly." He grinned as he took another bite.

I shook my head, sipping my wine. As he went in for another bite, I studied his profile, thinking about how Eckhart had described Grant earlier that morning. And wondering who of the two of us knew Grant better. Had he really been the type of cop who made up his own rules when he'd been in San Francisco? Was he now that he was in Sonoma? Or were Eckhart and I both just seeing what we wanted to in Grant—filling in the blanks that Grant's strong silent type demeanor created in the way we wanted them filled?

"What?" he asked.

"Hmm?"

"You were looking at me funny."

"Was I?" I glanced down at my plate to cover any looks I might have inadvertently been giving him, funny or otherwise. "I was just thinking."

"About?"

"Buckley," I said, half-truthfully. "And how I guess you never really know people."

He cocked his head at me. "How so?"

"Well." I sipped my wine, formulating my thoughts. "He seemed like a nice guy to me. I mean, when I interviewed him for the job. Only, it turns out his girlfriend was disappointed in him, her son hates him, his ex-wife *really* hates him. Even his partner has nothing good to say about him."

"His partner?" Grant's tone changed, suspicion suddenly clouding it.

"Or, you know, so it would seem," I quickly covered. "I mean, that his partner wouldn't have anything good to say about him."

I snuck a glance at Grant out of the corner of my eye to find him staring intently at me. As if trying to read between the half truths. I shoved more pizza into my mouth, chewing vigorously to cover any expression of guilt that might have been lingering on my face.

"Anyway," I said, once I'd swallowed the bite. "I just mean it makes one wonder what sort of judge of character they are." I snuck another glance his way. "I mean, how well do we really know anyone?"

"I'd like to think I know *you* pretty well." Grant took a sip of his wine, his eyes still holding a look of suspicion in them.

"You know what I *tell* you," I said. "But I'm sure we both have lots of things we hold back. Stories we haven't told each other." Like the apparently funny one about the scar on his backside that Lana had heard all about.

"Okay." Grant set his wineglass down. "So tell me a story, Emmy."

I licked my lips. "About?"

"What did you *really* do today?"

Oh boy. "Well…I, you know, did some work here at the winery." True. I had started out the morning with payroll I couldn't afford in front of me. "And…I had lunch at the Links. With David Allen."

It might have been my imagination, but I thought I saw his eyes narrow a little at the mention of David's name.

"And Ava," I added quickly, lest he get the wrong impression. "Lobster Bisque. It was delicious. I think they put thyme in it."

"Fancy." He sipped his wine again, and I had no idea if he was buying this.

"Well, it *is* the Links." I smiled halfheartedly.

"And what did you three talk about at lunch?" The suspicion was growing in his voice.

"Well…David's got his gallery showing tomorrow night," I said. "We're all going."

He nodded but didn't say anything.

"So…what did *you* do today?" I asked, hoping to move on from the parts I was leaving out.

"I told you." He licked a stray droplet of pinot from his lips. "Work."

"See, *that's* exactly what I mean." I put a hand on my hip.

Grant raised an eyebrow at me. "What?"

"That you don't give anything away that you don't want to. We're all just…giving an edited version of ourselves to each other." I hated how my mind immediately went to Eckhart's version of Grant.

He studied me for a moment. "Okay." He set his glass down on the counter. "I spent the morning with tech, finding out what was on Buckley's hard drive. And the afternoon with ballistics looking at the bullet they pulled from him."

"Either turn up anything useful?" I asked.

He shrugged, going in for another bite of pizza. "Not particularly. Buckley's computer had the usual mix of work and play—some invoices and info for freelance work he'd done. A couple of games. Some rather interesting internet searches."

"Oh? Such as?"

Grant grinned. "Let's just say Buckley's taste in pornography was a little on the daring side."

"Never mind." I held up a hand. "I don't want to hear it."

"I thought you wanted to get to know him," Grant teased, still grinning.

"What about ballistics?" I asked, changing the subject.

"Bullet came from a .22 LR. Long Rifle. Common shotgun, but the bullet was in good shape and they're fairly certain they could match the striation pattern to a particular gun if we had one."

"I'm guessing you checked if Buckley owned a Long Rifle?" I asked, thinking that would be very handy for Jamie to have laid his hands on.

But Grant shook his head. "No, nothing registered to him. But they're not hard to come by. You can basically walk into Walmart and buy one."

"So anyone could have gotten their hands on one," I said, my mind churning over this new info.

He nodded, sipping his wine. "They're mostly used for hunting small game."

"So you're still thinking this was an accidental shooting?" I asked. "Some hunter stumbles into my vineyard and mistakes Buckley for a deer?"

He shot me a look. "Or realizes he's been caught trespassing and poaching. Or Buckley startles him. Or the guy's high and shoots for any number of paranoid reasons."

I looked down at my plate, picking a piece of pepperoni off a slice. "You said the type of gun is used for hunting small game. Like, say, rabbits?"

"Sure." He ripped off a piece of his pizza crust and popped it into his mouth.

I licked my lips. "You know…Eckhart hunts."

He stopped midchew. "Eckhart," he repeated around the bite.

I could see the warning flashing in his eyes, but I forged ahead.

"He hunts small game. Rabbits specifically," I said, remembering the framed photo I'd seen on his desk that morning.

"Emmy…"

"So, it's quite possible he owns a Long Rifle."

"He also owns a service revolver and has access to a whole locker full of weapons, any one of which would have been a heck of a lot more convenient to shoot someone with," Grant said, an edge to his voice as if he didn't like this path we were going down at all.

"Sure, but those would all be easily traceable back to him," I reasoned.

Grant shook his head, his nostril flaring. "I knew I shouldn't have shared anything with you about this case. I give you an inch, and you take a mile."

"That's not fair," I shot back. "You're treating me like I'm some sort of child."

"No, if you were a child, I'd ground you."

I let out a humorless laugh. "Seriously? Do you know how chauvinistic you just sounded?"

"I'm not a chauvinist," Grant ground out, something flashing behind his eyes. "I'm a realist. And the reality is you are butting into something you know nothing about."

"Well then tell me about it!" I said, my voice rising to match the anger I could hear coloring into his. "Tell me why you're so sure Eckhart is innocent. Tell me how well you really knew Buckley. Tell me exactly how fabulous Lana is!"

"Lana?" Grant frowned.

I shook my head. "Never mind. My point is, stop treating me like I'm some idiot who can't handle the truth."

"Well now you just sound like Jack Nicholson."

"You're mocking me." I gave him a hard look. "And it's not attractive."

"You know what?" Grant said sliding off his stool. "Neither is the way you're trying to bait me into an argument."

"I'm not baiting you! I'm just tired of being underestimated by men who know it all."

Grant's eyes flashed again. He opened his mouth to say something but then apparently thought better of it, as he shut it again quickly, his jaw hardening as he shook his head and slipped off his stool.

"Thanks for the wine," he spat out before he turned and stalked out of the kitchen.

"Thanks for the pizza!" I shot to his retreating back, the words sounding more like an insult than good manners.

Though if he heard them, he didn't indicate it, his posture ram-rod straight, his stride long, and his head still shaking in anger as he disappeared down the hall.

I waited a moment, hoping he'd come back around the corner and apologize. But instead of his returning footsteps, I heard the engine of his SUV turn over and his tires spinning angrily on gravel as he sped out of my parking lot and back down the oak-lined drive.

So much for romance.

CHAPTER THIRTEEN

I awoke the next morning with a pounding headache. Which, in hindsight, might have had something to do with the fact the night before I'd single-handedly polished off both the rest of the large pepperoni pizza and the bottle of Pinot. And some ice cream. And chocolate. And more wine. What could I say? I didn't do rejection well. Bridget Jones and I had spent a long evening together, crying out our broken hearts until I'd fallen sleep somewhere mid *Edge of Reason*.

I groaned, rolling over to look at the clock on my bedside table. Just past nine. I hadn't meant to sleep in so late. But after the comfort food binge, the crying jag, and the Rom Com fest, it had been well after midnight before I'd passed out on my bed fully clothed.

I peeled back my blankets, thinking I definitely needed to send my wrinkled dress to the cleaners. It was a miracle I hadn't popped one of its seams after all the calories I'd consumed. I made a mental note to get Ava's recipe for green juice and turn over a healthier leaf that weekend.

I pulled myself out of bed and into a long hot shower. After downing a couple of Advil and applying enough mascara to make my lashes stand at attention, I started feeling human again. In an effort to cheer my headache away, I grabbed a pale yellow sundress from my closet, adding gold earrings and a pair of ballet flats. At least if my mood wasn't sunny, my outfit could be.

Though, I will say that as I made my way out the door of my cottage and down the stone pathway, the scents of freshly baked Cherry Vanilla Muffins and hot coffee that came wafting from the kitchen caused my mood to lift another notch. So did the cheery faces that greeted me as I followed the aromas into the kitchen. One face in particular that was a very welcomed sight that morning.

"Conchita!" I practically threw myself into her arms, ignoring the puff of flour that came up from her apron as I did.

"Emmy, *mija*!" She matched my fierce hug with her own. "Why didn't you call me?" she chided as I pulled away. "A murder in the vineyard?"

"Eddie told her," Ava said.

I pulled my attention from Conchita to find her and Eddie sitting at the counter, each nibbling from the plate of fresh muffins in front of them. Ava was dressed in a flowy white top with floral embroidery that screamed springtime. She'd paired it with a short denim skirt that gave the outfit the perfect blend of hard and soft. I would say she was the head-turner in the room, if Eddie hadn't been sitting next to her in head-to-toe pink seersucker. He looked like an overfed flamingo as he flapped his arms at me.

"Well, of course I told Conchita!" Eddie said. "I mean, a man died here. That doesn't happen every day."

"You're right," Ava agreed. "It's more like every other day."

"Ha. Ha. Very funny," I told her, grabbing a muffin.

Ava grinned at me. "Coffee?" she asked, moving to the espresso machine in the corner.

"Please," I said, instantly forgiving her friendly barb.

"How are you really, Emmy?" Conchita asked, her warm brown eyes full of concern. Her salt and pepper hair was pulled back into a tight bun at the nape of her neck, and the frown etched into the network of fine lines running across her tanned face pulled at my heartstrings.

"I'm fine," I lied, giving her what I hoped was a reassuring smile. "Really."

Her frown smoothed out some, but the concern stayed.

"I'm sure she's much more fine this morning than she was yesterday," Ava added, putting the espresso machine to work churning out heavenly smelling liquid. She turned to give the room a wicked grin. "Grant was here last night."

Just like that, my sunny mood went gloomy again.

"Oh really!" Conchita's frown disappeared completely, replaced by what I'd come to know as her meddling matchmaker smile. "How is our Detective Grant?"

"Fine," I said. Much less convincingly than the last time.

"Just fine?" Eddie asked, clearly having picked up on my unenthused tone. "Why do I get the feeling that's not a good thing?"

I sighed. "We kind of had a fight."

"Oh, honey." Ava handed me my coffee. "How bad was it?"

"Two-and-a-half Bridget Jones's bad."

"Ouch," Eddie said, being fully in the know on our Rom Com rating scale.

"What happened?" Ava asked.

I shook my head. "Nothing. I mean, it was just…" Him being pig-headed. Me being stubborn. Him being overprotective. Me being oversensitive. "It was nothing," I settled on. "A misunderstanding."

"These things happen," Conchita said. "Hector misunderstands me all the time. It's because we're from Venus and he's from Mars. I read a book about it." She nodded sagely. "But it doesn't mean Hector doesn't love me."

I gave her a smile, not having the heart to tell her that her marriage of twenty-five years to her first love was so not the same as the tentative maybe-relationship Grant and I had.

"Amen," Eddie, chimed in, clearly trying to be encouraging. "Curtis doesn't always understand me either." Eddie had been a house husband to his partner Curtis for twenty years before Curtis's health had prompted him to retire and prompted Eddie into the workforce and onto my doorstep. "Curtis misunderstands why I need to buy ascots, why I need Perrier over tap, why my shoes cost more than our rent…"

I couldn't help a laugh. "Thanks, guys. I'm…I'm sure it will be fine." I blew on my hot coffee, not at all believing my own words. "He's probably just under a lot of stress."

Conchita nodded. "Yes. Ava told me all about how he knew the man who died. They were police officers together?"

"Sort of," I hedged, not really sure myself how well they knew each other. Which made me feel no better about how we'd left things the night before. "Grant knew Buckley's partner."

"Who is one of our suspects in Buckley's murder," Eddie added.

I shot him a glance. I wasn't sure when they'd become "our" suspects, but I was pretty sure that if Grant heard him talking like that, it would do nothing to mend the fences we'd trampled the night before.

"I've been thinking about that," Ava said, sitting back at the counter and grabbing another muffin. "And I'm honestly not convinced Buckley's death has anything to do with his former police life."

"Really?" I sat on the stool beside her, taking a bite of my muffin. I was momentarily distracted by the sweet vanilla mingling with plump tart cherries bursting in my mouth. I'd missed Conchita.

"Really," Ava said, nodded emphatically. "Like Buckley's lawyer pointed out, there's really only one person who benefits from his death."

"The ex-wife!" Eddie said, stabbing the air with his index finger.

"Exactly," Ava said. "Carmen's halfway to being a millionaire with her—what did she call him?—'putz' of an ex-husband out of the picture."

I pursed my lips. "I wonder if she owns a Long Rifle."

Ava raised an eyebrow at me. "Is that the type of gun that killed Buckley?"

I nodded and quickly filled them in on the sparse few details Grant had given me the night before. Including the fact that a .22 LR was the type of gun one would use to hunt small game. "Like the rabbits Buckley's partner Eckhart hunts."

"See, I knew he was our number one suspect," Eddie said.

"I don't know," Ava said. "I mean, what does Eckhart have to gain by killing Buckley now?"

"Nothing," Conchita answered. "But maybe he had something to lose if Buckley remained alive."

"Like what?" Eddie asked, frowning.

Conchita chewed on that a moment before finally shrugging. "You got me."

"I still like Carmen," Ava decided, licking crumbs off her fingers. "She hated him, she has a non-alibi alibi, and she had a lot to gain by him kicking the bucket."

I had to admit, she made three very good points. And it would be a lot easier on my relationship with Grant if Carmen were the guilty party and not his former friend and fellow officer. "She *was* conveniently missing from work yesterday," I agreed.

"I wonder if she's in today," Eddie said, eyeing Ava's phone suggestively.

She grinned, taking the hint and picking it up to scroll through her recent calls. She tapped Nadia's Nails' number and put the phone on speaker, setting it on the counter as we all listened to it ring.

Four in I was beginning to think maybe we were calling too early for them to be open, when a familiar voice picked up on the other end.

"Nadia's Nails, how may I help you?" the same nasally receptionist answered.

"Hi. This is Ava calling again for Carmen. Is she in today?"

The woman on the other end sighed. "No. She's not."

"Out sick again?" Ava asked, sending me a knowing look.

"Beats me. She had a nine thirty appointment and just didn't show. Didn't even bother to call in today."

"Really?" Ava asked, wiggling her eyebrow up and down at us.

"Yeah. Really. So if she really is some friend of yours, when you see her, tell her she's fired if she doesn't show up tomorrow." With that, Nasally hung up.

"I'm beginning to think you might be right about Carmen," I said as Ava put her phone back into her pocket.

"You think she's hiding out at home?" Eddie asked.

I shrugged. "It's possible. The receptionist wouldn't give us her number."

Conchita blew out a puff of air between her lips in a *pft* sound. "Are you kidding me? You can find anyone on the internet these days."

I stifled a grin. Conchita had only discovered the internet about two decades after the rest of the world.

"Here, give me your phone." Conchita made a waving motion, indicating Ava should hand it over.

Which she did. One did not argue with the purveyor of the muffins in her own kitchen. "Why don't you use yours?" Ava asked as she forked it over.

Conchita waved her off. "I don't have a data plan. Too rich for my blood."

Was that a subtle dig at how much (or little) I paid her? I was beginning to feel like a scrooge in the boss department—minus the piles of cash.

"See, all you have to do is google the name and city of the person you want to find," Conchita went on, "and something will show up. A property record, a phone number, social media. It always does." She let her fingers do the walking, squinting at the screen to see the small print.

"What do you mean 'it always does'?" Eddie asked, narrowing his eyes at her. "How often are you invading someone's privacy?"

Conchita made the *pft* sound again. "Please. You think anything is private now? Alexa hears all, and Facebook practically reads my mind with their ads."

I chuckled. "So, any hits for Carmen Buckley in Napa?"

Conchita frowned. "Give me a minute. I'm not a miracle worker."

Eddie stifled a grin, sipping his coffee. "No, just nosy."

Conchita shot him a look. "You behave. Or the next time Curtis wants to know how much you paid for those fancy Italian shoes of yours, I'll show him how to search your browsing history."

Eddie gasp. "You wouldn't!"

Conchita grinned and winked at me. Clearly, she would not.

"You think Grant's looked at Carmen as a suspect yet?" Ava asked, rising to refill her coffee cup.

I shrugged. "He hasn't said anything to me." I paused. "Not that I'm sure he would." I shoved that uncomfortable thought down. "Why?"

"Just wondering if maybe that's why Carmen's hiding out. You know, afraid the police might suspect her and stop her insurance payment," Ava said as the coffee machine did its thing, gurgling and brewing.

"Could they do that?" Eddie asked.

"Oh yeah." Ava nodded. "If it turns out Carmen killed Buckley she wouldn't get the money at all."

"Really?" Eddie asked. "Who benefits from the insurance policy then?"

Ava shrugged. "I guess the insurance company. Someone had to be paying the premiums the last two years. But, yeah, if she killed him, she can't profit from the death. It's called…" She trailed off, looking at the ceiling as if trying to remember.

"Slayer Rule," Conchita supplied.

"How did you know that?" I asked.

"I just googled it." She held up Ava's phone.

"I thought you were googling Carmen's address," Ava chided.

"Give me a minute…" Conchita went back to squinting at the screen. I was about to offer to go get her reading glasses for her, when she let out a triumphant, "Ah-ha!"

"You find her?" Ava asked, coming to look over Conchita's shoulder.

"I did." She turned the phone around so we could all see the screen. She had a website called RapidPeopleSearch.com pulled up, with a listing page displayed for a Carmen S. Buckley nee Santiago, complete with a current address.

"How did you do that?" Eddie asked, appropriately impressed.

Conchita blew on her nails and buffed them against her collar. "I may be old, but I got skills."

I clicked on the address to show a map with a little red pinpoint near the freeway. "Looks like it's about halfway between Sonoma and Napa." I glanced up at Ava. "Kind of in the middle of nowhere."

"Sounds like a great place for a killer to hide out," Ava said, eyes shining with that unmistakable *Charlie's Angels* look. "Who wants to go for a drive?"

* * *

Half an hour later, Ava, Eddie, and I pulled off the freeway in my Jeep and into open farmland. And as we pulled onto Carmen's street, I instantly understood how badly she needed money. It was a one lane road, flanked on either side by small, dilapidated homes that looked like they'd originally been constructed for migrant workers who'd picked the grapes in this region by hand. Each dwelling was the same size and shape—little more than a squat square building with a front stoop and a roof—but they were a variety of dull, peeling paint colors, as if several people had tried over the years to cheer them up. Clearly none had succeeded, as every hue of blue, red, yellow, and even pale pink was dull and dingy in a way that said it had been years since anything had looked cheery here.

Carmen's number was halfway down the block, on a house that was part burgundy and part grey, just depending on how much of the old paint colors had been exposed in places. The cement stoop was cracked, the roof missing a few tiles in front, and the grass long ago dried and given way to hard packed dirt. A flowerpot sat to one side under a closed window, though the only thing planted in it was a couple of dead sticks and a faded flag that said *Happy Thanksgiving*. It was spring. Clearly Carmen had given up on décor as well. From the faded looks of it, the flag could have been there since last fall or Thanksgiving 1998.

I parked next to the patch of dead grass on the right side of the road and got out of my Jeep, locking the doors after Ava and Eddie did the same.

"This is depressing," Eddie said, eyeing the building.

"No car in the driveway," Ava noted, nodding to the left of the building. Though "driveway" might have been overstating it a bit. There was a patch of dirt at the side of the building, where a shiny black puddle of oil indicated a car had recently sat.

Ava led the way to the front door and rapped hard enough that I feared the faded wood might split in two.

I strained to listen, but no sign of life came back to us. No footsteps, no TV blaring, no shift of fabric as someone moved to peek out the peep hole.

Ava tried again for good measure, knocking loudly as I stepped to the left and peered in the window. Not that I could see much. The curtains were drawn so that only a sliver of the room was visible between them. I could make out a sofa, a coffee table, and a rug on the floor. No lights on. No movement.

"I don't think she's here," Eddie decided, coming to stand next to me. He squinted, pressing his pudgy face close to the window. "See anything?"

I shook my head. "Not really."

"Which means she's clearly not home sick," Ava said, giving me a pointed look.

"Maybe she went to the doctor's office?" I offered. "Or pharmacy?"

"Sure." Ava nodded. "Or maybe she's halfway to the Bahamas right now with the insurance money from offing her ex-husband."

"That is highly unlikely," I told her. Then added, "Insurance doesn't pay up that fast."

"Maybe she's just running scared," Eddie offered. "No cash, on the run, knowing her alibi stinks and it's only a matter of time before—hey, where are you going?"

Ava moved around the back of the house, ducking beneath a clothesline. "I just want to take a peek in the back windows."

"What if she has a dog or something?" Eddie asked, looking nervous as he followed a step behind us. Eddie had a teacup Pomeranian named Winky, but that was about as ferocious an animal as Eddie could stomach. I'd even seen him blanch at a feral cat once.

"Relax. If she had a dog, she'd have a fence."

"If she could afford a fence," I said, stepping over broken pottery and a lawn chair with a large hole where the derrière went.

"Lucky us—looks like she can't afford decent window coverings either." Ava nodded toward the back window—singular—which was adorned in crooked vertical blinds that had bent away from the window on the right side.

She took a step closer, putting both hands up to shield her eyes from the sun as she looked through the dusty pane.

"Any sign of Carmen?" I asked, starting to feel antsy standing in her unfenced yard where any of her neighbors could see us and report suspicious trespassers.

"Negative. In fact, no sign of anything really. Place looks dark."

"I think we should go," Eddie said, his gaze going to the next shack over on the right.

I followed his line of sight to find the face of a young girl staring out at us through a side window. "I agree."

Ava sighed but straightened up and followed our lead back around to the front of the house. Only, as she walked across the dead lawn back to the Jeep, she paused at Carmen's mailbox.

"What are you doing?" I asked.

She didn't answer, instead doing an over-the-shoulder glance before quickly pulling open the box and extracting its contents.

"Ava! Tampering with the mail is a federal offense," Eddie hissed at her.

"I'm not tampering. Just looking," she protested. "And look at this." She held out a bill from the water company.

"She has bills." I shrugged.

"Look at the postmark." Ava pointed to it. "Five days ago. From a local address. It would take three at max to arrive here."

"Which means it's been sitting in Carmen's mailbox for at least two days," I said, working it out in my head as I spoke.

"Which means Carmen hasn't been home in two days," Eddie said.

I met Ava's gaze as she voiced the same thing I was thinking.

"It looks like Carmen's skipped town."

CHAPTER FOURTEEN

At a dead end with Carmen, we drove back to the winery, where I dropped Eddie off to get some actual work done that day (feeling almost guilty that he may not have a job to work soon if I didn't fix our finances), and I followed Ava out to her car in the parking lot.

"You think we should tell Grant about Carmen leaving town?" Ava asked as she beeped her car locks open.

I shrugged. "I think he's still looking at all of this as a random shooting." I paused. "But, yeah, maybe we should send him a text or something."

I must have looked as enthused about that as I felt as Ava shook her head. "I'll do it."

I raised an eyebrow at her. "You?"

"It doesn't matter if he's mad at me," she reasoned. "I'll tell him I was that early nail appointment she skipped out on or something. I can leave you out of it."

"I hate all these half truths," I mumbled, thinking as much about what we were saying as how Grant had kept me in the dark about his relationship with Buckley.

"Grant's a good guy," Ava said as she pulled her phone out, fingers flying over the keyboard. "You guys will get through this."

I sent her a wan smile as I keyed Grant's number in for her, not confident she was right.

However, then I gave myself a mental shake. Moping around wasn't going to help anyone. "You know, there's one thing about all this that's been bothering me this morning," I said, changing gears.

"Oh? Just one?" Ava teased, glancing up from her text.

I grinned. "Okay, one *other* thing. I can't stop thinking about those photos that Buckley had in his files."

"Of Katy Kline and James Atherton," Ava clarified.

"And Grant," I added my stomach clenching at the thought.

"They could be nothing," Ava said. "I mean, totally unrelated. I have lots of random pictures on my phone," she said, holding up her pink sparkly case as if to prove her point.

"Yeah, but I bet you only *print* the important ones."

"Okay, you got me there." She hit the button to send her text and put her phone back in her pocket. "So, what do you think was important about those photos?"

"I don't know. But I'm wondering if maybe it would be worth talking to James Atherton. At least maybe ask him how he knew Buckley."

Ava glanced at her watch. "I don't have to be at the shop for another couple of hours. Wanna ride into town with me?"

* * *

James Atherton was a sales rep for Bay Cellars, and he and I had an almost civil relationship. I knew him through his ex-wife Leah, who I considered a close friend. James, on the other hand, I did not. I'd had the misfortune to meet him after his second wife had been killed, and James, along with the police, had put Leah in the role of prime suspect. I'd done everything I could at the time to try to help her clear her name, which had even at one point included looking at James as his wife's possible killer. In the end he'd been guilty of selfishness and poor judgment but innocent of her murder. We'd parted ways on tentative terms, and I wasn't totally certain he'd be happy to see me.

A thought I tried not to dwell on as we pulled up to Bay Cellars. It was one of the biggest wineries in the region, covering several sprawling acres just outside of town. Their employees numbered in the hundreds and, unlike mine, all had dental and 401K plans. Their wines were in every grocery chain in America, at moderate prices that just about every household could afford. They were the type of corporate winery that every small place like Oak Valley simultaneously envied and feared. More than once Bay Cellars in general, and James Atherton in particular, had offered to buy Oak Valley but at a fraction of what it was worth. And more than once I'd hesitated before saying no. Though that hesitation was longer and longer as my debt grew bigger and bigger.

I steeled myself against the green-eyed monster as Ava parked her GTO in the lot, and we made our way to the main entrance. Displays of beautifully labeled bottles and national ad campaigns covered the walls of the lobby, and to our right I could see several people mingling in the massive tasting room, laughing, sipping, and generally having a great time, even though it was barely noon.

A dark haired woman dressed in a sleek little black dress and thigh high boots stepped out from behind the stone reception counter as we approached.

"Welcome to Bay Cellars," she said, her voice pleasant and welcoming to match her smile. "Are you here for a tour or a tasting?"

"I was actually hoping to speak with one of your sales representatives. James Atherton."

"Do you have an appointment?"

"No." I shook my head, wondering if we should have called ahead. Of course, then it would have given him ample time to make an excuse not to see me. "But we're here from Oak Valley Vineyards," I added, hoping that lent us some credibility in her eyes.

"Of course," she replied, even though I could tell the name was lost on her. "Can I have your name please?"

"Emmy Oak. And Ava Barnett," I said, gesturing to my friend.

"Just a moment, please." She stepped back behind the counter and picked up a white telephone receiver, mumbling quietly into it. After a couple of exchanges, she set it down and turned back to us.

"I'm so sorry, but Mr. Atherton is just finishing up with another client right now," she informed us.

I wasn't sure if that was true or just what he'd told her in order to put us off. "That's fine," I said, matching her pleasant smile with a falsely cheery one of my own. "We can wait."

"Uh, he didn't say how long he'd be…" She trailed off. Clearly she'd been told to get rid of us.

"We're not in a rush," Ava piped up. She glanced over at the tasting room. "In fact, we can make ourselves comfortable in there until he's free."

"Um…sure," the woman said. To her credit, her smile only faltered a bit before going back into professional mode. "I'll let Mr. Atherton know."

We thanked her and stepped into the room on our right, where two sommeliers stood behind a large wooden bar, pouring small glasses for the crowd of tourists. Ava and I took a spot near the end of the bar and caught the attention of the wine steward closest to us.

"Hello, ladies," he said, giving us the same friendly smile the receptionist had started out with. It must have been standard issue to employees along with their health package. "What can I get you two to try today? We've got a full bodied Cabernet Sauvignon and an oaky Chardonnay uncorked?"

"How about the Cab?" I asked.

Ava nodded approval.

"Sure thing," the man said, reaching for a pair of glasses and pulling a bottle out from behind the counter. While he poured professionally enough, he lacked some of the dramatic flourish of Jean Luc's style. Though as he set the glasses in front of us, the fruity aroma and dark color was excellent.

I was just about to reach for my glass, when my phone buzzed from my purse. I quickly pulled it out, fearing a response from Grant.

Only, as I looked at the readout, it was David Allen's name that came up.

You're coming tonight, right?

"Who is it?" Ava asked, nodding a thanks to the sommelier as she picked up her wineglass.

"David. Wants to make sure we'll be at his show tonight," I said, texting back a reply.

Ava and I will be there.

Six. Sharp.

I grinned at his reply. David must have been really nervous about the showing. He'd never "sharped" me about anything before.

"This isn't bad," Ava said as she tasted from her glass.

I put my phone away and took a sip. I had to admit she was right. I wanted to hate it a lot more than I did. While it was a little more fruit forward than I would have liked, the sweet cherry notes and the bitter finish were actually a quite pleasing combination.

"They seem really busy," Ava noted as a new group of tasters entered the room, laughing and chatting animatedly as if this hadn't been their first stop that day.

"And our room was empty," I noted. I'd checked before leaving, making sure I wasn't shirking any vintner duties. Jean Luc had looked downright lonely behind our empty bar.

"Things will pick up," Ava said, putting a hand on my shoulder.

"I'm not sure it will be fast enough." I set my glass down on the bar. "As much as I hate the idea of giving up some of Oak Valley, I think Schultz is right. It's the only way to keep our doors open."

She gave me a sympathetic smile before taking another sip from her glass. "Schultz have anyone interested yet?"

I shook my head. "I haven't heard from him."

"Well, look on the bright side. Maybe you'll get lucky and some tech exec will be looking for some little winery to throw his billions at but be too busy to bother you with how it's run?"

"Oh, to have that kind of luck," I said, raising my glass in a salute.

Ava grinned, clinking her glass to mine in a cheers-to-that, before we both sipped.

"Wow, I have to say, this is really good," Ava said, licking her lips.

"Our Cab always is," came a male voice behind my shoulder.

I spun to find myself facing James Atherton's sparkling white veneers. His tan was darker than when I'd last seen him, and if I had to guess, I'd say he'd been spending his shutdown days either south of the border in Baja or under a tanning bed. His salt-and-pepper hair was a little more salty than when I'd last seen him, though he looked like he'd had some work done—his forehead was as smooth as a baby's and his eyebrows didn't seem to move at all.

"It's nice to see you again, Emmy," he said, shaking my hand.

I found that phrase hard to believe, but I matched his salesman smile with one of my own. "You remember my friend Ava."

"Hi." She gave him a wave as she set her wineglass down on the bar.

"Of course. Lovely to see you too," he told her before addressing me in a voice that was way too excited for the occasion. "To what do I owe this pleasure?"

"I was hoping I could talk to you about a mutual acquaintance."

He raised an eyebrow (with difficulty) my way. "Oh? This isn't about Leah, is it?"

"No." I shook my head. "It's about someone who worked for me until recently. Bill Buckley."

The fake smiled faltered at the mention of the name. "Didn't I read that he passed away?"

"Unfortunately, yes. He, uh, died at my winery."

Atherton smirked. "That can't be good for business."

"No," I reluctantly admitted. "It's not."

"Well, I'm sorry, but I'm not sure how I can help you." Atherton shook his head. "I barely knew the man."

"But you did know him?" Ava pressed.

He was slow to answer. "Yes. I hired him for a couple of security jobs."

"When was this?" I asked.

"The last one was maybe three months ago," he responded, eyeing us both. "Why?"

"Because he had pictures," Ava said.

Atherton's fake tan paled. "Pictures." He looked from Ava to me. "Wh-what do you mean?"

"Photos. Of the party, I'm guessing. You were in them."

He made a sort of strangled sound in the back of his throat and suddenly looked ill. His eyes darted left and right, and he stepped in closer. "Come up to my office. We can't discuss this here."

"Can't discuss what—" I started to ask, but he'd already spun on his polished shoes, his long legs pumping with purpose toward the stairs.

Ava shot me a questioning look.

I shrugged and quickly hopped down from the barstool to follow him.

We finally caught up to him at the top of the landing, where he pushed open the doors to a large office on the right. Tall windows provided a breathtaking view of vineyards and rolling hills. A large desk sat in the center of the room, and several glass cupboards holding various vintages of wine bottles stood opposite the windows.

Atherton ushered us in and shut the door behind us, still looking concerned as he crossed behind his desk to a leather chair beneath a wall of commendations and awards. Ava and I sank into a pair of chairs in front of him. I'd barely sat with a soft hush of leather beneath my thighs when Atherton leaned on his desk, clasping his hands in an unconscious pleading motion in front of him.

"Where did you see the pictures?"

I opened my mouth to answer, but Ava put a hand on my arm and said, "Why don't you tell us what you know about Buckley first."

Atherton licked his lips. "Like I said, I hired him to provide some security for me."

"Were you threatened?" I asked, thinking I could see how Atherton's personality would lend itself to that.

But he shook his head. "No, no. Nothing like that. I just wanted some extra security for a couple of events I threw."

"How did you find Buckley?" Ava asked.

"A friend gave me his name. Said he'd done an event for him."

"When was this?" Ava asked.

"The first time I used him was for a New Year's party. Winery sponsored. I hired him to keep an eye on the door. You know—make sure no one drove home who shouldn't and everyone had Ubers. That sort of thing."

"And then?" Ava asked. "You mentioned a couple of events."

"Yeah." He paused, did more lip licking. "At my house. My birthday."

"And?" Ava pressed.

He took a deep breath, his eyes going from me to Ava. For a second I thought he wasn't going to say anything more. Then he finally looked down at his hands and opened his mouth to speak. "And about a week later, Buckley called me looking for money."

"Money? You mean, payment for the security work?" I asked.

"No, I'd already paid him for that." Atherton sighed deeply again. "He said he'd seen what happened at the party, and if I wanted him to keep his mouth shut about it, he wanted payment."

"Wait—are you saying Buckley was blackmailing you?" Ava leaned forward in her seat.

Atherton's head bobbed up and down. "Yeah. Some nerve, right?"

"How much was he asking?" I wanted to know.

"Two grand," Atherton said. His eyes lifted to meet mine. "At first."

"At first? You mean, you paid…and he asked for more?"

He worked his jaw back and forth, and I could tell his pride was taking a nice hit telling us this. "He said he had pictures." He paused. "I'm guessing that's how you saw them?"

I nodded. "They were among Buckley's possessions."

He grimaced. But luckily didn't ask what *I'd* been doing among Buckley's possessions. "Buckley said that if I wanted to keep them from getting out, I had to keep him happy."

"How happy?" Ava asked.

"Very. Several thousand dollars over the course of the last three months."

His meaning sank in. He'd been paying Buckley right up until the man had died. Conveniently. "When was the last time you talked to Buckley?" I asked.

Atherton let out a short laugh. "I don't think so."

"Excuse me?" I asked.

"I'm not helping you play Nancy Drew again." He shook his head. "I was nowhere near Buckley when he died. I just got back from a buying trip to Santiago, and I have several colleagues who can vouch for that."

"Tell me, exactly how much did you pay Buckley in all?" Ava asked.

He worked his jaw back and forth a little more before finally spitting the answer out. "Twelve grand."

I let out low whistle without meaning to.

Atherton turned his predatory glare on me. "Which I'm sure seems like a lot to someone at Oak Valley," he said on a sneer, "But it was worth it to me."

I was dying to know…"What exactly did Buckley see at the party?"

Atherton sucked in a long breath, eyes again going from Ava to me. "You said you've seen the pictures?"

Ava nodded. "We have. But indulge us."

He sighed. "He had a photo of me. With Harold Heimlich."

"Who?" I asked, glancing at Ava. The blank look on her face said the name was lost on her as well.

"He's the leader of the CANE."

"Cane?" I asked. "What's that?"

Atherton squirmed in his seat. "California Nazi Enthusiasts."

I blinked at him. "You're a Nazi?!" I hadn't thought my opinion of James Atherton could sink any lower, but I'd been wrong.

"No!" he practically yelled. He waved both hands in front of his face as if trying to magically wave away the idea. "No, nothing could be further from the truth."

"So, you just party with Nazis?" Ava shot him a look.

"No! No, listen—I didn't know who he was at the time." James sighed again and scrubbed a hand over his face. "He was introduced to me as a friend of a friend. We shook hands and had a couple of glasses of wine together. That's it."

"And his Nazism never came up?" Ava still looked like she wasn't convinced.

"No! And I swear to you, I had no idea who he was at the time."

"But Buckley did," I said, piecing it together.

Atherton nodded, looking practically ill again. "Look, I'm throwing my hat in the ring for the state senate this fall." He turned to me. "Senator Foxton's former seat is free. You remember him?"

I did. The entire scandal surrounding the death of Atherton's second wife had been what preceded Foxton's withdrawal from the reelection race.

"Anyway," Atherton went on, "Buckley threatened to go public with the photo. To say that Heimlich and I were friends! Friends!" He shook his head at the very thought.

"So you paid him twelve thousand dollars for his silence."

Atherton nodded.

"Until someone killed him," Ava noted.

"I told you, I know nothing about that. I was in Chile."

For once, I had the feeling Atherton was being totally straight with us.

"Now, if there's nothing else?" Atherton said, trying hard to infuse his voice with some of his usual pretension as he rose from his desk.

Ava and I stood too, following him to the door, which he held open for us. Only, as I was about to step through, he stopped me.

"By the way," he said, the pretension working up to usual speed now, "I heard through the grapevine, so to speak, that you're looking to take on a partner at Oak Valley."

I froze, that sick feeling immediately hitting my stomach again. "I'm looking at funding possibilities," I hated admitting.

He shrugged. "Frankly, I'm surprised you lasted this long. Small family operations can't compete with us in this market."

"We have a niche audience," I said, not able to help defending the place.

"Sure. Sure." He nodded, as if placating a child as Ava and I stepped out into the hall. "But uh, let me know if you don't find that partner. We'd be happy to make an offer on the acreage." He sent me a shark-like grin before shutting the door with an ominous click.

I cringed, praying it did not come to that.

CHAPTER FIFTEEN

Since it was lunchtime and we'd already each had a glass of Cabernet, Ava suggested we stop for something to eat before heading back to the winery. We chose Nick's Niche, one of our favorite local hole-in-the-wall delights to refuel and regroup. The server had brought us each a peach iced tea and a plate of Nick's Smashburgers and hand cut french fries, and after several moan-worthy bites of juicy burger smothered in sweet caramelized onions and spicy sauce, our conversation organically turned to what we'd learned in Atherton's office.

"So Buckley was a blackmailer," Ava said, licking sauce off her fingers.

I nodded. "So it seems." I sipped my sweet tea. "Though, it's not a huge leap from taking bribes to blackmail artist. I mean, he'd traded his silence for money in the past."

"Right. Sorta. I mean, he wasn't exactly silent in the end," Ava pointed out.

I nodded. "All the more reason for someone he's blackmailing *now* to feel nervous about Buckley actually keeping quiet."

"Only, Atherton has an alibi." Ava looked disappointed. "You think he's telling the truth about it?"

I nodded. "Seems too easy to check up on."

"Well, maybe Atherton hired someone to kill Buckley?" Ava offered.

"Maybe." I pushed a couple of fries around on my plate. "Or maybe Buckley wasn't just blackmailing Atherton."

"What do you mean?" Ava asked, sipping her tea.

"I mean Buckley had photos of Katy Kline too."

"That's right!" Ava nodded. "You think he was blackmailing her too?"

"It's possible."

"But over what?" Ava asked. "I mean, he already spilled the beans on her business two years ago."

I shrugged. "Maybe something else he knew about her from back then? Or some parole violation he found now?" I thought back to the pictures we'd seen. They'd simply looked like Katy interacting with a cookie customer. Like with the ones of Atherton, nothing had immediately stood out as nefarious about it.

"If Buckley had photos of people he was blackmailing," Ava said slowly, "what was he doing with pictures of Grant?"

The burger stuck in my throat. "I don't know."

Ava bit her bottom lip. "You don't think there's something from Grant's past that maybe…" She trailed off, and I could tell by the look on her face that she hated even thinking it.

"No." I shook my head, protesting more confidently than I felt.

"Right." Ava nodded agreement. Then paused. "It's just that the way Eckhart described Grant…and there *was* that IA investigation…I mean, maybe…"

"No," I said again, making a mental decision to stick by the man I knew despite the question marks being thrown my way. I sucked in a deep breath. "The photos of Grant have to be there for another reason."

"Okay." Ava didn't look convinced. But she was a good enough friend that she let it go. "Well, let's just say that Buckley was blackmailing James Atherton and Katy Kline, then."

"Right. Let's go with that," I told her, relieved.

"If Atherton has an alibi, then maybe it was Katy who didn't want to pay Buckley's asking price."

I nodded. "And she knows firsthand what the consequences are of Buckley not holding up his end of the deal. She paid him for his silence once and ended up in prison anyway."

"So, you think maybe this time she decided to silence Buckley before he could let whatever secret she's holding out?" She raised an eyebrow at me.

"I think it's definitely worth another trip to Katy's Cookies to find out."

* * *

Half an hour later, Ava and I pushed through the glass front door of Katy's Cookies, the bell above us jingling merrily. As it had been on our last visit, the place was empty. Baskets of baked goods lined the walls, and the scents of freshly made chocolate chip and peanut butter cookies linger in the air. But the white tables and chairs were again void of customers. The only sound in the place was the hum of a mixer from somewhere back in the kitchen, which ceased as soon as the bell signaled our arrival. A beat later, Katy's round frame filled the doorway.

"Welcome to Katy's Cookies, can I help—oh it's you again." Some of her friendly perk faded as recognition set in.

"Hi." I waved and gave her what I hoped was a friendly just-here-to-chat smile.

"What do you want?" She crossed her arms over her chest, her eyes narrowing beneath her feathered bangs.

"I, uh…"

"We wanted to check up on that cookie basket she ordered for her mom," Ava jumped in. She shot Katy a wide smile.

Katy's eyes pinged from one to the other of us before she finally answered. "Derek's delivering it today. It'll be there by four."

"Oh. Well, good," I said. I bit my lip, not sure where to go from there. I glanced at Ava.

"Was there anything else?" Katy asked, hostility lacing her voice as she arched an eyebrow at us.

"Actually, yes," Ava said, taking a step closer to the counter. "We wanted to ask you something."

"Did you." Katy's eyes narrowed again.

"I guess we might as well tell you." Ava sent a tentative glance my way.

I nodded encouragingly.

"We found out that Bill Buckley was blackmailing one of his former clients."

If Katy was surprised, she didn't show it, her face wearing a hard emotionless expression that I could well imagine she'd spent months in prison cultivating.

"He had pictures of this client," Ava went on. "Doing something…well, something he'd rather the public didn't see."

Katy's poker face broke just long enough to smirk. "I can only imagine."

"Anyway, Buckley was blackmailing the client with these photos." Ava paused, giving weight to her next statement. "And we also found pictures of you among Buckley's things."

"Me?" Katy frowned. "Can't imagine why."

"They were of you and a customer," I jumped in. "Here at your shop."

Katy's gaze slowly went from Ava to me. "And?"

I pursed my lips. "And we were wondering…Katy, was Buckley blackmailing you too?"

She scoffed. "Over what? Selling cookies?"

She had a point. Nothing in the photo had appeared untoward.

"Was it something about your past? About your escort business?"

"I told you, that all came out. I pled guilty. It's public record, and I paid my debt to society."

"Most of it," Ava mumbled.

Katy shot her a look.

"Well, you *were* sentenced to four years," Ava reasoned.

"Was he threatening to hurt your new business?" I fished. "Warning that he'd tell your customers what you'd done in San Francisco?"

"The only thing hurting my business right now is a couple of idiots with false accusations scaring off my customers," she said hotly.

I looked around. I hadn't seen a single customer.

"If he was trying to blackmail you, you're the victim here," Ava said, making her voice sound sympathetic.

But Katy just scoffed again. "Gee, thanks for the legal lesson, blondie."

"Was it something about your parole?" I asked, not ready to give up yet. "Did Buckley threaten to tell your parole officer you'd violated it somehow?"

"That's it!" Katy said, her voice rising with anger. "I've had enough of you two. Get out." She pointed an arm toward the glass doors.

"Look, I didn't mean to accuse you of anything—" I backpedaled.

But she didn't let me finish, stalking around the counter, still pointing at the door. "Out! I don't ever want to see you two in here again. Got it? Now get out!"

Ava and I quickly got out. What else could we do? Plus, I could see the hardened criminal coming out in her, and I had no desire to be shanked in a cookie shop. Even once we'd scurried out the door and were crossing the parking lot in the warm sunshine amidst the throng of shoppers filtering in and out of the CVS, I still had goosebumps at how threatening she'd looked.

"Is she watching us?" Ava whispered, clearly mirroring my thoughts.

I dared to glanced back at the shop window. Luckily, no sign of Katy Kline shooting death glares at us.

I shook my head. "She must have gone back into the kitchen," I said as we reached Ava's car.

She quickly unlocked it, and we slipped inside.

I let out a breath I hadn't realized I'd been holding, collapsing backward on the headrest.

"Okay, so what do we think?" Ava asked. "Was Buckley blackmailing Katy or not?"

I shrugged. "Hard to say. She did get very defensive." I paused. "But then again, an innocent person might get defensive too."

Ava pursed her lips as we both stared at the benign looking storefront. "The question is, what did he have on her?"

"I don't know." I shook my head, watching people walk past the cookie shop. No one went in. No one even gave it a second glance, really. "Honestly, whatever Buckley had on her, I can't imagine it hurting her business more than it's already hurting now."

"What do you mean?" Ava asked.

"I mean, I haven't seen a single customer go in there."

She frowned. "It does seem empty. But didn't she say most of her business was delivery?"

"Right." I glanced at the store again. "I wonder…"

"What?" Ava asked, pulling her lipstick out and touching up in the rearview mirror.

"What about her delivery guy. Derek. Do you think her nephew might know if Buckley was threatening her?"

Ava cocked an eyebrow at me. "Maybe. I mean, he works at the shop, so there's a good possibility he might have at least seen Buckley. Or would know if the two had been in contact." She glanced back at the shop. "Of course getting him alone to talk to us would be the trick."

"Actually, we know exactly where he'll be this afternoon," I told her, feeling the grin in my voice.

Ava's eyes lit up as she turned them on me. "Delivering cookies to your mom!"

* * *

Half an hour later Ava and I pulled up to Sonoma Acres and parked in the small visitor lot before giving our names to the receptionist in the lobby. She logged us in and gave us each a visitor tag to stick on our shirts before we made our way down the hallway of the east wing.

"Knock, knock," I said, actually saying the words as I did, in fact, knock on the door to my mom's private room.

I heard footsteps approaching, accompanied by my mom's voice. "Emmy, is that you?" A second later the door opened to reveal her confused features.

"Hi, Mom," I said, coming in for a hug.

"Hi, honey." She hugged me back before turning to Ava. "Ava, nice to see you too." She paused, the frown of confusion still on her face. "Did you tell me you were coming today?"

"No," I assured her. "This wasn't pre-planned."

She looked relieved at the fact she hadn't forgotten something else. "Oh good. Well, what a nice surprise. Come on in." She gestured to a pair of chairs by the window. I noticed one held an open paperback novel, facedown as if we'd interrupted her reading. "Are you here about the case?" she asked, moving the book to a side table and lowering herself into the chair.

Ava opened her mouth to answer, but I shot her a look that silenced her.

"Uh, case, Mom?" I asked. I hadn't discussed anything about Buckley with her, and as far as I knew, she hadn't heard the news yet.

"The thefts." She looked from me to Ava. "Here at the Acres. You did promise you'd discuss it with your detective."

"Thefts?" Ava gave me a raised eyebrow.

"Right. Yes, I did promise," I said. "And I did discuss it with him."

"You didn't discuss it with me," Ava chided, giving me an amused grin as she sat in the other chair.

"There's been a rash of thefts here," Mom explained to Ava. "Everyone is on edge."

"Do the staff know?" Ava asked.

I nodded. "They do. And I'd hardly call it a *rash* of thefts."

Mom and I quickly filled Ava in on the missing photo, the pillow, and Mrs. Pettigrew the stuffed cat. When we were done, Ava was barely containing her laughter.

"And you said *Grant* is on the case?" Ava said, amusement twinkling in her eyes at the thought.

I sighed. "I said I discussed it with him."

"Well, what did he say?" Mom asked.

"He said he'd look into it."

Mom smiled and looked so relieved that I didn't have the heart to tell her Grant thought the "burglar" was about as nefarious as I did.

"But he's really busy right now," I hedged. "On another case. It could be a bit until he can investigate."

Mom nodded. "Sure. I understand."

"So…what do you think they did with the cat?" Ava was still grinning. "The thief."

Mom shrugged. "Well, I don't know. Maybe they're just a kleptomaniac. Can't help what they steal."

Actually, that wasn't an altogether terrible theory. I made a mental note to ask the staff if anyone suffering from that affliction was among the residents.

I was about to say as much, when I was interrupted by a knock at the door.

Ava perked up and shot me a knowing look.

"I don't know who that could be," Mom said, getting up.

I knew exactly who it could be, but I didn't have a chance to tell her before she crossed the small room and opened her door again.

"Good afternoon! I have a delivery here from Katy's Cookies for a Ms. Laura Oak," Derek the Delivery Guy said, his white teeth gleaming in his tanned features as he held up the gift basket I'd picked out the day before.

"Wow, for me?" Mom asked.

"I guess so." Derek handed the basket to her.

"Who is it from?" Mom asked, turning it over to look for a tag.

I cleared my throat loudly. "Surprise!" I said, feeling slightly guilty that there were some ulterior motives behind the gift.

"You did this?" Mom asked. "What's the occasion?" I could see that small fear in her eyes again that she'd forgotten something important.

"No occasion," I quickly said. "Just…I saw this and thought of you."

"That's what the card says," Derek added with a smile. "*Thinking of You.*"

"Well, aren't you the best daughter in the world." Mom pulled the cute little teddy bear out of the basket, giving him a loving once-over.

"I hope you enjoy the cookies," Derek said and turned to go.

"Uh, wait," Ava said, jumping up from her chair.

Derek paused, eyes going beyond Mom to take in Ava for the first time.

"Uh, you're Katy's nephew, right?" she asked.

"That's right." His face broke out into a slow smile of recognition. "Didn't I see you at the shop yesterday?"

Ava gave him a flirty smile. "You sure did."

"Well, nice to see you again," he said, infusing the words with warmth as his gaze gave her a slow up and down, lingering just a little bit long on the short hemline of her denim skirt.

"Same," Ava said. "Do you have a minute?"

"I guess." He shrugged. "Was there something else?"

"Yyyyyyes." Ava nodded slowly, and I could see her trying to come up with a good cover story of why we'd be interrogating him about his aunt. "We were hoping to get a little more from you."

Something flashed behind his eyes, and he cocked his head to the side. "Wait, this was a regular delivery right?"

"Regular delivery?" I asked.

"I mean, usually Katy marks the basket if it's a special order." His eyes went from Ava to me to Mom. And back to Ava. "Did you pay for a special order?"

Something about the way he was looking at her suddenly had my mental wheels churning.

"What do you mean by special order?" I asked.

"Well, just…I mean…" His eyes darted from one to the other of us again. "Did you *just* order cookies?"

And suddenly it clicked. Why there were no customers in the cookie shop. Why Katy was so defensive. What Buckley had been blackmailing Katy over…

"Sex."

All three pairs of eyes spun my way.

"You're talking about sex, aren't you?" I asked the delivery guy.

Derek's mouth curved into a slow grin again. "So you *didn't* just order cookies. This *was* supposed to be a special delivery."

Mom's jaw dropped open. "You ordered me sex? With *him*?"

"No!" I shook my head. "No, we just ordered you cookies, Mom."

"Then who ordered me?" Derek asked, taking a step toward Ava.

"No one," I said emphatically.

It might have been my imagination, but I thought I saw disappointment momentarily cross Ava's features before she shook her head. "She's right. We just ordered cookies. But," she added, "that's not what most of Katy's customers order, is it?"

Derek still looked mildly confused, but he shook his head. "Look, I'm not supposed to talk about this to anyone. Katy could get in a lot of trouble."

"Again," Ava mumbled.

"We're not looking to make any trouble for Katy," I assured him. That is, as long as she wasn't a murderer. "But someone was trying to make trouble for her, wasn't he?"

Derek blew out a big breath. "So you know about that guy, too, huh?"

"What guy?" Mom asked, clutching the teddy bear to her chest, her gaze whipping from one to another of us. "What's going on here?"

"He's a gigolo," I explained, pointing at Derek. "He works for Katy Kline, who went to prison for running a female escort service out of her brother's butcher shop."

"And now," Ava added, picking up the narrative, "apparently, she's running a *male* escort service out of her new cookie shop."

Derek gave her a sheepish grin and shrugged. "A guy's gotta make a living."

Mom snorted. "Please. You're preying on lonely women."

"I don't prey!" he defended. "They come to Katy looking for some companionship. I'm a good listener. Women love that. They're willing to pay for it."

Like the woman we'd seen in the photo. It suddenly made sense. Buckley had taken a snapshot of the woman paying Katy for Derek's services.

"How much?" I asked.

"Huh?"

"How much did they pay Katy for your listening skills?"

He shrugged. "A grand per delivery. Sometimes more, depending on what kind of basket they ordered."

"Whoa." Ava gave Derek an up and down of her own.

He grinned, showing of those white teeth again. "What can I say—I'm a *really* good listener."

"I'll bet," Ava mumbled, and I had a bad feeling she was contemplating a cookie basket.

"What about Buckley?" I asked, pulling us back on track.

He frowned. "Who?"

"The guy who you said was making trouble for Katy," I supplied.

"Oh. Yeah, I dunno the guy's name. But Katy said she knew him from San Francisco."

"And he figured out her cookie shop was just a front just like the butcher shop?" Ava guessed.

"I don't know what he figured out, but I know I saw him in the shop arguing with Katy."

"When was this?"

"A few days ago. Like, maybe Friday."

The day Buckley had died. I felt the hairs on the back of my neck stand at attention. "What did they argue about?"

But Derek shook his head. "I didn't really hear. I just came in as the guy was leaving, but I could tell they'd had it out. Katy was practically fuming."

"Did she say anything?" Ava pressed.

"Just that I should keep my mouth shut about the whole thing." He looked from Ava to me. "You won't tell her I talked to you will you?"

Ava shook her head, and I could see her taking pity on him. Either that or still thinking about his listening skills.

Derek turned his imploring eyes my way. "And you won't tell your boyfriend, right?"

That hair on the back of my neck stood at attention again.

"My boyfriend?" I asked slowly.

"The cop," Derek supplied. "Katy said you were dating some detective or something."

I lifted my eyes to meet Ava's. I hadn't mentioned Grant to Katy. She'd clearly been looking into us and knew a whole lot more than she'd let on.

And a lot more than I felt comfortable with, considering she was a convicted felon and possible murderer.

"Look, I gotta go," Derek said, standing. "If this isn't my special delivery, I'm gonna be running late." He paused, pulling something from his pocket and handing it to Ava. "My card. You know. In case you want delivery sometime." He gave her a wink of his bright blue eyes.

Ava blinked at him, but before she could respond, he'd already turned and was walking out the door.

"Did I just get hit on by a gigolo?" Ava turned to me. "Or do I look lonely enough that I'd pay for it?"

CHAPTER SIXTEEN

By the time we'd left Mom with her cookies and at least a brief explanation of who Buckley was and what Katy Kline had to do with all of it, it was dark and we only had an hour before David's gallery showing. Ava dropped me back off at Oak Valley to get ready before heading home to do the same and promising to meet me at the gallery.

Since I'd abused my little black dress so horribly already the night before, I was short on dressy outfits. I opted for some skinny black jeans that, when paired with a white silk shirt, looked upscale enough that I could zhoosh it up with some jewelry. I draped a couple of silver chains around my neck, just above the open collar of the shirt, and went for long, dangling earrings that reminded me of a silver waterfall as they hung from my ears. A couple of silver cuff bracelets completed the look, along with some spiky black heels. While it wasn't evening wear, it was bordering on artsy, so I figured it would pass muster for the occasion. Besides, I didn't want to upstage the artist, right?

I was already running late by the time I parked in the pay lot next to the Groudin Gallery in downtown Sonoma. After finding an empty space near the back, I locked my Jeep up and click-clacked in my three inch heels to the gallery's front doors. I steeled myself against David's chiding at not quite being there at six sharp, but as I pulled open the glass doors and entered, I realized neither of us had needed to worry. The room was packed. Art lovers in dark suits and cocktail dresses crowded elbow to elbow, chatting animatedly about David's work, laughing as they sipped from champagne glasses, hopefully feeling fast and loose with their credit cards.

The gallery was a maze of white walls, providing lots of space for hanging art, and as I navigated them, I spied Ava right away, her floor length white gown hard to miss among the sea of subdued colors. With a slit up one side and pair of white sandals dressing it down just enough to feel boho chic, she looked like a Grecian goddess. Especially with the way she'd braided her hair and pinned it into a halo just above a pair of slim gold hoop earrings. She stood next to David with a glass of champagne in one hand. She waved to me with her free one when she spotted me.

I waved back, making my way toward the pair.

"Wow, this is a great turnout," I said as I approached.

David shrugged modestly. "It's not bad." He glanced down at my jeans. "You look nice."

"The LBD was in the wash," I defended.

The corner of his mouth quirked up. "I said it was *nice*."

"It feels casual," I said, glancing around at the other gowns and cocktail dresses. Even David was in a pair of slacks that night, paired with a white button down shirt and black sport coat. He looked practically grown up, even if the shirt was sans tie and opened at the collar.

"So what do you think." David nodded toward the canvas on the wall in front of us.

Like most of his art, it was done in dark hues, black and grey dominating the canvas in bold, decisive strokes, with just a little blood red color thrown in here and there for dramatic effect. While the style was abstract, it looked to me like some sort of mountain scene. Like a violent landscape that left me feeling almost antsy in its urgency.

"It's…nice."

David threw his head back and laughed. "You hate it."

"No, no!" I protested quickly. "It's just…dark."

He nodded. "It is."

"I think it's deep," Ava jumped in. "The red feels like an undercurrent of heat under the earth's crust. Sort of like what bubbles up inside all of us sometimes. The heat and anger. Right?"

David frowned and nodded his approval. "Not bad. I've had worse critiques."

I cocked my head at the painting.

David leaned in and whispered in my ear. "You still hate it."

I grinned. "I still think it's dark."

"Here." He grabbed me by the elbow, steering me to the left. "I have one that's maybe more your style. I just finished it last night."

"Is this the one you weren't sure if you were going to show?"

He nodded. "I'm still not sure it fits, but I took a chance with it."

I followed him around the corner to one of the other white walls. This one held a larger canvas. While the color scheme was similar to the last one—dominated by shades of grey—the subject matter was softer. It was a portrait of a woman, still abstract but more delicate in technique than the last one, and it almost felt like a black and white photograph in the subtle shading he'd managed to throw on the subject's face. The woman stood in profile, staring out at something just beyond the canvas's edge. The look of longing in her eyes was haunting, and I felt my breath catch in my throat at the emotion he'd captured.

"Wow. David, this is really good."

I glanced over to find him smiling at me. "I thought you might like it."

"I love it," I told him honestly. "It's so…different from your other work."

He chuckled. "You mean better?"

"No, no. All your work is good. It's just the emotion this one evokes is different. It's not so…angry.

He shrugged. "Guess I'm losing my edge." He grinned.

I was about to argue that maybe losing one's sharp edge wasn't a bad thing, when someone called David's name from across the room, hailing him with a wave.

David nodded and waved back. "That's Groudin. The gallery owner," he explained. "Duty calls." He gave me a wink before he threaded his way through the crowd to where a short guy with a mustache chatted animatedly to a couple in all black about one of David's works.

I turned my attention back toward the portrait and was admiring it more as Ava caught up to me.

"Hey. I snagged you some champagne." She handed me a glass.

"You are a goddess," I told her. "Almost literally, in that outfit."

"Thanks." She did a little twirl for me. "Thought it might appeal to the artsy crowd."

"Did you see this one?" I gestured to the painting of the woman. "It's really good."

Ava turned her attention to the canvas. "That's different for David."

"I think it's beautiful."

She studied it a moment. Then she turned to me with a funny look in her eyes. "You do know who that is, right?"

I looked from her to the portrait. "Who?"

Ava's lips curled back in a slow smile. "Emmy, that's you."

I blinked at her, my eyes going back to the haunting image. "No. That's not…no, there's no way David would…I don't look like that," I finally settled on.

"*That* is totally you." Ava nodded. "Look how David captured the line of your nose here. And your cheekbone." She pointed to the canvas.

I frowned at the painting. "I don't see it. And besides, why on earth would David paint me?"

"Maybe he has a thing for you," she teased.

I scoffed. "No chance."

She turned back to the painting. "It's kind of sad, isn't it? The way she's clearly yearning for something just outside the frame. Like whatever she needs will always be just outside of her reach."

I frowned at the picture. She'd described the feeling perfectly.

"It's powerful," Ava went on. "Who knew our boy had such a deep soul?"

I nodded, having thought much the same only a few minutes before. "It's definitely not me."

Ava grinned. "It's definitely you."

"She looks so…lost. I don't look like that."

Ava gave me a funny look. "Maybe that's how David sees you."

The thought of David seeing me as anything but the woman he regularly mooched wine off of and occasionally indulged in brotherly teasing with was unnerving. Like suddenly he knew something about my psyche that I hadn't given him permission to unearth.

"Uh-oh," Ava said, eyes going to a spot behind us. "Here comes trouble."

I didn't get a chance to ask her what kind of trouble before a familiar voice boomed behind me.

"Hi, Ava."

Grant.

I closed my eyes for a beat, taking a deep fortifying breath before I spun around to face him.

"Emmy," he said, his voice neutral enough that I had no idea if he was still upset at how we'd left things the night before.

"Grant," I countered.

We stood there staring at each other for a moment before Ava cleared her throat. "Okay, well, I'm gonna mingle. I'll catch up to you later," she told me before scurrying away.

"You look nice," Grant said when we were alone. He leaned in to plant a peck on my cheek.

"Thanks." I felt my shoulders relax some at the signal we weren't totally on the outs. "I didn't figure you for an art lover."

He glanced at the painting of the woman on the wall in front of us. "David invited me."

I gave him a raised eyebrow. Grant and David weren't exactly the best of friends. In fact, David usually had a habit of disappearing whenever he smelled law enforcement approaching. Probably the card shark in him.

"I think he was trying to fill seats, so to speak," Grant explained. "Figured I'd stop by to show support." He paused, his eyes roving the painting before turning back to meet mine. "And to see you."

"Me?" I asked.

He nodded and took a step closer to me. "I don't like how we left things last night."

"That makes two of us," I conceded.

The corner of his mouth tugged upward. "Glad we're on the same page."

About that at least. About everything else surrounding Buckley's murder investigation and our roles in it, I still wasn't so sure.

As if he could read my mind, Grant said, "I got Ava's text earlier. About Buckley's ex-wife *allegedly* leaving town."

"Oh?" I took a sip of champagne in an effort to cover any reaction I might have had.

"Yeah. I'm going to assume you were standing right there when she sent it?"

"Guilty as charged," I admitted.

He grinned in earnest. "So, here's the deal. I'm not gonna ask *how* you and Ava know that Carmen left town—"

"That's a good deal."

"—and you're going to promise that whoever you talked to and wherever you went to find this information out, you're not going there again."

I pursed my lips together. It sounded more like a directive than a deal now. However, it was a small step up from outright ordering me to stay away from all things Buckley. And, since I didn't intend to call the nasally receptionist at Nadia's Nails or visit Carmen Buckley's depressing shack outside of town again, I decided I'd take the small baby step forward with Alpha Male, and I nodded.

"Deal."

Some of the tension slipped from his posture as he turned to glance at the painting in front of us again. "This is David's work too?" he asked.

I nodded, sipping from my glass.

"It's not as violent as the other stuff," he noted.

"I guess he's trying something different. I like it."

Grant's eyes went from the painting to me. "Is that you?"

"What? No!" I scoffed. "No, not at all."

"Hmm." He cocked his head to the side. "Kinda looks like you."

"It is for sure not me. Why would David paint me?"

"I wonder."

"It's not me. It's…someone else. Probably imaginary. Who knows what goes on in the mind of a tortured artist? *That* could be anyone."

"Tortured artist?" Grant grinned.

Trust me, he would be when I was through with him. Especially if the painting really was of me.

"The only thing that seems tortured about David," Grant said, eyes going to the man in question who was laughing and drinking champagne, "is deciding just where to spend his trust fund."

"David isn't that shallow," I countered, not sure why I was defending him. "But I guess you just don't know him very well."

Grant gave me a funny look, his eyes flickering to the painting. "Do you?"

I frowned. "I'm not sure what you're implying—"

His eyes went meaningfully to the painting again.

"—but if this week has taught me anything, it's that none of us really ever know anyone."

"So you said last night." He crossed his arms over his chest, some of the tension returning. "What is that supposed to mean?"

I blew out a breath. "Nothing."

"Emmy, is there something I should know about you?"

"About *me*?" I let out a sharp laugh. "No, last night I was talking about *you*."

He frowned. "What do you need to know about me?"

"I-I don't know." Everything. Something. Maybe nothing. I felt the conversation slipping from tentative truce to emotionally confusing, and the larger-than-life portrait of a lost woman who may or may not be me staring at us wasn't making it any clearer. "How come you never talk about San Francisco?" I blurted out.

"San Francisco?"

"Yes. About what happened to you there before you were transferred."

His frown deepened. "Why would I want to talk about that? It wasn't a pleasant part of my life."

"But it *was* a part of it. A part of you. Who you are. What makes you tick."

He shook his head slowly. "No. That incident doesn't define me. It was bad, it's over, and there's no point in dwelling on it."

"So you're just going to pretend it never happened?"

"What do you want me to say, Emmy?" he asked, shifting his weight, the irritation in his voice clear.

"I want you to talk to me!" I said, getting worked up again. "I want you to tell me about your childhood, your past, your friends, your enemies, your hopes, your dreams, the moon shaped scar on your butt!"

That last part might have been said a little too loudly, as several pairs of eyes turned our way.

I took a deep breath, lowering my voice. "I want to get to know you. Really know you."

He gave me a hard look, the little gold flecks in his eyes dancing in a heated frenzy. "I thought you did know me."

Ouch. The undercurrent of hurt in that statement was worse than the heat in his eyes.

"That's not what I meant," I backpedaled. This was going all wrong. Again. "I just hate that you're hiding things from me."

"Hiding things?" The edge of anger was unmistakable in his voice now. "*I'm* not the one hiding things, Emmy. You're the one sneaking around town."

"You hid that you knew Buckley."

"No, I *told* you I knew him."

"But not until way later. Why didn't you want me to know about your connection to him?"

"Gee, I don't know, maybe because you have a habit of putting yourself in the middle of dangerous situations that don't concern you because of some cockamamie theories!"

"Cockamamie theories?" I narrowed my eyes. "First of all, what are you, ninety? Who says cockamamie?"

"Emmy—" his voice warned.

But I ignored it, too angry to care.

"And second of all, my theories are good. They're great, even. Better than yours about some random trespasser."

"Emmy—"

"And thirdly, I did not put myself in some dangerous situation. It showed up at my winery. So stop treating me like I'm some stupid little girl who can't take care of herself."

"I did not say that," he ground out.

"Your meaning was pretty clear."

Grant shook his head. "I'm not doing this with you again."

"Fine. Don't do it. Don't do anything with me!"

He looked from the painting to me one last time before he shook his head again. "Good night, Emmy."

While I was still trying to formulate a scathing parting remark of my own, he turned and stalked out of the gallery.

I watched him, my breath coming hard, my heart beating fast, and a hollow feeling forming in the pit of my stomach that I'd screwed it up again with him.

No, I refused to think that way. *He'd* screwed it up again. Why couldn't he just be straight with me? Give me that respect. Why did he have to play the strong silent type, trying to protect me from…I don't know. Everything. I was tired of it. Tired of being spoon fed only what he wanted me to know, tired of being marginalized, tired of fighting with him.

And as I let out a long breath of air, the anger fading, I realized I was just plain tired. The week was catching up to me, and as the rush of the moment flooded out of my system, I could feel the weight of everything taking its toll on me. All I wanted to do was go home and curl into a ball beneath my nice warm quilt and shut the world out.

I glanced around for Ava to tell her I was leaving, but I saw she'd joined David and the gallery owner, the three of them talking now to the couple, who looked interested enough in the violent mountain piece that they looked ready to pull out their black cards. I didn't have the heart to interrupt. This was David's night. I didn't want ruin it.

Instead, I sent Ava a quick text, letting her know I was going, and with a parting glance at the Lost Lady on the canvas, I set my champagne glass down on an empty table and headed for the door.

The cold night air hit me like a blast of ice as I stepped outside, though the instant chill was almost welcomed, calming down my heated nerves. I wrapped my arms around myself as I traversed the parking lot again.

I was about halfway across the lot when I heard it.

The loud roar of a motorcycle.

I spun just in time to see a figure in a black leather jacket tear away from the alley at the back of the Groudin Gallery building. I might have imagined it, but the rider looked a lot like Jamie Connolly.

I froze, watching his taillight disappear down the street. What had the teenager been doing there? Stalking me? Or David? Or generally just looking to make trouble wherever he could?

Or maybe I was just getting paranoid. A lot of people drove motorcycles. And wore leather jackets.

I quickly beeped my Jeep unlocked and got inside, cranking up the heater as I pulled out of the lot. I flipped on the radio, but as soon as I hit the main road, I turned it off again. Why did it seem every song was about some lost love? Not the subject I wanted to dwell on that night. Not that Grant and I were madly in love. I wasn't sure we were in anything at the moment. Except in a perpetual standoff.

Stress. It was the stress getting to us both. Grant's job was inherently high stress, and me...well, the sooner I could get the label of "deadliest little winery" off my back, the better chance Schultz could find a partner willing to funnel some disposable income our way. *If* that chance even existed. My phone had been conspicuously silent all day, and I was feeling less and less optimistic about this possible solution that I hadn't wanted in the first place. But it was better than losing the winery. I'd already lost my dad way too young, and time and illness were taking my mom away from me. I couldn't lose Oak Valley too.

I felt my eyes tear up. And then there was Grant. Had I lost him too? To be fair, I'd never really had Grant. I wasn't sure he was the type of guy to be had. I sniffed. But I'd enjoyed his company. I wondered if that was it. I'd never enjoy it again. Our easy dinners eaten at the kitchen counter were a thing of the past.

Then again, had I even known the guy I'd been eating with? Eckhart had painted a really different picture of who Grant was. Even Snow White had seemed like she'd had her own version of him—a very flirty one who liked to talk about his butt. And what version had I had?

One who'd been trying to bury his connection to a dead man from the beginning.

A dead man who had pictures of Grant.

I tried to focus on the road and not that unnerving thought. The lights of downtown were long behind me, and trees rose up on either side of the two lane road, vine covered hills resting in the shadows just beyond. I eased off the gas and pumped my foot on the brake, coming to a curve in the road.

Only, nothing happened.

My thoughts were immediately jarred from my pity party to the present as I pressed down again, thinking maybe my heel had gotten caught on the floor mat or something was stuck under the brake pedal.

But my foot had free range, and the pedal went down to the floor with ease when I hit the brakes again.

Only, again, nothing happened. The car didn't slow.

If anything, I picked up speed on the slight downhill grade. Panic surged through me as I veered right, taking the curve in the road at a much faster speed than I'd hoped. I felt the back end of the Jeep fishtail as I struggled to maintain control of the vehicle. Tall, dark trees loomed ahead of me, the stretch of road illuminated only by my headlights, whipping a wild path in front of me. My foot was pounding on the brakes, pressing for dear life even though it was clear they weren't going to help me. I gripped the steering wheel with both hands, knuckles going white as another turn threatened ahead.

My breath came in hard, fast pants, my heart hammering against my rib cage as the turn approached at frightening speeds. I tugged the wheel to the left.

Only, this time, the curve was too sharp, and I was going too fast.

I felt my wheels veer off the pavement, careening over the embankment, the road disappearing to the left as my car plunged straight ahead.

Right toward a tree.

CHAPTER SEVENTEEN

I pulled the steering wheel to the right with everything I had, I felt my tires bumping over rocks, dirt, and fallen tree branches, and I heard a loud, piercing scream of terror.

Which, in hindsight, was probably mine, as I watched the landscape rush up to meet my windshield before the car came to a stop with a sickening crunch of twisted metal and broken glass. It all happened in a matter of seconds, my air bag inflating like a punch in the chest as the crescendo.

My heart was pounding a mile a minute, and my entire body felt like it was frozen in place. I could hear the sound of my engine still on, my breath coming fast, the hiss of air from the slowly deflating bag coming out of my steering wheel. But they all felt like they were ringing in my ears in slow motion. I closed my eyes and focused on breathing, finally pulling my adrenalin back down to a functional level. I pried my hands from their death grip on the steering wheel and slowly moved my head from left to right. My neck felt stiff, but at least it swiveled normally. My head was starting to ache, and my chest felt heavy, but my arms and legs all moved fine.

It took a couple of tries to get my driver's side door open, the metal crushed just enough to make it stick. Finally I shoved hard enough to move it, stumbling out of the car and onto the cool damp earth.

I looked back at my car and almost cried. While I'd avoided a head-on collision which had likely saved my life, the right front fender seemed embedded in a large oak tree, and I had a bad feeling my poor Jeep would never be the same again. I grabbed my phone from my purse and pulled up a call screen, though I hesitated when it came to who to call.

9-1-1 came to mind, but any real emergency had passed. And I was sure they'd dispatch an EMT, who would take one look at my car and want to drive me to the emergency room. I could barely afford a Band-Aid, let alone an ambulance ride to Sonoma Valley Hospital. I could already feel my muscles tensing up after the jarring experience, signaling I'd be sore tomorrow, but I was pretty sure I'd escaped any real damage.

Ava was still at the gallery with David, and I already felt bad enough about skipping out on his night without pulling Ava away too.

There was Grant, but the last thing I wanted to incur at the moment was more of his hard stares and pointed questions. Especially when I had no answers. Clearly my brakes had stopped working. What wasn't so clear was why. While it was entirely possible there had been some mechanical error, my mind immediately flashed to the figure on the motorcycle that I'd seen peeling away from the gallery just moments before I had. Had it been Jamie Connolly? And, if so, had he done something to my car as a warning? A threat? Or worse…to make sure I ended up like Buckley?

In the end, I dialed Eddie's cell, hoping I didn't wake him up or interrupt a romantic date night with his husband.

Three rings in he answered with his usual cheeriness. "Hi Emmy, what's up?"

"Hi. I hope I'm not disturbing you?"

"No, no. Curtis and I were just finishing dinner. Why? Everything okay at the winery?"

"Yeah. I mean, I think so. I just…" I looked at my poor Jeep and had to bite back tears. "I had a little car accident."

"Accident?" I could hear Eddie moving. "What happened? Are you all right?"

"Yes, I'm fine." Mostly. "But my car isn't."

He must have heard the crack in my voice on that last word, as he gave me a sympathetic, "Oh, honey! Where are you?"

I glanced around. "I'm somewhere along Sonoma Highway." Which was dark and deserted at this time of night. While I knew my car would need a tow, it was clearly in no condition for a thief to drive off in, so that unpleasant task could wait until morning. "Any chance I could bother you for a ride home?"

"Of course! I'm on my way now."

"Thanks," I said, fully meaning it. "I'll text you my location," I promised before I hung up and pulled up my map app.

Once I'd sent that off, I gathered the few personal items I had in my car, shoving them into a reusable shopping bag I always kept in my trunk, and sat on my back bumper to wait for Eddie.

By the time he pulled up in his powder blue Honda Civic, I was chilled to the bone and feeling about as sorry for myself as I could get. My car was totaled. My love life was in shambles. My winery about to go under. Even David Allen apparently saw me as a lost soul.

"Oh Emmy," Eddie said, grabbing me in a hug and handing me a handkerchief. An actual cloth handkerchief, God bless him. I hadn't realized I'd been crying, but I gratefully took the indigo paisley printed square of fabric and dried my cheeks with it.

"Thank you. For everything." I hugged him back. "I don't know what I'd do without you."

"Well, luckily you won't have to find out," he reassured me, blissfully unaware that in a couple weeks' time, I wouldn't be able to afford to keep him around anymore.

A fact I almost blurted out then and there, but before I had the chance, Eddie grabbed my shopping bag in one hand and steered me by the elbow with the other, helping me into his car.

"Come on. Let's get you home, hon."

I just sniffed and nodded gratefully.

* * *

The next morning I woke up feeling like I'd been hit by a truck. Or a tree. My head ached, my chest was sore, and my neck felt tight and strained when I tried to turn it very far. I scowled at my reflection in the mirror as I dragged myself out of bed. My eyes were puffy and swollen from crying. Something I was determined not to do any more of that day. I was not a victim, and I was tired of feeling like one.

After I'd exhausted the hot water in my shower, I threw on worn blue jeans, a light sweater, and a pair of sneakers. Comfort clothes were definitely in order that day, but I added a pair of silver hoop earrings and extra mascara to take the outfit up a notch.

Once I felt mostly human and mainly presentable, the first thing I did was call Bob's Garage and let them know where my car was. Part of me had been tempted to just leave it there—fearing that the cost of a tow might be more than the car was worth at that point. But, once I'd made my second call, to my insurance company, they assured me that they'd be in touch with the shop and find out if my car was salvageable or not. I said a silent prayer that insurance might pay for some of that salvaging.

Unfortunately, that still left me temporarily without wheels, so once I'd fortified myself with a cup of coffee, I went in search of Eddie to beg to borrow his Honda for a quick trip into town.

Because I had a teen on a motorcycle to interrogate.

* * *

I rapped my knuckles on the door to 2C, the anger at the situation having built up on the ride from Oak Valley to the Shady Meadows. I waited impatiently on the doorstep, my right foot tapping a sharp staccato on the cement. I heard movement from within the apartment, though when the door opened it was Sheila Connolly on the other side, not her juvenile delinquent son. She had a purse on her shoulder and her apron in her arms, as if I'd caught her on her way out.

"Can I help you?" she asked.

I took a breath, trying to rein in my heated emotions. "Hi again. Uh, Emmy. I was here a couple days ago. From Oak Valley Vineyards."

"I know who you are," she said, impatience lacing her voice as she leaned against the doorframe. "What do you want?"

"Right. Well, actually, I wanted to talk to your son," I said, squaring my shoulders against her irritation. If anyone here had a reason to be irritated it was me.

"Jamie?" She frowned. "Why?"

"Because I suspect he…" Killed his almost stepfather, stole bribery money, tried to kill me by tampering with my brakes. "…damaged my car," I settled on.

The frowned deepened and she sighed. "What has that kid done this time?" she mumbled, almost more to herself than me. Then without waiting for an answer, she turned and yelled into the apartment. "Jamie! Jamie, get out here!"

"What?!" I heard the teen yell back, his voice laced with just as much impatience as his mother's.

"Out here. Now!" She turned back to me and gave me an apologetic smile. "It's always something with him."'

I tried to look understanding. "I'm sure it's hard being a single mom."

"You have no idea," she said, full meaning behind the words. Then she turned and yelled behind her again. "Jamie!"

"What do you want?" Jamie said, scowling as he came up behind his mother. The sight of me did nothing to soften the hard look in his eyes.

"This lady says you did something to her car." She gave him an accusatory glare.

"No!" He scrunched up his face. "I never touched your Jeep."

"How did you know I drive a Jeep?" I gave him an *I told you so* look.

He just continued to scowl.

Sheila sighed impatiently again. "Look, I have to get to work. I'm on the early shift today. How much is the damage?" she asked me.

"I'm not sure yet. It just went into the shop." I paused, looking past her. "But I'm happy to work this out with Jamie if you need to go."

Jamie narrowed his eyes at me. "There's nothing to work out," he mumbled.

"Oh, I think there is," I argued. "I have some questions for you."

"Questions?" Sheila's eyebrows drew together in a frown. "What kind of questions?"

I almost didn't want to answer, feeling a pang of sympathy for her. Especially if her troubled teen had murdered her troubled boyfriend. "About why he's been following me."

"Following you…" Sheila spun on her son. "Like, stalking?"

"No!" Jamie protested. "Why would I do that?"

"Indeed." I gave him a pointed look.

Sheila's gaze bounced from me to Jamie to the apron in her arms, clearly weighing priorities.

"If you need to go to work, I'm sure Jamie and I can work this out," I repeated, thinking I was going to get little from the teen in her presence anyway.

Sheila turned to me. "Are you sure?" She sounded dubious, as if she knew how hard it was to work anything out with her son.

I nodded. "It's fine," I told her. I gave Jamie a hard stare. "I'm sure we can come to an agreement."

Sheila didn't look so sure, but the pressure of getting to work must have outweighed whatever trouble she imagined her son was in this time, as she slid out the door past me. "Thanks. I'll…I'll swing by your winery later and we can work out payments or something."

I nodded, giving her a smile. "Thanks."

As soon as she was gone, I turned to Jamie. Who was still frowning at me, eyes narrowed, mouth set in a grim line, chin jutting forward in clear disdain.

That made two of us, pal.

I matched his surly look with one of my own. "So. You want to tell me what you were doing at the Groudin Gallery last night?"

He crossed his arms over his chest, looking menacing even in his sweatpants and bare feet. "Maybe I'm an art lover."

"Why do I find that hard to believe?"

"Because you have no imagination?" His mouth curved into a sly smile at the dig.

"I can easily imagine it was *you* who tampered with my brakes last night," I countered.

"Hey, if you've got bad brakes, that's on you."

"Hmm." I cocked my head to the side. "I wonder if the police will see it that way?"

At the mention of the authorities, his demeanor changed, fear flashing behind his eyes. "No way. You're not pinning anything on me. I didn't touch your stupid car!"

"You were at the gallery. And you seemed to take off pretty quickly when you saw me."

"Yeah. 'Cause the last time I chatted with you, it was delightful."

He had me there.

"Look, I'm giving you a chance to come clean before I go to the police," I told him.

"It wasn't me," he said, taking a menacing step toward me. "Why don't you ask that old dude, huh? The cop. He was hanging around outside the gallery too."

"Grant?" While I could see how someone Jamie's age might consider Grant mature, I'd never heard him labeled "old" before.

But Jamie shook his head. "Nah, not the guy that came to tell us about Bill. That other cop. The one with the mustache. Bill's old partner."

"Wait—Eckhart?" I asked my mind suddenly working overtime. "Are you saying Eckhart was at the gallery last night?"

Jamie nodded.

"Why was he there?" I asked.

"How should I know! It's not like I'm all chummy with the cops."

"But you saw him there. Outside?" I asked, trying to process the information. Had he been there following me…or Grant? And why? Were we getting too close to the truth? Is that why he'd tampered with my brakes?

"Yeah, he was there." Jamie nodded, looking a little more smug now that the heat was off him.

"What was he doing?"

Jamie shrugged. "I dunno. He was just kind of hanging out in the parking lot. Smoking a cigarette. Kinda looked like he was waiting for something."

Or someone.

"When was this?" I pressed. I hadn't seen any sign of Eckhart when I'd left.

"I don't know when he got there, but he left right before you did."

I bit my lip. Grant had left right before I did too. Had Eckhart been following him? Warning him that some truth from the past was about to come out? Buckley had had pictures of Grant—did his former partner know? Or had the officer been there to warn me off. Had Ava and I asked too many questions that hit too close to home?

Then something occurred to me. I'd been in Buckley's apartment—searched it pretty thoroughly actually. And nowhere had I seen any photos of Buckley in uniform, let alone with fellow officers. "How did you know the guy in the parking lot was Buckley's partner?"

"What do you mean?"

"I mean, how did you know what Eckhart looked like?"

Jamie frowned. "Well, the dude looked exactly like he did last time he was here."

"Last time he was *here*?" I felt my mental hamster perking up on his wheel. "Like, here, as in at this apartment?"

"Yeah." He frowned. "Why?"

Because Eckhart had told me he hadn't seen Buckley in years.

"When was this?" I pressed.

"I dunno. A couple weeks ago."

"And he saw Buckley while he was here?"

"Yeah. It was my day off, and the two were arguing so loudly they woke me up. I came out and told them to shut up, and Bill told me to get lost and mind my own business."

"What were they arguing about?" I asked.

"Beats me. I didn't stick around. Let Bill fight his own stupid battles, you know?" He sneered as if something about Buckley's death had proven he was incapable of that.

"Did you hear how they left things?" I asked.

Jamie shook his head. "Nah. But Bill was slamming stuff around the apartment for a good hour afterward. Whatever went on between them, it left Bill pretty cheesed off."

Which was interesting, but I was more interested in how it had left Eckhart. Had he been upset too…possibly upset enough to come back and kill his former partner over it?

* * *

Since I'd skipped breakfast in my haste to get to Jamie Connolly, I stopped at the Half Calf coffee shop and grabbed two blueberry scones and a couple of caramel flan lattes before heading to Ava's place. I knocked on the door to her loft with my goodies in hand. When she didn't answer immediately, I suddenly hoped I hadn't shown up too early. I was just about to turn around and let her sleep in, when I heard shuffling on the other side of the door and the security latch being thrown.

"Hey," Ava said, pulling the door open. She looked like she'd just gotten up, still wearing the pink sweats I knew she slept in, her hair piled on the top of her head in pre-shower messy bun.

"Sorry. I hope I didn't wake you," I said, stepping inside.

"No." Ava yawned, stepping back to allow me entry to her loft. "We've been up for a little bit."

I paused. "We?"

"Hey, Ems."

I looked past Ava to find David Allen sitting on Ava's futon. Wearing another pair of Ava's sweats—lavender ones—that barely went past his knees, a T-shirt that read *Girl Power* beneath a sparkly unicorn, and a grin that spanned from one ear to the next.

Oh no. Don't tell me…

"You spent the night?" I asked, raising an eyebrow David's way.

Ava nodded. "We'd both had way too much champagne to drink last night. Like *way* too much." She giggled, and she and David shared a look like they were in on some secret.

I tried hard not to picture what that might be. "I guess the showing was a success."

David nodded. "I sold almost every piece."

"Wow, good for you," I said, thoroughly meaning it. I wasn't sure what that meant in monetary terms, but I could see the hint of pride under David's usual sardonic grin.

"We might have celebrated just a little too hard," Ava said. "We shared an Uber here, and it was just easier for him to stay," she finished, making it sound casual.

Even if David's perma-grin was saying otherwise.

I glanced at the futon. The usual throw pillows sat there, along with a blanket, neatly folded. Impossible to tell if anyone had used it or if he'd had accommodations elsewhere...like in Ava's bedroom.

"You brought coffee?" David asked, rising from the sofa and nodding toward the cup in my hand.

"Uh, yeah. I brought one for Ava. I didn't know you'd be here."

David shrugged, but the grin stayed in place.

"You are a lifesaver," Ava said, taking the cup from my hand. "I'm not ashamed to admit, I'm a little hung over today." She took a long sip.

"Ditto." David reached over and took the cup from her hand, taking a long sip himself. "Delightful."

Sharing a cup of coffee. That felt a little more intimate than a couch sleepover. I tried to catch Ava's eye for some sort of confirmation or denial of just what I'd walked in on. But it seemed she was avoiding my gaze as she took the bakery bag from my hands and we all settled at the kitchen table.

"Blueberry scones. Be still my beating heart," Ava said, nibbling off a piece before handing half to David.

I tried to shake off the unease at seeing the two of them share food.

While David wore Ava's clothes.

After a sleepover.

"You left the showing early," David noted, popping a bite of scone into his mouth. "Everything okay?"

I nodded, so not wanting to rehash what had gone on with Grant. "Yeah, sorry. I...was just really tired." I licked my lips. "But I did have a sort of accident on the way home."

"Accident?" Ava's head popped up from the coffee cup she'd just reclaimed.

"What happened?" David asked. "You okay?"

"I'm fine." Mostly. I quickly filled them in on my faulty brakes and the collision with the oak tree.

"Ohmigosh, you could have been killed!" Ava leaned over the table, giving me a fierce hug.

I winced. "Not so tight. Airbag. Boobs. Bad combo."

"Sorry," she said, pulling back. "Why didn't you call me?"

"I didn't want to ruin David's night." I glanced over at him.

A deep frown was etched on his features. "You said your brakes stopped working?" he asked.

I nodded. "They did. I mean, when I first left the gallery they seemed okay, but about halfway home, they just stopped."

"Could be a cut brake line," he mused. "If the leak was slow enough."

"You think someone did it on purpose?" Ava asked.

I shrugged. "I had it towed to Bob's Garage. I guess the mechanic will be able to say for sure." I paused. "But, I did coincidentally see Jamie Connolly outside the gallery before it happened."

Ava turned to David. "I didn't see him at the showing. Did you?"

David shook his head. "Was he near your car?" he asked me.

"No. I mean, not when I saw him, but I don't know how long he was there. He claims he's just an 'art lover.'"

"So you talked to him?" Ava asked.

"This morning." I quickly filled them in on the conversation I'd had with Jamie, including the fact that, at least according to Jamie, he wasn't the only one of our suspects who had been hanging around the gallery. "And," I ended with, "Jamie Connolly also said he saw Eckhart arguing with Buckley a couple of weeks before he died."

"Wait—didn't he tell us he hadn't seen Buckley in years?" Ava said.

"Exactly." I popped a piece of scone into my mouth.

"So the detective is a liar," David pointed out, licking crumbs from his fingers.

"Officer," I corrected. "Eckhart hasn't made detective because of the scandal involving his former partner."

"He's also a hunter who may own the same type of gun used to shoot Buckley. He hunts small game," Ava told him. "Like rabbits."

David tsked his tongue. "Poor Bugsy."

"Aww. You softie," Ava teased.

He grinned at her.

Their exchange felt enough like morning-after banter to make me feel distinctly like a third wheel.

"Uh, anyway," I said, trying to ignore the odd sensation in my stomach. "If Eckhart did kill Buckley, and mess with my brakes, where do you think Buckley's blackmail scheme fits into all of it?"

"Blackmail?" David gave us both a questioning look. "What did I miss?"

"Oh, and gigolos!" Ava said with a grin.

"You girls have been busy while I've been toiling away on my art," David teased. "Do tell."

I quickly filled him in on what we'd found out from James Atherton and Derek the Delivery Guy.

"Come to think of it," Ava said when I was done, "I'm starting to wonder if that guy really was her nephew."

"Dear naïve Ava." David patted her hand.

"You know, I wonder," I said, thinking out loud. "If Buckley really was sitting on the original bribery money, why would he need to blackmail Katy and James for cash?"

"Maybe he actually did spend the original money," Ava said.

"On what?" I asked. "According to everyone, he's led a modest lifestyle."

"Maybe he lost it," David offered. "Could be the guy had a gambling problem."

Ava and I both turned to look at David. He *had* been the one who'd referred Buckley to me.

"Oh no. David, please don't tell me you played poker with him..."

"No!" David laughed and shook his head. "No, I would have told you that. I don't *know* that he had a gambling problem. It's just a theory."

"Well, whatever the reason, he took James Atherton for twelve grand," Ava said. "Who knows how much he was demanding from Katy."

"Sounds like Katy had the most to lose in the here and now if Buckley didn't keep quiet," David mused.

"Okay, but what about the gun?" Ava asked. "Where would Katy get that?"

David shrugged. "She's a former inmate. I'm sure she could figure out how to get a shotgun from Walmart."

Ava frowned. "Good point."

"But," David went on, "don't forget that while both Katy and Eckhart might have wanted Buckley gone, Carmen is the only one who has actually benefited from his death financially."

"And benefited big," I added.

"And she's missing." David popped a bite of scone into his mouth, grinning like he'd made his point.

"But there's still Jamie Connolly," I said. "I mean, really, we only have his word that Eckhart was anywhere near Buckley. And Jamie was at the gallery last night when my car was possibly tampered with."

"But if Jamie is telling the truth, then Eckhart was at the gallery too. And it could have just as easily been him tampering with your car," Ava pointed out.

"Which brings us full circle and no closer to knowing who killed Buckley." I sighed, feeling defeated again.

David must have noticed, as he said, "Let me throw some clothes on and I'll grab my car to drive you home."

But I shook my head. "I'm fine. Besides, I borrowed Eddie's car."

"You sure?" Ava asked, rising from the table with me.

"Yeah." I grinned, loving them both for offering. But I felt like I'd already intruded enough on their whatever-this-was. "I'm fine."

"Are you heading back to the winery?" David asked.

I nodded. "Unfortunately, I've got to make a decision about my employees. Schultz hasn't found me a partner yet, and

I'm losing faith he'll be able to with all of this hanging over our reputation. I think it's time to make some hard choices."

"You sure you're out of options?" David frowned.

I shrugged. "Unless a miracle lands in my lap."

"Miracles can happen," David said.

"Since when did you become an optimist," I teased.

David chuckled and nodded toward Ava. "She must be wearing off on me."

Hmmm. Ava and David. That was a pairing that I might need to take some time to get used to.

"Something good will happen. I'm sure of it." Ava gave me a sympathetic smile and squeezed my hand as she walked me to the door.

"See what I mean?" David called after us.

Ava ignored him. "I'll call you later?"

I nodded my thanks and gave her a hug before heading back to my borrowed car.

CHAPTER EIGHTEEN

My mind was whirling with a hundred jumbled thoughts as I made the drive back to the winery. Ava and David together or not together. Grant and me on the outs. Buckley and everyone in his life who'd apparently had great reason to want him dead. His almost stepson hated him, his former partner argued with him and lied about it, his ex-wife was half a million dollars richer with him dead, and Katy Kline had just avoided paying Buckley a second time for his silence. Even James Atherton had been out several thousand dollars thanks to Buckley, though I had to admit his alibi put him out of the running as far as a would-be killer was concerned.

The problem was everyone had motive, most had no alibi, and it was all too easy to see any one of them finding Buckley alone on my vineyard and ending their problems. The more I'd found out, the less the finger pointed in any one direction.

I rolled down the window of Eddie's Civic, letting cool air wash over me. Scents of blooming jasmine and baking grapes instantly made me feel at home, and I tried to ignore the small ache in the pit of my stomach that this may not be home for much longer. I was fighting wet eyes again at the thought when my phone rang, my mom's name lighting the display.

I swiped to take the call, putting it on speaker.

"Hi, Mom," I said. "Everything okay?"

"Hi, sweets. I just wanted to thank you again for the cookies. Though, my scale kinda hates you."

I grinned. "You're welcome. And I'm sure your scale will get over it."

"Who knew a pimp could make such good oatmeal raisin," she joked.

I couldn't help a laugh. "Well, at least one part of her front is real."

"Anyway, there's something else I want to tell you." I could hear the hesitation in my mom's voice and suddenly feared the worst.

"What's wrong?" I asked, trying to remember if she'd had any tests scheduled recently.

"Not wrong, really, but…okay, well, you're going to laugh at me."

"I promise not to laugh," I said, relieved at least it wasn't health related. I couldn't bear to face that right now on top of everything else.

"Sure, but you're going to break that promise."

"Okay, I pinky promise not to laugh, but if I do I could use one today. How's that?"

She sighed. "You were right about Mrs. Pettigrew."

"The cat?" I clarified. "What was I right about?"

"She wasn't stolen."

"So, Oscar Worthington found her?"

"Yeah. Well, actually one of the staff found her. In another resident's room."

"And I'm guessing this other resident did not steal Mrs. Pettigrew?"

Mom sighed again. "No. Well, I suppose technically, yes, but it wasn't on purpose. Mrs. Henning gets…confused sometimes."

"Don't we all," I joked.

"Very funny, Em. But apparently she had a cat once that looked very much like Mrs. Pettigrew, and she had a moment where she, well, she kind of got pulled back in time and thought Mrs. Pettigrew was Buster."

"Buster was her old cat, I take it?"

"Yeah. Anyway, she's been enjoying Buster's company for the last few days, stashing him under her bed at night because the Acres does not allow pets."

"Very sensible," I said, trying my darndest to uphold my pinky promise and keep the laughter bubbling up in my throat at bay.

"Anyway, Donny, the night nurse, finally found her."

"Well, I'm sure Oscar is relieved."

"Mostly. Mrs. Henning kind of petted a bald spot into Mrs. Pettigrew's back, so she's going to need some repairs."

I stifled a laugh.

"You promised you won't laugh!"

Okay, I guess I didn't stifle too successfully.

"Sorry. But it is a relief to know that there isn't a thief at Sonoma Acres."

"I didn't say that," Mom hedged. "The photo and the pillow are still missing, you know."

"You don't think that maybe those will just turn up too? I mean, did they do a thorough search of Mrs. Henning's room?"

"Yes, and the other items were not there. I'm telling you, those really were stolen." She paused. "Just not the taxidermy cat."

"Okay, okay," I said, figuring it was better to humor her than argue it at this point. "Well, thank you for the cat update," I told her, turning left into the winery's oak-lined driveway.

"You'll pass that along to Detective Grant, right?" Mom asked.

Oh boy. That was a whole other conversation I didn't want to have. "I'll let him know when I see him." When that would be, I had no idea. "But," I added, "I'm just pulling up to the winery now."

"Okay. I'll let you go. Give Conchita a hug for me."

"Will do."

"And you're still coming for dinner this weekend, right?"

"Wouldn't miss it for the world," I promised her before we said our goodbyes and hung up.

* * *

As soon as I got to my office, I was greeted by a message from Gene Schultz. No luck on the partner front. Ditto the venture capitalist front and bank front and any private investors front. He did find one loan shark who was willing to give me a short-term loan, but I had a bad feeling it came with a hefty interest rate and my kneecaps as collateral. Meaning I was pretty darn sunk.

I spent a depressing afternoon processing my last month of payroll and even went so far as to leave James Atherton a message to inquire just how much Bay Cellars might offer for Oak Valley's vineyards. I was about to go drown my sorrows in a bottle of wine from our cellars—possibly our last run at this rate—when Eddie popped his head through my office door.

"Hey, boss. I'm clocking out for the day."

"Hi, Eddie. I parked your car in the front lot," I said, reaching into my purse to extract his keys. "Thanks so much for the loan."

"Anytime," he said, taking them back from me. He must have sensed my mood, as he paused in the doorway. "You okay?"

"Fine." I nodded, lying through my teeth. "It's just been a long day," I added, infusing some truth into the statement.

"Well, don't worry," Eddie said, giving me a wide smile that dimpled his pudgy cheeks. "Things are bound to pick up soon."

I tried to match his smile, but I was pretty sure it didn't reach my eyes as I shut the top on my laptop, lest he see just how not-bound-to-pick-up things were. I didn't like hiding our status from him, but I was dreading how I would tell him. And Jean Luc. And Conchita and Hector.

I pushed those thoughts to the back of my mind as Eddie waved goodbye and I traversed the short hallway to the tasting room. Jean Luc had apparently gone home for the day already as well, as it was dark but cleaned and organized. Not surprising—Jean Luc was fastidious, and with a nearly empty tasting room the past week, he'd had a lot of time on his hands. I pulled a bottle of our small run Petite Sirah from the chiller behind the bar. A 1997. If I was drowning my sorrows, I was going to do it in style. I was just reaching for the corkscrew when something outside the picture window caught my eyes.

Movement.

I froze, peering out into the dusky evening. While the sun had set, the sky was still a hazy blue, leaving the vineyard and surrounding areas shrouded in shadows.

And one of those shadows was moving.

I set the bottle down on the bar top and crossed to the French doors that led to the courtyard, peering out the glass panes. Standing at the edge of the patio was a woman in jeans and a navy sweatshirt. She had her back to me, but I recognized her immediately. Sheila Connolly.

I let out a breath I hadn't realized I'd been holding. She had said she'd stop by to discuss the damage to my car.

I unlocked the back door, stepping out onto the patio.

"Sheila?" I said, approaching her.

She turned to give me a sad smile over her shoulder. "Beautiful place."

My heart clenched. She meant the place where her boyfriend had spent his last moments. "Thanks," I told her. "It's been in my family for generations."

She nodded, her gaze going back to the dusky hills. "Lucky you. Only thing my family left me was debt."

"I'm sorry." I cleared my throat awkwardly, knowing full well Buckley hadn't left her with anything either. "I, uh, didn't hear you at the door. My manager just left for the day."

"Yeah, I passed a couple of cars leaving. Did you talk to Jamie?" she asked, eyes still on the vine covered hills spanning the horizon before us.

I nodded. "I did."

"And?"

I licked my lips. While I wasn't 100% sure Jamie had tampered with my brakes, I wasn't 100% sure he hadn't either. "And I think we can wait and see what my insurance company says about covering the damages to my car," I hedged.

"He's not a bad kid, you know."

I had my doubts, but I just nodded. Even though I realized her full attention was still on the scene in front of us where Buckley had died and not me. "He seems…troubled."

She gave a snort of laughter. "That's putting it mildly. But if you had to live the life he has, it would be a miracle not to be troubled." She shook her head. "All I wanted was to give him something better, you know? I thought Bill would be better."

"I take it he wasn't an easy man," I said, knowing now what he'd really been up to.

She shook her head slowly in the negative. "Do you know what he got Jamie for his seventeenth birthday?

"Uh, no," I said, feeling almost like I was intruding on some grieving moment between her and the vineyard.

"Slippers. Fifteen dollar slippers from Target." She shook her head. "Jamie's friends were getting cars."

"Jamie has a motorcycle," I pointed out.

"He does. I worked double shifts all summer to buy it for him. Used." She paused. "Bill refused to chip in at all."

I bit my lip. "Well, it's been a tough financial year for a lot of people," I hedged.

She turned away from the hillside just long enough to give me a *get real* look. "You seem to be doing okay here."

"Appearances can be deceiving," I mumbled.

Though if she heard me, she didn't delve deeper into that statement, clearly lost in her own thoughts. She drew in a deep breath of air, as if drinking in the serene landscape. "It's almost magical here, this time of day. Somewhere in that hazy in-between light and dark. It's softer than it felt at night."

While the statement was true, the wording in it made me freeze. "At night?" I asked slowly, my mind suddenly whirling.

She nodded. "It was so cold then." Her voice was wistful and haunting.

"Sheila," I said, feeling my body tense. "When were you here at night?"

She turned to fully face me for the first time, and I realized she was holding something in her hands.

A gun.

A small wooden rifle.

And suddenly it was clear to me when Sheila had been at my winery before. In the dark. At night.

When she'd killed Bill Buckley.

CHAPTER NINETEEN

"Sheila, put the gun down—" I started.

But that was as far as I got before she cut me off.

"Don't." The one word was a command and threat all in one. "Don't speak. Don't move. And don't even think of crying for help."

I licked my lips, eyes riveted to the gun. While crying for help had admittedly been my first thought, my second was that there was no one at the winery to help me anyway. Jean Luc and Eddie had gone. Hector and Conchita's cottage was far enough down the road they'd never hear me. And even if anyone had been on the premises, there was no way help would arrive before a bullet would.

So, I slowly nodded my head in agreement.

"Good." Sheila took a step toward me. "Now let's go for a little walk, shall we?" she asked, her eyes flitting to the tasting room doors.

Doors I longed to lunge for.

She must have read the emotion in my eyes, as she commanded, "Now!" She inclined her head to the right. Toward the deserted vineyard. Where she'd killed Buckley.

I did some more lip licking, feeling my mouth go suddenly dry.

"Sheila, maybe we should just talk about this," I said, putting my hands up in a surrender motion.

"No talking." She took another step toward me. "Just walking." She lifted the gun barrel even with my midsection.

What else could I do? I walked. Even though I felt as if I were being marched to my doom.

"You killed Buckley," I said, stating the obvious as I stepped off the paved patio and into the soft dewy grass of the meadow beyond.

Sheila's voice was hard and void of any sadness I'd associated with her in the past as she answered. "You know I did. Don't play dumb now."

If only I'd been playing. Sheila had been the one person in Buckley's life who *hadn't* benefited from his death in one way or another. Or so it had seemed. "Why did you do it?" I asked, genuinely curious as much as trying to stall for time.

She scoffed. "If you'd known Bill, you'd be asking why I didn't do it *sooner.*"

Fair point. The more I learned about him, the more I'd realized he was far from a model citizen. But… "Something must have put you over the edge."

"Every day I spent with him put me closer to the edge. You have no idea what I put up with. He was a bully." She paused, infusing the next word with clear anger. "And a liar."

"Liar?" I asked. "What did he lie to you about?"

"Everything!" she said, her voice rising.

I glanced back at the fading lights of the winery, hoping against hope that Eddie would come back for a forgotten handkerchief or David would pick that moment to come mooch a glass of wine, and someone would hear her yelling.

"Do you know how many shifts I work a week?" she asked, shoving me forward with the butt of the gun in my ribs.

I winced. Not from physical pain but from the menace of the object, having seen firsthand what it was capable of.

"Do you know how many *hours* I work?" she went on. "Every dang week?"

I shook my head. "No," I answered, hating how shaky my voice sounded.

"Sixty. I pull three doubles. Making minimum wage and crap tips from jerks who call me sweetheart and honey and complain about runny eggs."

"Sounds terrible," I said, trying at sympathy.

"What would you know about terrible?" she spat back. "In your posh winery drinking your fancy merlot."

I hesitated to point out that there was nothing fancy about merlot, and my "posh" winery was actually going under.

"I still don't understand why you killed Buckley," I said instead.

"I told you," she hissed, marching me farther along a row of vines toward the crest of the hill. "He lied to me."

And finally it clicked. "About money."

"Yes, about money. I thought we were broke. That we had nothing. He let me work my butt off while he sat around 'looking for work' for months." She made air quotes with her hands, the gun momentarily leaving my personal space as it waved in the air.

I stopped walking, but before I could do any more to capitalize on the momentary reprieve from the weapon, the gun was staring me back in the face again.

"And all the while," she continued, "it turns out he was sitting on a mountain of cash."

"The bribery money," I guessed.

She nodded.

"So he did lie about having spent it all," I continued. "Not just to IA but to you as well."

More nodding.

"But if he had thousands of dollars, why didn't he use it to…"

"To give Jamie and me a better life? Move us out of squalor at Shady Meadows? Help me quit my soul-sucking job?" Sheila asked, not without a modicum of sarcasm lacing her voice. "Yeah, I asked him those questions too. He said he couldn't spend it without getting caught. That the police were still watching him. Liar *and* a coward."

The irony. He was sitting on a hundred thousand dollars he couldn't spend.

"Surely he could have used just a little to make your lives better?"

"Right?!" Sheila threw her hands up, the gun momentarily leaving my person again. "That's what I said. But no. He was selfish. Selfish and mean." Her eyes narrowed, and the gun swooped back into my orbit, freezing any thoughts of escape. "He said he couldn't spend any of it without the police getting wind and realizing he'd lied. He'd be facing criminal charges for sure then."

"How did you find out he'd been hiding the money?" I asked, trying to keep her talking.

"Jamie told me."

"Jamie?" I asked, pieces staring to fall into place.

She nodded. "He overheard some fight. Between Bill and his former partner."

"Eckhart," I supplied. The argument Jamie had told me about. He hadn't been making it up. He had, however, left out some key details about what he'd heard that day. "Are you saying Eckhart knew Bill had the money still?"

She nodded. "Eckhart knew all about it. In fact, Bill said he was in on it from the beginning."

I blinked at her, processing this. "Wait—Eckhart was taking bribes too?"

"Surprise, honey. Cops aren't always the good guys." She gave me a wry smile. "They were both taking cash to look the other way, but when Bill got caught, Eckhart paid him to take the fall for them both."

I shook my head, trying to wrap my brain around this. "Why wouldn't Katy Kline have said something?" I asked. "I mean, Buckley sold her out. Why didn't she roll on Eckhart?"

Sheila shrugged. "Maybe she didn't know. Bill said he was the muscle but the idea had all been Eckhart's."

"Bill confessed all of this to you?"

The corners of Sheila's mouth turned up in a sinister grin. "Amazing what one will admit to when staring down the barrel of a gun."

I swallowed hard, not having to stretch my imagination much for that one.

"But all of this took place two years ago," I pointed out. "What was Eckhart arguing with Buckley about two weeks ago?"

Sheila shook her head, scoffing. "Money. Bill wanted more of it for his *continued* silence."

"He was blackmailing Eckhart," I said, putting it together. It made sense. He'd been blackmailing Katy Kline and James Atherton. Why not his former partner too?

Sheila nodded confirmation. "Bill told me he was sure he could make Eckhart pay up. That he'd take care of me from now on. He'd make up for the past." She shook her head.

"You didn't believe him?" I asked, taking a small step backwards, feeling my back come up against a tall oak tree as I tried to put any distance I could between the gun and me.

She shook her head again. "Why should I believe him? He'd already lied to me for years." She grinned. "Besides—why settle for him 'taking care of me' when I could have it all?"

"*It all* being the bribery money. He told you where it was?"

She nodded slowly. "He had it all in cryptocurrency."

And here Ava and I had thought Cayman Islands was too sophisticated. Appeared I'd underestimated Buckley. Or Charlie's Angels had to catch up to the times. "You mean like Bitcoin?" I asked.

More nodding. "It was all easily accessible on an app on his phone."

Which is why Buckley'd had his phone out when he'd been killed. He hadn't been calling for help. He'd been forced at gunpoint to access his cryptocurrency account.

"I'm guessing the money is now in *your* cryptocurrency account."

Sheila grinned. "*Bill* couldn't spend money without coming under scrutiny. But who's gonna pay attention to me?"

"You were the one who tripped the security system here that night," I said.

"I wanted answers. Real answers, not that bull he spun me at home."

I looked at the rifle in her hands. "So you bought a gun?"

"Borrowed. Bill's pal Eckhart is a hunter. Did you know that?"

Actually, I did. I glanced down at the rifle. "This is Eckhart's gun?" At least I'd been on the right track about one thing.

"Yeah. Turns out, he's also a really deep sleeper, and he doesn't lock his bathroom windows at night." She shook her head, that sinister grin on her face again. "Way too trusting."

"You stole Eckhart's gun," I said, following her plot, "because you knew even if it led the police back to him, he wouldn't incriminate himself by telling them about the money."

Her spreading grin confirmed I was on the right track.

"You went where you knew Buckley would be alone, at night, in the dark. You convinced him to tell you everything. Then you killed him."

"Then all I had to do was wait until this all blew over, and Jamie and I could go start a new life somewhere else. A better life."

"With Buckley's money."

"With *my* money! He owed it to me!" she shouted back. "I put up with that man for two years! I earned every penny of it!"

While one could argue that point, I didn't intend to. Not with the gun still pointed at me. I glanced back at the winery, hoping against hope to see any sign of life. Unfortunately the only lights shining in the window were the ones I'd turned on before stupidly walking out the door to approach Sheila alone. The winery was deserted. The vineyard still. Not even a crow or squirrel in sight to witness my confrontation with a murderess.

"It was a perfect plan," Sheila went on. "With just one little snag." She leveled me with a hard stare.

Oh boy. "Which was?"

She narrowed her eyes at me. "You. I don't know what your deal was, but you just couldn't leave us alone."

I licked my lips. "I-I honestly had no idea," I tried to tell her.

"Sure. You just *happen* to come by the apartment asking all kinds of questions. About Bill. About money. About where I was the night Bill died."

Actually, I'd been asking where *Jamie* had been, but in hindsight I could see how Sheila's answer had failed to give her an alibi as well. I really wished I'd noticed that sooner. "We were just offering our condolences," I said.

"Then," she went on, "you show up at Jamie's work, harassing him."

"We were just having lunch."

"And today? What exactly where you 'just' doing when you showed up to interrogate Jamie about damaging your car, huh?"

She had me there. "Were you the one who tampered with my brakes?"

She frowned. "Why would I tamper with your brakes?"

"Why do you have me at gunpoint?" I countered.

Her eyes narrowed again. "You ask way too many questions."

In that moment I had to agree with her. I pursed my lips shut, watching as she took a purposeful step toward me.

"I'm tired of all the questions. And I'm tired of you." She raised the gun barrel flush with my belly. "It's time for the nosey vintner to go."

I swallowed down fear, trying not to panic. "You don't have to do this."

"No?" She shook her head. "I'm sorry, but I think I do. You know way too much."

Little did she know, I'd been clueless when she'd shown up. "You won't get away with this," I said, not totally believing that statement myself.

"Maybe not." She shrugged. Then a hard look hit her eyes. "But it's worth a try. What have I got to lose? A crappy apartment and a job that's slowly killing me?"

"What about Jamie?" I asked, my eyes scanning the vineyard behind her again for any means of escape. I thought I saw some movement to our right, but as the wind kicked up, I realized it must just be the rustling of the leaves.

"Who do you think I'm doing this for?" Sheila shouted, suddenly losing her cool demeanor again. "I have to get Jamie out of here. Out of this life. He deserved something better. Bill could have given us that." She sneered, shaking her head. "But he was too selfish."

"This isn't the way to do it," I said, desperate for anything I could say to calm her. Stall her. Appeal to any sense of humanity she might have left.

"No?" she mocked. "Well, I think it's the perfect way to do it."

She took another step toward me. Lips set in a grim line. All talking done now. Her eyes were cold and angry, as if picturing Buckley standing in front of her, having cheated her of the life she felt she deserved.

My breath stopped. My heart clenched.

And the leaves to my right rustled again.

Louder.

I sucked in a breath, my eyes shooting to the vines just behind Sheila.

She must have heard it too, as she spun as if on instinct.

But her instincts were a moment too late, as a bottle of 1997 Petite Sirah came crashing down on her head with a dull, painful sounding thud. She made a sort of strangled noise in the back of her throat before crumpling into a pile on the soft earth at my feet.

I let out a long breath, panic flowing from my heart out through my fingertips as I took in the person attached to the bottle of wine.

David Allen.

His breath was coming hard, his eyes wide as he stared down at the prone form of my would-be killer.

"Geez, Emmy. You really know how to make friends," he joked.

I would have agreed, but in that moment all I had energy for was to collapse into a puddle against the oak tree beside me and burst into tears.

CHAPTER TWENTY

Emergency vehicles lit up the night sky, red and blue lights strobing across the vineyard. The sounds of crackling walkie-talkies and wailing sirens filled the air as the fields filled with men and women in police uniforms. And I sat shivering on a wrought iron chair on the patio, watching it all unfold.

"You okay?" David asked, occupying the chair beside me. Both of us had been mostly silent as we'd called 9-1-1 and waited for help to arrive. EMTs had been first on the scene, strapping Sheila to a gurney and wheeling her away. I was pretty sure her final destination would be jail, but I was glad to see she'd just been unconscious and not the second body in my vineyard that week.

"Yeah, I'm good," I told him.

"You're shaking," he countered.

I wrapped my arms around myself, trying to stave off the chill. "I'm just a little cold."

"We could go inside," he offered.

I shook my head. "I'm fine." Truth was, it would take me a long time to be anything close to fine after having a rifle pointed at me, but something in me couldn't pry my eyes from the scene.

"He'll be here soon."

I turned to David. "He?"

"Grant. You're waiting for him to show up, aren't you?"

I licked my lips. Until David had voiced the thought out loud, I hadn't been sure, but I nodded.

"He'll be here." David put an arm around my shoulders. "He's into you, kid."

A laugh escaped me. "Thanks."

"Sure. Besides, it's kind of a crime scene here, and we both know that's his jam."

A longer laugh escaped me. "Oh, the lengths a girl will go to to get noticed by a guy."

"It's pathetic, really," David joked. "You poor, desperate thing."

We were silent a moment before I turned to him. "Hey, David?"

"Yeah."

"Thanks for coming by to mooch my wine tonight." His timing could not have been better. As I'd heard him tell the first responding officer on the scene, he'd walked into the tasting room just in time to see Sheila and me crossing the meadow. From that angle, he hadn't seen the rifle in her hands, or he said he would have followed us sooner. But he had thought it odd enough that after a few minutes, he'd picked up the only thing that felt handy as a weapon—the bottle of wine I'd left on the counter—and walked out into the vineyard to see where we'd gone. That's when he'd come upon Sheila and me, just in time to hear the tail end of her confession, where she made it clear what her intentions toward me were.

Something I would be eternally grateful for. Even if my Sirah was now considered evidence.

David chuckled. "Anytime, Ems." He paused. "But I actually came by tonight to give you something."

"Oh?" I asked. "A present?"

"Something like that."

For some reason my mind flitted to the portrait he'd painted. "What is it?"

But he shook his head, his eyes cutting to the tasting room door. "It will keep. Looks like your knight in shining armor is here."

I followed the line of his gaze to find Grant standing in the doorway, a stoic look of concern on his chiseled features.

Before I could do more than relish the relief that washed over me, he had crossed the patio and was at my side. "Are you okay?" he asked, the urgency in his voice betraying how much the answer meant to him.

I felt tears back up in my throat and nodded. "Yeah. I'm good. Thanks to David." I nodded to my companion, who was rising from his seat.

"Just good timing is all," David said, playing at modesty. He looked from Grant to me. "I'm gonna go inside and call Ava."

Grant and David did a manly nod thing, silently acknowledging each other's presence, before David disappeared inside the tasting room.

As soon as he was gone, Grant turned to me. "Are you really okay?"

I grinned, even though I felt those tears backing up so far they leaked right over my eyelids. "Yeah. Almost."

He reached down and pulled me into his arms, the warmth of his embrace washing over me like a comforting blanket. I leaned my cheek against his chest, feeling his heartbeat against my skin, and inhaled deeply the subtle woodsy scent of his aftershave. I never wanted to move.

I wasn't sure how long he held me there, but by the time we finally stepped apart, the tears had subsided, and I'd almost stopped shaking.

"Can you tell me what happened?" he asked softly.

"I can try," I said. Then I quickly filled him in on Sheila's confession, how Buckley had lied about the bribery money, and Eckhart's role in it all. "I'm sorry," I ended with. "I know he was your friend."

Grant inhaled deeply, nodding. "Well, like you said, I guess we don't always know people as well as we think."

"Sheila had planned to frame him by using his rifle."

"I suppose you were right about that one, huh?" he conceded, giving me a lopsided grin.

"So not all my theories are cockamamie, are they?"

He laughed. "No. Not all of them." He reached a hand out and tucked a strand of hair behind my ear, the gesture simple but more intimate than I'd felt from him in a while. "Accept my apology for that one?"

"Did I miss the actual apology?" I teased.

That lopsided grin appeared again. "I'm sorry I didn't take you seriously. I humbly apologize."

"Forgiven," I told him, standing on tiptoe to plant a light kiss on his lips.

His arms went around me, and the light kiss might have turned a little heavier. Grant made a low moaning sound in the back of his throat. "You're making me really sorry I'm going to be up all night processing your crime scene."

I pulled away, the moment of reprieve from all that had happened that evening fading as I became aware of our surroundings again. I glanced toward the ambulance where I'd seen the EMTs wheel Sheila. "What's going to happen to her now?" I asked.

"Once she's medically cleared, we'll charge her with first degree homicide, as well as your attempted homicide. Then she'll be going to jail for a very long time," he promised me.

"And the money?" I asked. "What happens to the cryptocurrency now?"

"I'll let the guys in tech figure out how to access that. But once they do, it will all be seized as police assets now." His gaze went out over the hillside. "Likely to be tied up in court for a while. Especially if Sheila goes to trial."

"I think she really was doing it all for her son, in the end," I told him, almost feeling sorry for Sheila.

Almost.

She *had* been threatening me at gunpoint, after all.

Grant nodded. "We picked Jamie up an hour ago."

I frowned. An hour ago, Sheila had still had me in the vineyard. "What did you pick him up for?" I asked.

"Putting a hole in your brake fluid line." He gave me a pointed look.

"How did you know about…" I trailed off. Then it dawned on me. "Ava?"

Grant nodded. "She called me this morning."

I shook my head. "I should have never given that girl your number."

Grant laughed. "What you *should* have done was call me yourself." He took a step forward, arms going around me again. "Why didn't you tell me about the accident, Emmy?"

I blew out a sigh. "I don't know. Thing were going so sideways between us. I just… I just didn't want to add another layer."

He cocked his head to the side. "Things were never *that* sideways."

I felt a smile snaking across my face. "Good." I took what felt like the first deep emotion-free breath in days. "But how did you find out for sure that it was Jamie who tampered with my car?"

"Well, I visited the garage you had it towed to. They confirmed there was a hole in the brake fluid line. Looked like it had been covered with some sort of putty."

"Putty?"

He nodded. "Designed to melt as the engine turned on and the car got warm, causing the brake fluid to only leak out once the car was already on the road."

I shuddered. "So he meant to kill me."

"More likely to cause you to run off the road, like you did. He's not talking, but my guess is he was trying to scare you away from his mom."

"She honestly didn't seem to know anything about the brakes," I said. "But it sounds like Jamie knew his mother killed Buckley?"

"Or at least suspected," Grant confirmed.

"You think that's why he was here at the winery the next day? Checking to see if his mom left any evidence behind?"

"It's quite possible." Grant nodded. "Like I said, he's not saying much right now. We've charged him as a juvenile, but the DA could easily push to try him as an adult for attempted murder if Jamie doesn't cooperate."

I glanced at the ambulance Sheila's gurney was resting in. "I don't think he's going to help you put away his mom."

Grant shrugged. "And I couldn't blame the kid there. But she's not the only one who will be facing charges in all of this."

I pursed my lips. "Eckhart?"

Grant didn't answer right away, the little gold flecks in his eyes moving in a frantic rhythm that told me how conflicted he felt. Finally he broke my gaze and looked out over the hills where crime scene techs were converging. "I'll call it in to SFPD. Let them handle it. Whatever happens, it's out of my hands."

"Sorry," I said again, putting a hand on his arm.

He gave me a sad smile.

"But Eckhart wasn't the only person Buckley was blackmailing," I told Grant.

"I know."

That one got me. "Wait—you know?"

He nodded. "We went over all of Buckley's bank transactions. He'd been depositing large amounts of cash that didn't coincide with any invoices for jobs he'd done."

I sighed and closed my eyes. Of course Grant knew. He was a cop. And a good one. "So you know about James Atherton?" I asked.

Grant nodded. "We paid him a visit this afternoon."

I couldn't help a small grin. "Bet he loved that."

"Almost peed his pants." Grant grinned too.

"And Katy Kline?" I asked.

Grant nodded again. "Wasn't too hard to put that one together. Though what he was blackmailing her over, we're still not sure."

"Derek," I supplied.

Grant frowned. "Derek?"

"Her delivery guy. She says he's her nephew, but he's really her gigolo."

Grant let out a small laugh. "So, she's in the male escort business now?"

I nodded.

"How did you find out?"

"I sort of ordered him for my mom."

"Wait..." He shook his head.

"Long story. But Katy's oatmeal raisin cookies are actually fantastic."

Grant looked as though he'd like the longer version of that story, but for the moment he let it go. Thankfully.

"There's something I have to tell you," I said, hating to ruin the moment but needing to come clean.

"Something more than hiring a gigolo?" Grant raised an eyebrow at me.

I nodded, licking my lips. "The way I found out about James Atherton and Katy Kline was that Buckley had photos of them. I confronted James, and he told me everything."

"Where did you see these photos?"

"Can we gloss over that?' I asked.

He raised the other eyebrow, but he didn't say anything, so I took that as a good sign.

"Anyway," I said, dreading to say it. But I couldn't not. "I saw that Buckley had photos of you too."

"You did?" he said.

I nodded. "Look, I don't know how well you knew Buckley or what went on between you two, but I..."

Grant's frowned deepened.

I forged ahead. "...I know he wasn't blackmailing you. I know he wouldn't have any reason to, and I know you wouldn't bite."

Some of the creases between his eyebrows smoothed out. "You do."

I nodded. "I know you better than that," I decided.

The left corner of his mouth quirked up in a half smile. "I'm glad to hear you say that." He took a deep breath. "But I know about the photos."

"You do?" Relief rushed through me.

He nodded. "His bank records were our first clue he was blackmailing someone, but the photos were what put us on to James and Katy. We found copies on his computer. Along with notes."

"What sort of notes?"

"Notes he'd kept about comings and goings, people he'd seen them with. Anything he thought they'd pay to keep quiet."

I licked my lips. "So, why did he have photos of you?"

"Well, according to his notes, he was hoping to find something he could hold over me."

I let out a breath. "So he did intend to blackmail you."

He nodded. "Look, Buckley knew about my past incident in San Francisco and the run-in with Internal Affairs. Only, he assumed—incorrectly—that, like him, I was dirty and lucky to get away with a transfer. Buckley thought if he looked hard enough, maybe he could find something here in Sonoma that was similar. Something he could hold over me. Apparently he'd been digging into my life and..." He paused, glancing down at me. "And that's why he took the job here."

"Wait—are you saying the only reason he was at my winery in the first place was to get some dirt on you?"

He nodded. "It appears that way. His notes indicated he felt I might let my guard down around my girlfriend and spill something usable."

While my mind was whirling with that new information, it somehow homed in on one part of that statement. "Did you just call me your girlfriend?"

Grant chuckled. "*That's* the part you're fixating on?"

"Answer the question, Detective Grant," I said, not able to wipe the grin off my face for anything.

He took a step forward, closing the gap between us. Then he leaned down, his lips skimming mine in a seductively soft kiss. "Does that answer your question?" he whispered, sending a shiver down my spine.

Oh, yeah. I felt myself melting into his embrace as he swooped in for another kiss.

"There's just one more thing I need to know," I mumbled onto his lips.

"Hmm?"

"How did you get the moon shaped scar on your butt?"

He chuckled, his lips going to my neck. "I'll tell you all about it." He paused. "At your place. Tomorrow night."

That was one bedtime story I couldn't wait to hear.

* * *

Heroic local artist saves the day!

I glanced down at the headline in the *Sonoma-Index Tribune* and shook my head.

"What?" David asked, grinning from ear to ear. "I think it's a very accurate portrayal of the harrowing events last week."

"You would," I teased, slapping him on the arm with the newspaper. An actual printed newspaper. David had cleaned out every machine downtown and was even threatening to frame a copy of Bradley Wu's very flattering article.

Flattering to David, at least. It still made our winery look like a haven for criminals and those with murder on the mind. Which, sadly, had done nothing to bolster sales that weekend, the tasting room holding only a couple of people, despite it being happy hour on a Saturday.

While David had been touted as the man who had saved the life of the "most unlucky vintner in Sonoma" and brought to justice the "killer among the vines," Bradley Wu had also been able to secure an exclusive interview with Carmen Buckley, the "long-suffering" first wife of the victim.

According to Wu, Carmen Buckley had, in fact, left town as we'd suspected. But it had not, however, been because she'd been guilty of killing her ex-husband but because she'd been celebrating her upcoming windfall from his life insurance policy. She'd given the guy who'd stood her up the night of Buckley's death a second chance, and, being that he ended up being as cute in person as his pictures online, the two had spent a whirlwind long weekend in Las Vegas, making a dent in Carmen's insurance payout. A small dent. She was, after all, a half millionaire now.

Wu had also reported that Sheila Connolly was pleading not guilty by reason of insanity, having claimed that living with a man like Buckley had driven her over the edge. While I had to admit that residing in Shady Meadows seemed pretty depressing, I had a hard time seeing an actual insanity plea stick.

Unlike his mother, Jamie had admitted his guilt in it all. He'd confessed to Grant that he'd cut my brake line at the gallery, saying he'd watched a couple of YouTube tutorials on how to do it. Though he insisted he'd only hoped to scare me into backing off his mom and not actually harm me. While he wasn't saying much about his mom and whether he actually knew she'd been guilty or only suspected, he had agreed to tell the police everything he knew about Eckhart and Buckley's arrangement in exchange for being charged as a juvenile. Which I was actually pretty okay with. While Jamie had, in fact, scared the bejeezus out of me that night and caused the several thousand dollars' worth of damage to my beloved Jeep (thankfully most of which had been covered by insurance), he'd done it to protect his mom.

I didn't want to think what sort of things I might be capable of in the same position.

Like Jamie, Eckhart had also had the good sense to come clean once faced with the evidence of his crimes. However, according to Eckhart's version, it had been Buckley who'd been the mastermind behind the bribery scheme and Eckhart had only gone along for the ride. When Buckley had been caught, Eckhart paid him everything that he hadn't spent in order to keep Eckhart's name out of it. Only, he hadn't counted on Buckley coming back for more two years later. He claimed that's what the argument Jamie had overheard had been about—Buckley looking for more money and Eckhart telling him he had none. After Buckley had died, Eckhart had discovered his rifle missing and had hoped it was just coincidence. Until I'd shown up in San Francisco asking questions about Buckley's death. Eckhart had erroneously thought Grant had sent me, which was why he'd been following Grant that night when Jamie had seen him at the gallery. He'd been trying to find out if Grant knew the truth about the bribery and his part in it. When IA had arrested him, he'd been partly relieved that at least it had only been for bribery and not a successful frame-up for Buckley's murder.

"So," I said to David, "did you just show up to gloat at your newfound fame and drink my wine?" I gestured to the glass of Zin in his hands.

David grinned. "Wow, a *thanks for saving my life, David* would be nice."

"Thank you," I said with all sincerity. "You know I am forever grateful."

"Twice." He held up two fingers. "This is twice I've saved your cute little bacon, Ems," he said, eyes flitting to my derriere.

"Thank you *twice*," I told him. "I am twice as in your debt."

His grin widened. "I like the sound of that. Remind me to collect on that someday." He winked at me.

I cleared my throat. "So, I've fawned over you and you have your wine, so I'm going to go serve the other customers," I said, gesturing to a couple at the end of the bar who clearly already had full glasses.

"Just a minute," David said, holding up a hand and setting his glass on the bar top. "I actually stopped by to give you something."

I bit my lip. The something he'd mentioned the other night when he'd "saved my bacon." I'd had a full week and a half to contemplate just what it was David was giving me, and only one dreaded thought had come to mind.

"David, I don't want the painting," I blurted out, the words rushing from my mouth before I could stop them.

David frowned. "The painting?"

"The one you made of m—" I stopped myself from saying *me* just in time. "Of the woman. The lost woman," I amended. While it was hauntingly beautiful, the fact that everyone seemed to think David had painted me was even more haunting. And unnerving. And brought up emotions I wasn't sure I wanted to have. "It's beautiful, but it's…just not for me."

David's frown slowly dissolved, a grin taking its place. "Emmy, I'm not giving you a painting," he said. "Do you know how much my paintings sell for?"

I shut my mouth with a click. "I guess not."

"A lot more than you could afford," he said, grin widening. "Besides, I sold that piece at the showing."

"Oh." I pursed my lips together, feeling a blush creep into my cheeks. "Well, good for you."

He cocked his head to the side. "Why did you think I was giving it to you?"

I licked my lips. "No reason. I just…I mean, you said you had a present for me…and I sort of thought maybe…well, you know, because I said I liked it…and it sort of looked like it could have been…" I trailed off, going absolutely nowhere I wanted to be with that sentence.

David raised a questioning eyebrow at me as if daring me to finish the thought.

I took a deep breath. "Okay, I have to ask you something."

"Yes?" David asked, arching the eyebrow further, grin still punctuating his cheeks as he swirled his Zin in his glass.

I took another deep breath...and realized I didn't want to know the answer to *that* question. Instead, I chickened out and went with, "Did you sleep with Ava?"

David's wineglass paused halfway to his lips. "What?!"

"The other night. After the gallery opening. You spent the night."

"On the couch," David said with a chuckle.

"You were in her clothes."

"I spilled champagne on my blazer."

"You drank from her coffee cup."

"I'm rude and needed caffeine," David said, laughing in earnest now. "Ems, Ava and I are friends."

"I know, but how good of friends are you?"

"Not *that* good."

"Really?" I asked, giving him the side-eye.

"Really. I slept on her lumpy futon. Like a gentleman. Had an uncomfortable rod in my back all night."

I gave him another dubious look.

"Would you like to see the mark it made?" he asked, lifting the hem of his T-shirt.

"No!" I gave him another playful swat with the newspaper. "Do not disrobe in my tasting room!" I glanced around at the sparsely populated room.

"You prefer I should I disrobe elsewhere?" He winked at me.

"There will be no disrobing. Here, there, or anywhere."

"You're no fun." He picked his wineglass back up and took a sip, the smile still present on his lips. "But you're adorable when you're flustered."

I took a deep breath and shook my head at him. "You said you were here to give me something?"

He nodded. "I am." He set his wineglass down on the bar and reached into the back pocket of his jeans, extracting a folded sheaf of papers. He slid them across the bar to me.

I glanced from him to the papers. "What's this?"

"Read it." He leaned back in his chair and sipped wine around his smile again. Which was practically wicked enough that I suddenly feared what was on the pieces of paper.

I reached out and unfolded them, seeing a document in small font. I read the first few lines silently before their meaning hit in. "David, what is this?"

"It's a partnership agreement."

I shook my head. "Partnership?"

"You said you needed to take on a partner here. Someone to infuse the place with a little capital."

An odd mix of hope and dread filled my chest. "Are you saying you want to invest in the winery?"

He shrugged. "Why not? It's a nice place. Lots of history. I fully endorse the product." He held up his glass. "And I happen to know the owner very well." He gave me another wink.

My mind was whirling, eyes scanning the paperwork in front of me. Which looked perfectly legit and perfectly enticing. "You're serious?" I asked. "I mean, you can afford this?"

David threw his head back and laughed. "Well, not if you're going to bleed me dry. I mean, I do expect to see a return on my investment. Eventually," he added.

"Eventually could be a while," I hedged, looking around at our mostly empty happy hour.

David shrugged. "Wedding season is coming up. Hector said he expects a good harvest this year. I mean, as long as you can keep the place out of the headlines and yourself out of any more trouble," he teased, nodding toward the newspaper, "I think a profit isn't out of the realm of possibility, do you?"

"I-I don't know what to say," I told him, honestly meaning it.

"Say yes," he said, sipping from his glass again. "You need the cash."

"And what do you get out of it?" I asked, dubious.

He shrugged. "A nice little hobby. A sound investment."

A license to show up and drink my wine anytime he wanted. A say in anything that happened at Oak Valley Vineyards. A permanent fixture in my life.

I glanced over at him, casually sipping Zinfandel at my bar, in his ripped jeans, T-shirt touting some band, combat boots, and a sardonic smile. I wasn't sure if I was looking at my savior or my undoing.

But I took a deep breath and made a decision.

"Yes."

"Yes?" he asked, raising his eyebrows up into his too long hair.

I nodded. "It's a deal." I stuck my hand out toward him. "Partner."

His grin widened again. "Partner," he said, shaking my hand.

I shoved all thoughts of second-guessing out of my head, instead focusing on what David's lovely money could do for me.

For *us*, I mentally amended, thinking of Eddie, Jean Luc, Hector, and Conchita, and all of the employees at Oak Valley who were more like family. If adding David to that family was the price I'd pay, so be it. Every family had that quirky, black sheep of a cousin, right?

"By the way," I said, refolding the paperwork that I'd look over in more detail later. "Who was the woman in the painting? The lost looking one?"

David turned his attention to his glass, swirling the remains of the red liquid. "Just a girl I know. No one in particular." He took a sip.

I watched him, not sure what to think of that answer. And the fact he wasn't making eye contact. I was about to woman-up and ask more, when my phone rang from my back pocket. I pulled it out to see Mom's name lighting the display and swiped to take the call.

"Hey, Mom," I said, stepping away for a little privacy.

"Emmy, I'm so glad you picked up. You won't believe what happened!"

"Mom, are you okay?" I asked, a flutter of panic washing over me at the urgency in her voice.

"Yes, I'm fine. But…well, it's all been so terrible."

"What's been terrible?"

"It's Oscar Worthington."

I racked my brain for the name. "You mean the guy with the stuffed cat?"

"Yes. Emmy, I *told* you there was trouble here. I just can't believe it's come to this. There are police officers everywhere."

"Police?" Now she really had my attention. "Mom, slow down and tell me what's happened."

I heard her take a deep breath on the other end. Which might have calmed her but did nothing to slow the escalating panic in my belly.

Especially when she said the next line.

"Oscar has been murdered!"

"Murdered?" I said before I could stop myself. I clamped my lips shut, glancing down the bar where my new partner was sitting, hoping no one had heard me.

"It's true! Emmy, what are we going to do?"

I closed my eyes. There was only one thing I could do. Say goodbye to my promise from a moment ago to stay out of trouble.

"I'll be right there."

RECIPES

Walnut Mushroom Au Gratin Copycat

2 tablespoons olive oil, divided
1 cup walnuts, coarsely chopped
1 medium onion, cut into quarters and thinly sliced
8 ounces small button mushroom, halved or quartered into small chunks
3 cups thinly sliced broccoli stems and bite-sized florets
1 8-ounce can sliced water chestnuts
1 clove garlic, minced
2 tablespoons sherry
2 tablespoons soy sauce
1 cup sour cream
6 ounces dry spinach fettuccini
1 cup shredded Monterey jack cheese
1 cup shredded cheddar cheese

Preheat oven to 375°F.
Cook the spinach fettuccini until barely tender, about 10 minutes.

Heat a large skillet over low heat, add walnuts and stir until lightly toasted and fragrant, then remove and reserve the nuts and return the skillet to the stove.

Add one tablespoon oil to the hot skillet, add onions and mushrooms and cook until just beginning to brown, then remove with a spoon and reserve. Add the remaining tablespoon of oil to the pan and sauté the broccoli until crisp-tender, about 10 minutes. Stir in the reserved onions, mushrooms, water chestnuts, garlic, and spinach fettuccini. Remove from heat and add the sherry, soy sauce, and sour cream. Stir gently to coat without breaking the noodles.

Place mixture in a greased, shallow 2½ quart baking dish. Sprinkle evenly with the reserved walnuts and then the cheeses. Bake until cheese melts, about 15–20 minutes.

Tips!
You can bake the mixture in any type or combination of casserole pans you wish. If you use large individual ramekins, bake only until the casserole is hot and the cheese melts, about 10–12 minutes.

Wine Pairings
Best served with wines that complement the cheese of the au gratin, like an oaky Chardonnay or a full bodied Cabernet Sauvignon. Some of Emmy's suggestions: River Road Double Oaked Chardonnay, Heitz Napa Valley Chardonnay, Dry Creek Vineyard Cabernet Sauvignon

Creamy Pork Marsala

1 tablespoon olive oil
6 boneless pork loin chops (4 ounces each)
2 cups sliced fresh mushrooms
⅓ cup chopped onion
3 garlic cloves, minced
1 cup Marsala wine
1 cup reduced-sodium chicken broth
1¼ cup heavy cream
1 teaspoon cornstarch
2 tablespoons water
Fresh chopped parsley for garnish

In a large nonstick skillet heat oil over medium heat. Add pork chops and cook about 4–5 minutes on each side or until browned and internal temperature reaches 145°F. Remove from pan; keep warm.

In same skillet, add mushrooms, onion, and garlic and cook 2–3 minutes or until onions are soft. Add wine and chicken broth and bring to a boil, stirring to deglaze the pan. Then add in heavy cream.

In a small bowl, mix cornstarch and water together then add to pan and let simmer until it's slightly thickened, for about 5 minutes. Add the pork back to the pan for the last 2 minutes before serving. Sprinkle plate with chopped parsley for garnish.

Tips!
The alcohol in the dish will cook out, however, if you prefer not to use alcohol at all, you can substitute more chicken broth. If you don't have Marsala wine on hand, you can get close to the same flavor by using a dry white wine and a splash of brandy.

Wine Pairings

Best served with a full-bodied white or a light bodied red like a Pinot Noir that won't overwhelm the sweetness of the Marsala sauce. Some of Emmy's suggestions: LOLA Chardonnay, Willamette Valley Vineyards Pinot Noir, Fogdog Pinot Noir

Oatmeal Raisin Cookies

1 cup butter
1 cup brown sugar
1 cup granulated sugar
2 eggs
1 teaspoon vanilla
1½ cup white flour
1 teaspoon salt
1 teaspoon baking soda
3 cups quick-cooking rolled oats
½ cup chopped walnuts
1 cup raisins

In a large mixing bowl, combine all ingredients. Roll dough into logs then wrap in waxed paper, and chill in the refrigerator for 1–2 hours or until firm.

Preheat oven to 350°F.

Slice logs into ¼–½" pieces. Place on an ungreased cookie sheet and bake for 8–9 minutes, just until the edges of the cookies start to turn golden brown. Makes about 5 dozen cookies.

Tips!
Add 1 teaspoon of cinnamon for a warmer flavor. Or for those who are not raisin fans, substitute 1 cup semisweet chocolate chips or M&Ms for raisins. If in a hurry, the dough logs may be put into the freezer for 10–20 minutes or until just firm enough to slice.

Wine Pairings
Best served with sweet dessert wines or a Riesling or fruity Chardonnay. Some of Emmy's suggestions: S.A. Prum Riesling, Clean Slate Riesling, Butter Chardonnay

Lobster Bisque

2 tablespoons butter
1 tablespoon olive oil
1 onion, finely chopped
2 carrots, peeled and finely chopped
2 stalks celery, finely chopped
½ teaspoon sea salt
¼ teaspoon black pepper
2 cloves garlic, minced
2 tablespoons tomato paste
2 tablespoons all-purpose flour
4 cups seafood or fish stock
1¼ cups dry white wine
1 bay leaf
3 sprigs fresh thyme
½ cup heavy cream
4 cooked lobster tails, chopped
Finely chopped chives for serving

In a large pot heat butter and olive oil over medium heat. Add onion, carrots, and celery and cook 5–7 minutes or until soft. Season with salt and pepper then stir in garlic and tomato paste. Cook 2–3 minutes. Sprinkle the flour over the vegetables and cook for an additional minute.

Pour in seafood stock and wine and then add the bay leaf and thyme. Reduce heat and let simmer, stirring occasionally, for about 30 minutes.

Remove bay leaf and thyme and use an immersion blender to purée until the consistency is smooth. Return to low heat and stir in heavy cream and lobster meat, cooking just until warm, about 5 minutes.

Garnish with chopped chives before serving.

Tips!
If you'd rather make your own stock, boil 2–3 fresh or frozen lobsters for 10 minutes, strain, discard the shells and use the meat. If lobster tails aren't available or you want a more affordable option, you can substitute 1 pound of lobster claw meat.

Wine Pairings
Best served with Chardonnay that brings out the sweetness of the lobster or Viognier. Some of Emmy's suggestions: Stag's Leap Viognier, La Crema Chardonnay, Fruit & Flower Chardonnay

Cherry Vanilla Muffins

1¾ cup all-purpose flour
⅓ cup sugar
1 teaspoon baking powder
½ teaspoon baking soda
½ teaspoon sea salt
1 cup buttermilk
2 large eggs
2 tablespoons pure vanilla extract
1 tablespoon Patique California Cherry Liqueur
2 ounces butter, melted and cooled, plus a little more butter for greasing the pan
1 cup finely chopped cherries, either sweet or sour

Preheat oven to 400°F.

Lightly grease muffin tins with butter.

Whisk together the flour, sugar, baking powder, baking soda, and salt in a large bowl. In a separate bowl, whisk together the buttermilk, eggs, vanilla extract, and cherry liqueur.

Pour the wet ingredients into the dry, followed by the butter and cherries, stirring the ingredients together until just combined. The less you mix, the more delicate the muffins will be.

Scoop the muffin batter into the greased cups, filling about ¾ to the top.

Bake for 20–22 minutes or until cooked through. A toothpick into the center of a muffin should come out clean. Allow to cool for 5 minutes then remove carefully from the pan.

Tips!
Our *bonita* Conchita took the time to handpick and pit the cherries using a sharp knife. But frozen, thawed, and drained pitted cherries may be substituted.

Wine Pairings
Best served with a light sweet dessert wine like a Gewürztraminer or a Moscato. Or for brunch, try the fun Cherry Mimosa recipe below!. Some of Emmy's suggestions: Caposaldo Sparkling Peach Moscato, Rosatello Moscato, Chateau Ste Michelle Gewurztraminer

* * *

Cherry Mimosas

12 ounces chilled Champagne
2 ounces cherry liqueur
Rosemary sprigs

Place a few leaves of rosemary in each Champagne flute. Pour 1 ounce cherry liqueur over rosemary, add Champagne to fill the glass. Garnish with rosemary sprigs.

Makes 2 cocktails.

Nick's Smashburgers

4 Brioche hamburger buns (most will want seconds)
1 pound 80/20 ground beef (or other meat)
4 slices American cheese
1 yellow onion, sliced
2 tablespoon butter
3 tablespoons vegetable oil
3–4 tablespoons Vermouth
Sea salt
Fresh ground pepper

The biggest secret is in the sauce:
2 tablespoons mayonnaise
1 tablespoon siracha ketchup
1 tablespoon Coleman's mustard
2 tablespoons diced dill pickles or dill relish
Sea salt and freshly ground pepper

Mix well.

In a small frying pan, sauté onions until soft. Just when looking almost perfect, add Vermouth and continue until onions are slightly golden.

Without working meat together too well, leaving little air pockets (very important!), form ¼ pound balls, salt and pepper all the way around each ball, and place on hot oiled flat grill. Then with a spatula (or two if necessary) push down hard to smash into very flat patties. When juices start to pool on top of the burgers and the edges start to get brown, loosen gently from the grill and flip the patties. Top each burger with a slice of cheese and continue to grill until cheese is well-melted.

Butter tops and bottoms of buns and place on grill, butter side down, until toasty.

To construct the burgers, put a generous tablespoon of sauce on the bottom buns, then 2 burger patties with melted cheese, then top with onions and the top of the buns. Prepare to be impressed!

Makes 2 burgers.

Tips!
To lessen the heat a bit, use regular ketchup in the sauce. Nick likes Kewpie Japanese Mayo, but any mayonnaise may be used.

Wine Pairings
Best served with wines that pair well with red meat, such as a Cabernet Sauvignon or an earthy Pinot Noir. Some of Emmy's suggestions: Cakebread Cellars Cabernet Sauvignon, Apothic Cabernet Sauvignon, Coeur De Terre Vineyard Pinot Noir

ABOUT THE AUTHOR

Gemma Halliday is the #1 Amazon, *New York Times* & *USA Today* bestselling author of several mystery series. Gemma's books have received numerous awards, including a Golden Heart, two National Reader's Choice awards, three RITA nominations, a RONE award for best mystery, and two Killer Nashville Silver Falchion Awards for best cozy mystery and readers' choice. She currently lives in the San Francisco Bay Area with her large, loud, and loving family.

To learn more about Gemma, visit her online at www.GemmaHalliday.com

The Wine & Dine Mysteries

www.GemmaHalliday.com

Made in United States
North Haven, CT
12 May 2022